Useful English Expressions
for Communication

如何提升
英語溝通能力
關鍵句1300

崎村耕二◎著　劉華珍◎譯

眾文圖書股份有限公司

一本強化英語與溝通雙重表達能力的實用書籍

英語溝通能力其實包括了兩個層面，一個是英語的能力，一個是溝通的能力，因此要提升英語溝通的能力就必須同時加強英語與溝通的能力，雙管齊下才能達成目標。根據筆者多年來在英語溝通的教學專業理論與實務的經驗來看，《如何提升英語溝通能力：關鍵句 1300》一書的作者以不同情境整理出常用而且實用的英語句型，加上將句型依主題分類，附上句型解說與重點提示，的確能夠幫助有心改進英語溝通能力的讀者──包括擔任有關英語溝通課程的教師、高中和大專院校在學學生，以及公民營機構公司的涉外事務從業人員等等──在此一領域中強化英語與溝通的雙重表達能力。

如果讀者要善用本書的話，筆者建議，在充分理解了英語句型以後，還要大聲朗讀這些句型，以角色扮演與互動演練的方式應用在教學或未來出席國際會議及國際談判的場合當中，將平面靜態的文本轉換爲立體動態的呈現，主動積極實踐英語溝通，以還原在人生舞台上的揮灑空間，讓參與者藉著不同情境的語意行爲成功地進出這個舞台，施展抱負，回應期許。

在應對今天 21 世紀國際化與全球化的各項議題中，例如經貿、環保、科技、政治、社會、文化、氣候變遷等議題，放眼所及，最新的相關資訊幾乎都還是以英語來建構、傳送與接收，因此，提升英語溝通能力是每一位進入國際社會 (International Community) 的成員，尤其是英語非母語的人士，無法規避的職責與志業。也因此筆者樂於推薦本書，也衷心盼望讀者經由本書精心設計的體例結構與涵蓋不同的內容主題策略應用，眞

正吸收本書關鍵句型的精華，然後運用正確流暢的英語溝通能力，昂首闊步，充滿自信，全力以赴，立足世界寰宇。

國立臺北大學應用外語學系專任教授
兼國際談判及同步翻譯中心主任

陸彥豪

前言

　　本書的目的在指出非英語母語者使用英語溝通的各種情境，並針對不同情境整理出常用的句型和實例。為方便讀者使用，特別將句型依主題分類，並附句型解說和重點提示。

　　所謂的「溝通」始於不同的立場和見解。由於立場不同、看法各異，雙方在溝通的過程慢慢理出頭緒，獲得共識，進而解決問題。溝通有許多形式，如交涉、討論、爭論甚至是面對質疑做出回應和反駁等等，這些都是溝通的一部分。

　　在英語系國家工作或求學，想當然一定要用英語和當地的人溝通。就算不是長時間住在國外，總是有出國旅遊的機會，這時候難免也要用到英語。而即使待在國內，學校或職場使用到英語的機會也愈來愈多。具體來說，到底什麼情況下必須用英語溝通呢？我們舉幾個例子來看。

(1) 在國外生活或旅遊：出門在外，遇到問題在所難免，可能是生活上的不便，可能是捲進某個麻煩，也可能是發生意外等等。這時候如果不適時用英語來捍衛自己的權利，可能會造成莫大的損失。

(2) 與外國企業交涉：不論是任職跨國公司或與外國企業交易，流利的英語表達能力是必備條件。

(3) 到英美地區求學：需要用英語和老師、同學討論課程內容或研究主題。

(4) 參加國際會議：參加國內外各種以英語發表的研討會時，與會者都需具備一定程度、特別是專門領域的英語能力，以便進行各種討論、發表論文、回答問題。

(5) 外交談判：身為政治家或外交官，與他國交涉時能否具體陳述議題，事關國家利益。

在上述場合，非英語母語者往往因為語言問題在討論一開始便居於劣勢。儘管對某個主題有一定程度的了解，但只要一用英語表達就無法發揮原有的實力。問題就出在「說英語」。筆者見過太多動不動就被外國人的言論駁倒，或自己的話被誤解而不知所措的人。筆者也有相同的經驗。雖然努力試著把話說清楚，但詞不達意，對話變成爭論，弄得雙方都不愉快。如果只是生活上的小事當然無傷大雅，但如果關係到生命、財產甚至是國家安全，問題可就非同小可了。

對非英語母語者來說，用英語溝通就像跑在滿是碎石子的路上，腳步踉蹌、跌跌撞撞。似懂非懂聽著的同時，一邊說著不甚標準的英語，不僅對發音斤斤計較，在動詞變化、名詞的單複數等細節上也是小心翼翼，還要注意和自己的母語截然不同的構句方式。表達某個概念前，總是先把要說的話在腦中想過一次，這是最麻煩的一點。如果英語夠流利，想都不用想就自然而然脫口而出了吧。換言之，討論事情時，大腦一部分的活動都耗費在跟談話內容無關的思考上。

非英語母語者面臨的另一個難題是，不擅長英美國家特有的論證方式。基本上，東方人有刻意避開討論的傾向。不是說東方人不討論事情，而是通常希望能「大事化小，小事化無」。這與其說是一種美德，倒不如說是對於和他人正面交鋒感到猶豫。即使在學校教育上，討論的比重也不高。中小學教育是如此，就連討論比率應該加重的高等教育依然由教師主導課程進行。反觀英美國家，從中小學開始便讓孩子學習討論的方法，到了大學，以討論形式為主的課程變多，學校不僅鼓勵學生互相討論，更藉

此培養學生主動積極的態度。

以英國牛津大學的學生會會議爲例，會議不但模擬英國議會的開會方式而進行，校方更定期邀請知名的政治家和學者參與討論，與學生站在對等的立場上正面交鋒。另外，牛津大學的導師制度亦值得借鏡。導師制度的目的是讓教師與學生透過討論激發出前所未有的新意、並樂在其中。由此可見，眞正的討論絕對不是毫無意義的辯駁。

「內容」固然是溝通討論的重點，但現在的英語學習者多半抱持著「只要有內容不怕說不好」的想法，不願意積極學習如何表達。然而內容再豐富，如果沒有正確、合宜的表達方式也無法傳達給對方。因此，把語言學好並且有條理地說出來是溝通的另一大重點。

本書除了收錄各種溝通場景的常見句型，也盡可能爲讀者整理出意義相近但語感上有些微差異的句型，並說明其異同。此外，既然是溝通討論，必定有一個或多個對象，爲了幫助讀者更清楚了解句型的用法，筆者特別設計了幾個日常生活中可能發生的情境，並以所介紹的句型編寫例句和對話。

本書從事前準備、執筆到付梓，獲得許多人的幫助。會話方面，特別感謝 Michael Mainwaring 及 Roger Nunn 的建議與指教。此外，正如前一本拙作《英語論文寫作技巧》，若沒有創元社矢部文治社長以及編輯部猪口教行先生的勉勵，筆者實在毫無自信能順利完成本書，在此由衷感謝。最後，如果本書能爲讀者帶來助益、幫助各位提升英語溝通能力，將是筆者最大的榮幸。

崎村耕二

本書結構與表記方式

本書依主題分為 12 章，每章細分為 7 到 38 個不等的項目，共 210 個。每個項目之下再依情境劃分句型，項目組成如下：

項目標題　即項目名稱。

使用情境　該項目下各種情境。

　　句型　各種情境下的常用句型。這個部分也會整理出相似但意義有些微差異的句型。至於句型中使用的註記，請參考下方的「句型表記方式」。

　　中譯　英文句型中譯。本書收錄的句型多為日常生活常用句型，因此翻譯上也會偏向口語。另外，由於採中英左右對照，中譯部分盡量符合英文的呈現方式，方便讀者比對參考。

句型解說　具體說明句型重點，包括文法、意思解釋、類似說法等，並提供例句或情境對話，幫助讀者了解句型的使用方式。

重點提示　提供每項句型概括性的解說。

句型表記方式如下：

1. ... 表示可以按照情況填入恰當的字詞。
2. [ ] 當中的字詞可用來取代 [ ] 前的字詞。
3. 若 [ ] 當中包含多個說法，則用 / 區隔。
4. ( ) 當中的字詞可以省略。
5. 句型中第一人稱單數的 I 或複數 We 都可當主詞用，為求統一，本書一律以 I 為主詞。然而，如果某些例句較常以 We 為主詞，則以 We 取代 I。
6. 拼字統一為美式英語。

Contents

Contents

第4章　責備 ·························· 79

第5章　交涉 ·························· 103

第 6 章　表達意見 ······················· 151

Contents

第 7 章　有技巧地討論 ………………… 195

Contents

第1章
贊成

與他人溝通討論時,最重要的就是針對對方的意見表達自己的看法,換言之,是持贊成意見還是反對意見。本章從單純表示贊成的句型出發,語帶委婉或部分認同的句型都有著墨。

Useful English Expressions
for Communication

表示贊成 (I)

■ 我贊成你的意見。

1. I agree with you.	我贊成你的看法。
2. I agree with your opinion.	我贊成你的意見。
3. I go along with you [that].	我支持你〔你的看法〕。
4. I couldn't agree more.	我完全贊同。
5. I'm in favor of...	我贊成……。
6. I'm of the same opinion.	我的看法也一樣。
7. I feel much the same way.	我也這麼認為。
8. I agree with all you've said.	你所說的我都贊同。
9. I agree with you on all points.	你的見解我全都認同。
10. I agree with you there [on that point].	關於那點，我完全認同。
11. We agree on this point.	關於這點，我們都贊同。
12. We all agree on that.	我們都贊同那件事。
13. That's exactly what I was trying [going] to say.	這正是我想〔要〕說的。
14. That's my idea, too.	我的想法也是那樣。
15. That's what I'm saying.	我所說的就是那樣。
16. That's exactly how I see it.	我的看法就是那樣。
17. That's exactly what I think [what I was thinking].	和我想的完全一樣。

■ 句型解說

1. 也可以直接說 I agree.。如果要加強語氣,可在 agree 前面加助動詞 do,變成 I do agree with you.。除了 do 之外,還可以用 entirely(完全)、totally(完全) completely(徹底地)、certainly(當然)等副詞來修飾動詞 agree,加強同意 語氣,例如 I entirely agree with you.(我完全同意你。)

   同意並接受他人意見,或因認同對方而委婉表達協助的意願時,可以用 agree to...,to 後面不能接「人」,只能接「事情」。例如 I agree to the terms.(我 接受那些條件。)

2. 除了認同「人」,也可以認同對方的「想法」,這時 with 後面可以接 opinion (意見)、argument(論點)、what you say(你所說的)、idea(想法)等表示意 見、想法的名詞(如句型 8)。
   - *I agree with* your argument.
     我贊成你的論點。
   - *I agree with* what you are saying.
     我認同你所說的。
   - *I agree with* the overall idea of the plan.
     我贊成整個計畫。

3. go along with 和 agree with 一樣是「同意」的意思。

4. 直譯是「我不能同意更多」,也就是「完全贊同」的意思。

5. in favor of... 是「支持,贊成…」的意思,表示有若干選項,其中有一個特別 喜歡的。
   - *I'm in favor of* the first plan.
     我贊成第一個提案。

7. 了解對方的意見或心情,婉轉地表示同意。

10. there 指的是對方所說的內容、所提出的論點。而 on that point 明確點出了「那一點」，表示對方所提的各種論點裡，自己贊成其中一個論點。換句話說，使用這個句型時，清楚地陳述自己支持的觀點非常重要（句型 11, 12 亦同）。

11, 12. we 指的是「我方」。

■ 重點提示

　　仔細聽對方陳述意見，如果肯定對方的看法，就直接給予正面評價。亞洲人通常不會直接表示贊同或反對，只是露出微妙的笑容，常常讓西方人摸不著頭緒甚至感到不悅。上面介紹的句型中，有一些表達同意的說法比較委婉，講話比較含蓄的讀者不妨多加利用。總之，遇到表示贊同的情況時，請盡量避免什麼也不說只是猛點頭，或不停地說 Yes. Yes.。適當使用 I agree. 等說法，讓對方清楚知道你的立場。

▦ 表示贊成 (II)　　　　　　　　　　　　　⦿MP3 003

■ 你說的沒錯。

1. (Just) As you say...	正如你所說的……。
2. You're talking sense.	你說的有道理。
3. I share your point of view.	我想的跟你一樣。
4. I'd like to echo what ... has said.	我想要呼應……說的。
5. I don't really have much to add to...	對於……我沒有其他意見。

■ 句型解說

3. 認同別人的觀點。

4. 自己沒有意見，而且也同意他人的意見。

5. 贊成他人的論點，而且沒有其他要補充的意見。

表示認同 (I)

◉MP3 004

■ 你是對的。

1. You're right.	你是對的。
2. You're right in saying [thinking]...	你那樣說〔想〕沒錯。
3. You're right in your judgment [assumption].	你的判斷〔假設〕是對的。
4. You're right when you say [said]...	你說……，確實沒錯。
5. How right you are!	你說的一點也沒錯！

■ 說到重點了。

6. That's the point.	說到重點了。
7. That's it.	沒錯，就是這樣。
8. That's a good point.	這想法不錯。
9. You have a point there.	你那樣說有道理。
10. Your suggestion [remark] is very much to the point.	你的建議〔意見〕非常切重要點。
11. There's something in what you say.	你說的有理。

■ 就是那樣。

12. That's (very much) the case.	（差不多）就是那樣。
13. That seems to be the case.	似乎是那樣。

■ 句型解說

1. 善用副詞，就能表達不同的語氣。

- *You're* quite *right.*
  你說的很對。

- *You're* absolutely *right.*
  你說的一點也沒錯。

6, 8, 9. 對方「說到重點了，說的有道理」，表示認為對方所提到的很重要，但不等於絕對的贊成。

12, 13. the case 指的是真相或事實，可以用在對方所說的內容和事實相符的情況。

■ 重點提示

上述的句型，主要是針對對方所提出的看法進行主觀評判時使用。

❖ 表示認同 (II)　　　　　　　　　　　　　◉ MP3 005

■ 正是……。

1. ... rightly...	……確實是……。
2. ... justly...	……公平地……。
3. ... and rightly so.	……一點也沒錯。

■ 句型解說

1. 例如：

- Professor Jones *rightly* pointed out that the experiment was unreliable.
  瓊斯教授指出該實驗是不可靠的，確實是這樣。

也可以說 ... is [was] right when he [she]... 。

- Professor Jones *was right when he* pointed out that the experiment was unreliable.
  瓊斯教授指出該實驗是不可靠的，確實是這樣。

- -

2. 例如：

- Mrs. Thatcher has been criticized, *justly* I think, for not spending enough money on education.
  柴契爾夫人被批評沒有投入足夠的教育經費，這批評我覺得不過分。

- -

3. 例如：

- Picasso has always been praised as the greatest artist of the twentieth century, *and righly so.*
  畢卡索經常被譽為 20 世紀最偉大的藝術家，這話一點也沒錯。

- -

■ 重點提示

上述句型用來表示第三者的意見。

⠿ 表示肯定 ◉ MP3 006

■ 沒錯，就是這樣。

1. Yes (indeed).	確實沒錯。
2. Certainly.	的確。

3. Sure.	當然。
4. Absolutely.	一點也沒錯。
5. My answer is yes.	我的答覆是「沒問題」。

■ 句型解說

1. 要做出肯定的答覆時，除了 Yes 以外，也可以多用 Yes indeed.、Yes, I am. 或 Yes, I do.。

情境對話

A: Do you agree?

B: *Yes, I do.*

A：你贊成嗎？

B：我贊成。

2. 請看以下對話。

情境對話

A: Did you see the man entering the building?

B: I *certainly* did.

A：你有沒有看見那個男人走進大樓？

B：確實看到了。

3. 簡略的說法，常用來承諾對方。

4. 也是簡略的說法，語氣比 Yes. 或 Certainly. 更強烈。

情境對話

A: Do you think he is right?

B: *Absolutely.*

A：你認為他是對的？

B：那當然。

基本上認同

■ 基本上我贊成。

1. I agree with your main point.	我贊同你的主要論點。
2. I agree with you on the whole (,but...).	總的來說，我同意你的看法（，不過⋯⋯）。
3. I agree with the basic point you made.	我認同你提出的基本論點。
4. I would support the concept behind that.	我支持那個看法背後的概念。
5. I understand your view [point].	我了解你的看法〔論點〕。
6. I agree in principle.	原則上我同意。
7. I agree [It's all right] in principle (,but...).	原則上我贊成（，不過⋯⋯）。

▪ 句型解說

4. 不完全同意對方的看法，但認同該看法背後的概念或發想。

7. 例如：

- *I agree in principle*, *but* I'd just like to add something to what you said.
  原則上我贊成你說的，不過我還想補充一下。

▪ 重點提示

　　基本上同意對方看法的表達方式，由於並非全盤接受，這些句型後面常常接 but...。

大致上認同

■ 或許沒錯，但是……。

1. That may [could] be (so), but...	或許是這樣，不過……。
2. You may [could] be right, but...	你或許是對的，不過……。
3. That may be true.	那或許是對的。
4. I see your point, but...	我了解你的意思，不過……。
5. That's all very well, but...	那樣很好，不過……。
6. Yes of course, but...	當然沒錯，不過……。
7. You could put it that way, but...	是可以那樣說，不過……。
8. I respect your opinion, but...	我尊重你的看法，但是……。

■ 我漸漸同意……了。

9. I find myself agreeing with...	我漸漸同意……了。

句型解說

1. 如果要在認同的前提下表達其他意見，可以加入 well，說成 That may well be, but...（話是沒錯，不過……。）

2. 也可以這樣用：Come to think of it, you may be right.（這樣想的話，你或許是對的。）

4. 並非全然同意、但大致上接受。如果只是要表示讓步，也可以用 I'll give you that.（我承認這一點有理。）

7. 認同對方的說法，但句中的 could 給人不照單全收的意味，意思是「要這麼說也可以，但是……」。

8. respect 是「尊重」的意思，在這裡是指尊重對方的看法。

情境對話

A: From every point of view, it is quite dangerous to invest in the venture. I'm not sure whether we can finance the budget.

B: Well, you are an experienced accountant and *I respect your opinion* as such, *but* it is important for us to take action now.

A：從各方面來看，投資這項事業的風險很大，我不確定我們是否能夠提供這筆預算。

B：嗯，你是個經驗老到的會計師，所以我尊重你的看法，不過我們現在真的得採取行動了。

- -

9. 開始認同對方的看法。find oneself ...ing 是「發現自己漸漸變得……」。

- -

■ **重點提示**

　　上述句型大多用來表示部分同意的情況，換句話說，儘管肯定對方的論點，卻不是全盤接受。這類的句型通常先表達贊同，之後再說出反對的部分。

消極地認同　　　　　　　　　　　⊙MP3 009

■ 應該沒什麼大問題。

1. I don't see anything wrong with that.	我不覺得那有什麼不好。
2. I don't see why not.	沒什麼不好啊。
3. I see no objection to...	對於……我沒什麼要反對的。

■ 句型解說

1, 2. 都用了 I don't see...，表示對方的論點沒什麼大問題，雖然不十分贊成，但也沒什麼好反對的地方。這種句型有時能達到催促對方的效果。

情境對話

A: Do you think I should consult a lawyer?

B: *I don't see why not.*

A：你覺得我該找律師談談嗎？

B：沒什麼不好啊。

有限制的認同 ⊙MP3 010

■ 我認同……，不過……。

1. You're right except that...	除了……之外，你是對的。
2. You're right in one respect.	就某一方面來看，你是對的。
3. You're right in the sense that...	就……而言你說的沒錯。
4. I take your point as far as ... is concerned.	就……來看，我認同你的看法。
5. I agree up to a point.	就某個程度而言，我同意你的看法。
6. I agree with the first [last] point (that you've made).	我同意你一開始〔最後〕（提出）的論點。
7. I agree with your other points.	我同意你其他的論點。
8. In some ways it's quite a good idea.	就某些方面來看，這確實是個不錯的點子。
9. I agree with most of the points that you've made, but...	你提出的觀點我大多認同，但是……。

10. I agree with most of what you said, but...

你說的我幾乎都贊同，不過……。

11. I agree with you completely on that point, but...

就那一點來說，我百分之百同意你的看法，但是……。

12. I agree that ... Nevertheless,...

我贊成……。不過，……。

13. I agree with part of what you said.

我同意你部分看法。

14. I agree with A, but I don't agree with B.

我贊成 A，但無法認同 B。

15. That's true, at least in..., but...

至少就……來看是那樣沒錯，不過……。

16. I agree with you to some extent, but I still can't understand why [how/what]...

某種程度上我同意你的看法，但我還是不能理解為什麼〔怎麼會／是什麼〕……。

17. It is true that..., but...

……是對的，不過……。

18. That's all right for you, but...

對你來說或許沒問題，但是……。

19. ... is reasonable [acceptable] if..., but...

如果是……的話，……是可以理解〔接受〕的，不過……。

■ 句型解說

8. it 指的是對方剛剛提出的意見。

9, 10. 意思相同，另一種說法是 You're right in most respects, but...（你說的大部分都沒錯，但是……。）

- *I agree with most of the points that you've made, but* there is one thing that I find difficult to accept.
  你提出的論點我大部分都同意，但有一點我很難接受。

13

19. 在某個條件或範圍內同意對方的看法，基本句型是「某個論點在條件 1 之下是成立的，但是在條件 2 之下不成立」。也可以說成 It is ... with..., but it is ... with...（……是……，但……是……。）

情境對話

A: Why don't you try to change the old system?

B: Your question *may be reasonable if* you ask it as an outsider, *but* it just doesn't make sense to us.

A：為什麼不試著改變舊的方法？

B：從局外人的角度來看，你的問題確實不無道理，但對我們來說並非如此。

■ 重點提示

除了完全贊成和完全反對，有時也會有部分贊成的情況。換言之，雖然無法認同對方所有的想法，但可以接受某部分的觀點。這個時候便要表達有限度的支持。例如，某個意義上是贊成，另外的意義上則是反對。又或是反對某些細節，但大體上是贊成的。

此外，有的句型乍看之下表示贊成，但其實是為了帶出反對意見，例如句型 9 到 12 和 15 到 19。這些句型都用 but... 接反對意見。

表示理解   ◉MP3 011

■ 我了解。

1. I see what you mean.	我懂你的意思。
2. I know what you mean.	我了解你的意思。
3. I see your point.	我知道你的想法。
4. I see [I can see...].	我明白〔我能明白……〕。
5. In a way I see what you mean.	我大概了解你的意思。
6. I see what you're trying to say.	我知道你試圖表達什麼。
7. I see what you want to do.	我知道你想做什麼。

■ 句型解說

1. 後面也可以接 but 再接反對意見，例如 I see what you mean, but...（我懂你的意思，但是……。），表示能理解對方的論點，但無法同意。

2. I know... 表示了解對方所說的內容。

4. 請看以下對話。

情境對話 1

A: That's what happened in Japan toward the end of the Edo period.

B: Now *I can see* the general idea of the political situation at that time.

A：那就是日本江戶時代末期的情況。

B：我想我現在對當時的政治情勢有大概的了解了。

情境對話 2

A: So I want to have additional funding to continue my research.

B: *I can see* what your needs are, but I'm afraid there's nothing I can do.

A：因此，希望能有其他的經費，讓我能繼續做研究。

B：我可以了解你的需求，但我恐怕幫不上忙。

5. 例如：

- I don't share your opinion, but *in a way I see what you mean.*
  我的看法跟你不同，不過我大概了解你的意思。

  也可以對調，改成：

- *I see what you mean*, but I don't share your opinion.
  我了解你的意思，但我的看法跟你不同。

■ 重點提示

　　上述句型用來表示可以理解對方所說的話，或可以體會其心情與立場，但並不見得贊成，可能有其他看法。

同情對方的處境或立場

●MP3 012

■ 我了解你的感受。

1. I understand your problem [concern/ worry/objection/position/situation].	我了解你的問題〔顧慮／擔憂／ 反對／立場／處境〕。
2. I can imagine how you...	我能想像你有多麼⋯⋯。
3. You may well...	難怪你會⋯⋯。
4. I have some sympathy with your position [situation].	我蠻同情你的立場〔處境〕。
5. ... is understandable.	⋯⋯是可以理解的。

■ 句型解說

1. 對他人的處境或問題有同理心。雖然帶著同情的心情，不代表願意伸出援手。 這個句型後面常接 but...。
   - *I understand your problem, but* I'm afraid there is nothing I can do to help you. 我了解你的問題，但我恐怕幫不上忙。

2. 能體會他人的心情，但不等於同情。

   情境對話

   A: ... and last week the president told me to leave the company within a month. I was very depressed and didn't know what to do.

   B: *I can imagine how you* feel.

   A：⋯⋯然後上禮拜老總要我一個月內走人。我很沮喪，不知道該怎麼辦才好。

   B：我能想像那種感覺。

3. 考慮到他人的狀況或立場，進而表示理解。
   - *You may well* say so.
     也難怪你會這麼說。
   - *You may well* be angry.
     也難怪你會生氣了。

5. 對別人的看法表達理解。

- Your objection *is understandable*.
  你會反對是可以理解的。

重點提示

如句型解說所示，上述的句型不是用來表示贊成與否，而是對他人的情況、行爲、情緒或立場，以客觀角度表達理解的態度。

同意但提出另一種見解　　◉ MP3 013

■ 我承認……，但……。

| 1. I have to admit it (, but...). | 我不得不承認（，不過……）。 |
| 2. I admit that is true (, but...). | 我承認那是對的（，但是……）。 |

句型解說

1. 雖然不認同，但事實的確如此。

情境對話

A: I failed the examination. I am very disappointed.

B: But you didn't work very hard, did you?

A: No, *I have to admit it*.

A：考試被我搞砸了，我覺得很難過。

B：不過你也沒有很用功吧？

A：是沒有啦，這我不得不承認。

admit 後面也可以接 that 子句為受詞，例如：

• *I have to admit that* it makes sense.
  我不得不承認那很合理。

■重點提示

　　不得不承認某個事實，或討論出現不利自己的情況時，可使用上述句型。有時句子後面也會接 but...。

02

第 2 章
反對

第 1 章介紹了「贊成」的各種說
法，本章則要介紹「反對」的句
型。等各位讀到第 3 章「指出錯
誤」的部分，就能學到溝通討論
中「攻」的技巧。

Useful English Expressions
for Communication

表示反對

■ 我不贊成。

1. I don't agree with you.	我不贊成。
2. I disagree with you.	我反對。
3. I have a different opinion.	我有不同的看法。
4. I don't think so. [Do you think so? I don't think that...]	我不這麼認為。〔你這麼認為嗎？我不認為……。〕
5. I can't [don't] accept...	我無法〔不〕接受……。
6. I see things differently.	我有不同的看法。
7. That's not my idea of...	我對……的看法不是那樣。
8. I don't like the idea of...	我不認同……。
9. I think something else.	我有其他看法。

■ 恐怕無法苟同。

10. I'm afraid I can't [don't] agree with you.	我恐怕不能〔不〕同意你的看法。
11. I'm afraid I have to disagree.	我恐怕無法認同。
12. I beg to differ.	抱歉，我不贊同。

■ 完全不贊成。

13. I entirely [totally] disagree with you.	我百分之百反對。
14. I couldn't agree less.	我完全無法認同。
15. I find it difficult to agree with you.	我很難認同你的看法。

■ 我反對……。

16. I'm against...	我反對……。

17. I'm opposed to...　　　　　　　　　　我反對……。

18. I'm not in favor of...　　　　　　　　我不支持……。

■ 我無法理解……（你所說的）。

19. I don't see the point of...　　　　　　我不了解……有什麼意義。

20. I don't see why...　　　　　　　　　　我不能理解為什麼……。

21. It's difficult to see why [how]...　　　很難理解為什麼〔怎麼〕……。

22. I'm not convinced by your argument.　你的論點無法說服我。

■ 對於……，我持保留態度。

23. I have some reservations about...　　對於……，我持保留態度。

■ 我不認為如你所想的那麼……。

24. I don't think it is as ... as you think.　我不認為事情如你所想的那麼
　　　　　　　　　　　　　　　　　　　……。

■ 句型解說

1, 2. with 後面除了接人，也可以接事情。

- *I don't agree with* what you said about…
  你剛剛說的跟……有關的部分我不同意。

- *I disagree with* the first [last] point that you've made.
  我反對你一開始〔最後〕提出的論點。

- *I disagree with* your interpretation of the poem.
  你對這首詩的詮釋我無法苟同。

4. 以反問的方式來暗示自己並不這麼認為，和 I disagree. 相比較為婉轉。如果要帶點諷刺的語氣，可以加上 You don't really think...?（你該不會真的認為是……吧？）或 Do you really think so?（你真的這麼想？）。

5. 例如：

- *I can't [don't] accept* that view.
  我不能接受那樣的看法。

---

6. things 泛指所有事情，整句話是指「看事情的角度不同」。

---

7. 避免針鋒相對，委婉地表示自己的看法不同。

情境對話

A: In my opinion, a university is a place where professors apply themselves to their own academic objectives.

B: *That's not my idea of* a university.

A：我認為大學是教授專注於自己的學術研究的場所。

B：我對大學的看法不是那樣。

---

8. 當他人的言論消極且充滿偏見時，用來表達自己主觀上無法認同。I don't like the idea 的意思是「我不喜歡那個看法」。

10, 11. 婉轉地表示反對。雖然討論時必須堅定立場、正面迎擊，但顧及對方的心情，委婉地表達反對意見也是很重要的。類似的說法還有：

- I don't know if I agree (with you).
  我不知道是否贊成（你的看法）。

- I'm not sure I agree (with you).
  我不確定是否贊成（你的看法）。

- I wonder if I agree.
  我也不確定我贊不贊成。

---

12. beg to differ 表現的是一種明確的反對態度，通常用於反對權威者或地位較高的人物的言論。

---

14. 直譯是「我無法贊成更少了」，也就是「完全不贊成」的意思。

---

16. 請看以下對話。

情境對話

A: We should impose economic sanctions on the country.

B: *I'm against* that.

A：我們應該對該國施以經濟制裁。

B：我反對。

---

23. 對事情仍有疑慮，reservations about the idea [plan] 是「對某個想法〔計畫〕所持的保留態度」。

• *I have some reservations about* introducing the computerized system in our school.

對於學校引進電腦系統一事，我持保留態度。

---

24. 雙方對於事情的程度有不同的看法，類似說法有 I don't think it is so... （我不認為有那麼……。）

情境對話

A: Our experiment was quite successful, wasn't it?

B: *I don't think it was as* successful *as you think.*

A：我們的實驗蠻成功的，你不覺得嗎？

B：我不認為有你所想的那麼成功。

否定對方的意見 ◉MP3 015

■ **不是那樣的。**

1. That's not true.	不是那樣的。
2. What you're saying is not true.	你說的和事實不符。
3. That's not the case.	不是那樣的。
4. It's not ... at all. [It's not really..., is it?]	完全不是／沒有……。〔其實不是／沒有……，對吧？〕

■句型解說

4. 表示對方所說的內容或意見與事實不符。

情境對話 1

A: It's obvious that the Japanese economy will recover soon.

B: *It's not* obvious *at all*.

A：看來日本的經濟很快就會復甦了。

B：看起來並非如此。

情境對話 2

A: The bright blue color of the background makes a contrast to the dark shadows which lie here and there in the picture.

B: But the color of the background *is not really* that bright, *is it?*

A：背景的亮藍色襯托出整幅畫各處的陰影部分。

B：但背景的顏色並沒有那麼亮，對吧？

▓ 不確定是否同意   ◉MP3 016

■ 我不確定。

1. I'm not sure.	我不確定。
2. I don't know.	我不知道。
3. I don't know about..., but...	我是不太清楚……，但是……。
4. You never know.	誰知道呢。
5. So you say.	話是這麼說，但誰知道呢。

■句型解說

1. 後面也可以接名詞子句。

* *I'm not sure* if it's the best solution.
  我不確定這是不是最好的解決方法。

- -

2, 3. 雖然看法不同，但沒有直接表達出來，帶有「不發表個人意見」的意味。

情境對話　1

A: He must be a genius!

B: *I don't know.* He may just be very clever.

A：他一定是天才！

B：我不知道耶，他可能只是腦筋動得快而已。

情境對話　2

A: The watch is accurate and it has a good design.

B: *I don't know about* the design, *but*, yes, it has a good reputation for accuracy.

A：這支手錶的時間很準，也很有設計感。

B：有沒有設計感我是不清楚啦，不過時間確實是出了名的準。

- -

4. 雖沒有直接反對，但抱持其他看法，特別是對於未來的預測而言。

情境對話

A: The price of the stock will rise soon.

B: *You never know.*

A：股票不久就會漲了。

B：難說啊。

- -

5. 表示不贊同。

- -

意見相左

● MP3 017

■ 你怎麼說都不要緊，但……。

1. Say all you want about..., ...	無論你怎麼說……，……。
2. Say what you like, but I think...	你怎麼說都不要緊，不過我認為……。

■ 看法不同。

3. That's a matter of opinion.	那是意見不同的問題。
4. That's what you say.	那是你的看法。

■ 句型解說

1, 2. 帶有婉轉的語氣。

- *Say all you want about* his personality, Wagner was a great composer.
  你要怎麼說華格納的個性都無所謂，他就是一位偉大的作曲家。

4. 說話時重音放在 you，用來強調自己和對方看法不同。

■ 重點提示

　　各有各的見解，想要表達「話不投機半句多」的感覺時，可以使用上述句型。

出乎意料　　　　　　　　　　　　◉MP3 018

■ 我很意外。

1. I'm surprised that (you)...　　　　我很驚訝（你）……。

2. I hardly expected ... to...　　　　我完全沒預期……會……。

3. I wonder...　　　　　　　　　　　我很納悶……。

4. You (do) surprise me.　　　　　　你（真的）嚇到我了。

■ 我從沒想過……。

5. I never thought that...　　　　　　我從沒想過……。

6. That's never struck me before.　　我從來沒想過會是那樣。

■ 句型解說

1. 感到出乎意料。

情境對話

A: Studying English is a waste of time.

B: *I'm surprised that* an English teacher would say that!

A：學英文根本是浪費時間。

B：我沒想到一個英文老師居然會這麼說！

其他的說法還有 I am surprised to find that...（我很訝異地發現……。）或 I'm
surprised at...（我對……感到震驚。），例如：

• *I'm surprised at* your comment [remark].
　你的意見〔發言〕嚇了我一跳。

• *I'm surprised at* your comment about the possibility of taking over the
　company. Do you really believe it's possible?
　我很訝異你居然提出接管公司的意見，你真的相信有可能嗎？

2. 感到出乎意料或和現實不符。

- *I hardly expected* you *to* refuse.
  我完全沒想到你會拒絕。

---

3. 例如：

- *I wonder* why he didn't run for the election.
  真不知道他為什麼沒有參選。

---

4. 對於對方的發言或行為感到意外，助動詞 do 用來加強語氣。

---

5. 例如：

- *I never thought that* the prime minister would decide to step down so soon.
  我從沒想過首相會這麼快就決定下台。

■ 重點提示

　　聽到的內容不符合自己的期待、特別是因此而做出某些反應時可以用上述句型。若驚訝中帶著責備，通常會把對方的話複述一遍。

情境對話

A: I suggest we cancel the plan.

B: Cancel the plan! How on earth could we do that?

A：我建議不如取消這項計畫吧。

B：取消計畫？怎麼可以這麼做？

表示否定　　　　　　　　　　　⊙ MP3 019

■ 並非如此。

1. Certainly [Surely/Absolutely] not.	當然不是。
2. ... never...	從未…，絕非……。

3. ... not ... at all. 絕對不是……。

4. Nothing [None] at all. 完全沒有。

5. Far from it. 差得遠了。

■ 句型解說

1. 全盤否定。

情境對話

A: Do you support him?

B: *Certainly not!*

A：你支持他嗎？

B：當然不支持！

2. 堅決否定。

情境對話

A: You said the manager was a cunning old man, didn't you?

B: I *never* said that!

A：你說經理是個老狐狸，是吧？

B：我從沒說過那種話！

4. 請看以下對話。

情境對話

A: Is there anything about the plan that you find objectionable?

B: *Nothing at all.*

A：你對這項計畫有任何反對意見嗎？

B：完全沒有。

5. 簡略的說法，表示對方的話與事實不符。

情境對話

A: I think his work was a success.

B: *Far from it.*

A：我覺得他的事業很成功。

B：一點都不成功。

■ 重點提示

要否定對方的說法，或是說出否定的回答，除了單純用 No. 之外，也可以依據不同的情況使用其他字詞，表達出不同程度的否定。

情境對話

A: Did you steal the wallet?

B: No.

A：你是不是偷了錢包？

B：沒有。

也可以回答 No, I didn't.（不，我沒有。）或 Of course not!（當然沒有！），強調自己並沒有做那件事。另外，語氣也是個重點。鏗鏘有力地說出來才能表達堅定的態度。

▓ 委婉地否定 ●MP3 020

■ ……並非絕對。

1. ... not exactly...	……並不完全是……。
2. ... not necessarily...	……不一定是……。
3. ... not really...	……並非……。
4. Not [Nothing] particularly.	不是非常……。
5. I can't say...	我不能說……。
6. I wouldn't say...	我不會說……。

▪ 句型解說

3. 請看以下對話。

情境對話

A: What's the name of his wife?

B: It's Mary. Well, um … she's *not really* his wife. She's his girlfriend.

A：他太太叫什麼名字？

B：瑪莉。嗯，其實那不是他太太，是女朋友。

6. 請看以下對話。

情境對話　1

A: Somerset Maugham is a great novelist. What do you think of him?

B: He is one of the most popular storytellers, but *I wouldn't say* he is a great novelist.

A：毛姆是個出色的小說家，你對他有何看法？

B：他很會說故事，但我不會說他是個出色的小說家。

此外，也可以用 not in my opinion（我不覺得）來表示自己和他人看法不同。

情境對話　2

A: He is an able teacher, isn't he?

B: *Not in my opinion.*

A：他是個有能力的老師，不是嗎？

B：我不覺得。

▪ 重點提示

　　既然有堅決否定的情況，也就會有模稜兩可的否定情況。為了不破壞人與人之間的關係，語帶模糊的否定方式常常出現在我們的生活裡。事情也是，並非只有黑與白這麼簡單，這時候就可以適時利用上述表示委婉否定的句型。

肯定 vs. 否定　　　⊙MP3 021

遇到 Yes/No 問句時，中文和英文的表達有時是相反的，除了多加留意，更要經常練習。

情境對話

A: You haven't been abroad, then?

B: No, I haven't.

A：所以你沒出過國？

B：對，沒出過國。

英文以事實為中心來回答 Yes 或 No，中文則是以問話者所說的話為準，做出肯定或否定的答案。

興趣缺缺　　　⊙MP3 022

■ 我不感興趣。

1. I'm not interested in...	我對……沒興趣。
2. I'd rather not...	我寧可不要……。
3. I'd prefer not to...	我希望不要……。
4. I don't really want to...	我不太想……。
5. I don't really feel like it.	我不太想。
6. I don't think I will [can]...	我不認為我會〔能〕……。

■句型解說

1. 對於他人的邀約興趣缺缺時，可以直接回答 I'm not interested.（我沒興趣。）

2, 3. 沒有意願去做某件事。

■重點提示

　　面對他人的熱情邀約，直接拒絕似乎太不禮貌，不過，曖昧不明的回答反而會把情況弄得更複雜，尤其在跟西方人士打交道的時候，正確傳達 No 的態度十分重要，因此先說 No 較爲恰當。善用上述句型，便能在不傷感情的情況下拒絕他人。

提出疑問　　　　　　　　　　　　◉MP3 023

■ 為什麼……？

1. What's the point of...?	……有什麼意義？
2. I don't understand [see] the point of...	我不了解……有什麼意義。
3. I don't understand [see] why...	我不明白為什麼……。
4. But why...?	但是，為什麼……？
5. But what for?	但目的是什麼呢？
6. What's wrong with...?	……有什麼問題？
7. I can't help wondering why...	為什麼會……呢，我不得不感到納悶。

■ 句型解說

2. 類似的說法有 I don't [can't] see the advantage of...（我不知道……有什麼好處。）

情境對話

A: We should sue the company for damages.

B: *I don't understand the point of* trying to settle the problem with a lawsuit because it will take too much time and money.

A：我們應該對那家公司提起損害賠償的訴訟。

B：我不了解用打官司的方式解決問題有何意義，因為那太浪費時間也太花錢了。

3. 也可以說 What I can't understand is why...（我不能了解的是為什麼……。）

4. 請看以下對話。

情境對話

A: ... and, John, you will go to New York to see some of our VIP clients.

B: *But why* should I go to New York to see them when I could just phone or send an email to them?

A：……另外，約翰，你得去紐約和一些 VIP 客戶見面。

B：但為什麼非去紐約不可？我可以用電話或 email 和他們聯絡呀。

6. 請看以下對話。

情境對話

A: I wouldn't recommend Gary for the post. Surely there must be someone more suitable for the job.

B: *What's wrong with* Gary? He knows his job. He has been doing very well since he came here.

A：我不建議讓蓋瑞接這個位子，一定有其他更適合的人選。

B：蓋瑞哪裡不好嗎？他很清楚自己的本分，來到公司後工作表現一直都很出色。

讓步但同時提出其他看法　◉MP3 024

■ 即便如此，……。

1. Even so,...	就算這樣，……。
2. Even then,...	即使如此，……。
3. But I still think...	但我還是認為……。
4. In spite of..., I still think...	儘管……，我還是認為……。
5. All the same,...	儘管如此，……。
6. But again I (would) think...	不過，我一樣（會）認為……。
7. But I still can't help feeling [thinking]...	但我還是忍不住會覺得〔會認為〕……。

■ 句型解說

1. 請看以下對話。

情境對話

A: Why do you oppose the reconstruction of the building? Everyone knows that the building has become too old.

B: Of course it is dangerous to keep it as it is. *Even so,* wouldn't you agree that it is an interesting building from an architectural point of view? I suggest we keep reconstruction work to a minimum.

A：為什麼你反對改建呢？大家都知道這棟房子已經太老舊了。

B：如果都不整修當然是很危險的。但就算這樣，你不覺得從建築的角度來看，這棟房子真的很有趣嗎？我認為改建要控制在最低限度內。

3. 請看以下對話。

情境對話

A: So we'll decide to adopt Mr. Smith's plan. Is there any objection to that?

B: I wouldn't say I'm against it, *but I still think* that my plan is better.

A：所以我們打算採用史密斯先生的企劃，有任何異議嗎？

B：我並不是反對，不過我還是認為我的企劃比較好。

---

5. 簡略的說法，意思是「儘管如此」。

---

6. 這裡的 again 表示「和之前提出的想法相同」。

---

7. 請看以下對話。

情境對話

A: We decided that we should compensate the client for the damage. You don't have any objection to that, do you?

B: No, *but I still can't help feeling* that it's not 100 percent our fault.

A：我們決定賠償顧客的損失，沒有人有異議吧？

B：沒有，但我還是會覺得不全是我們的錯。

提出反對意見的技巧　　◉MP3 025

(1) 先確認對方的意見再表示反對。

➡ Do you think so? ... indeed, but I don't think that...
　你這麼認為？雖然確實是……，但我不認為……。

情境對話

A: He is a genius.

B: *Do you think so?* He is a talented playwright, *indeed, but I don't think* he is a genius.

A：他是天才。

B：你這麼認為？他確實是個有才華的劇作家，但我不認為他是天才。

(2) 直接使用否定句型表達反對的態度。

➡ It's not ... at all.
　完全不是……。

雙方意見相左時，除了「我反對」或「你錯了」等說法，也要確切指出反對哪一部分的論點。

情境對話

A: It's obvious that Japan is going to come out of its recession soon.

B: *It's not* obvious *at all*.

A：看來日本很快就能從不景氣的狀況中復甦。

B：看起來並非如此。

(3) 出現不確定或矛盾的情況時，直接提出疑問（善用疑問句）。

(1) 直接發問

情境對話　1

A: That's a foolish plan.

B: *In what way do you think it's foolish?*

A：那是個愚蠢的計畫。

B：哪裡愚蠢了？

情境對話 2

A: Are you suggesting that women don't need to find a job?

B: I don't mean that.

A: *What do you mean, then?*

A：你的意思是說，女人不需要工作嗎？

B：我不是那個意思。

A：那你是什麼意思？

(2) 指出矛盾處

常用的說法有：

➡ If..., why [what]...?

　　如果是……，為什麼〔是什麼〕……？

➡ Why [What]..., then?

　　這樣的話，為什麼〔是什麼〕……？

情境對話 3

A: There's nothing wrong with the treatment.

B: *If* the treatment's OK, *how* do you explain his sudden turn for the worse?

A：治療沒有任何問題。

B：如果治療沒問題，你要怎麼解釋他突然惡化的原因？

(4) 用疑問句表示不贊同。

➡ But don't you think...?

　　可是你不認為……嗎？

➡ But wouldn't you agree...?

　　可是你不贊成……嗎？

➡ But isn't it true...?

　　可是難道不是……嗎？

A: I think we should give up this project.

B: Why do you think so?

A: Well, sales fell sharply last year, and they have never turned around since then.

B: Yes, I know. *But don't you think* we should wait and see for a while longer?

A：我認為我們應該放棄這項企劃。

B：為什麼你這樣認為？

A：嗯，去年的銷售額急遽下降，而且一直沒有好轉。

B：我了解，不過你不覺得我們應該再觀察一陣子嗎？

(5) 指出問題點。

⟹ But...? That's the question.

但是……？那才是問題所在。

A: This will make an interesting new business.

B: It sounds interesting enough. *But* is it going to be profitable? *That's the question.*

A：這會是個有趣的事業。

B：聽起來確實頗有趣的，不過會賺錢嗎？那才是問題。

(6) 加入其他問題。

⟹ But what about the question of...?

但是，……的問題呢？

⟹ But there is another way of looking at it.

不過，還可以從另一個角度切入。

情境對話

A: I think we should help them relax before the tournament. A sight-seeing tour would be a good idea.

B: *But what about the question of* the morale of the team? Won't they lose their focus?

A：我們應該讓他們在比賽前放鬆一下，觀光旅行挺不錯的。

B：但全隊士氣的問題呢？他們會不會因此鬆懈了？

(7) 認同對方看法之餘，藉由自己不同的觀點來凸顯事實。

⇒ That's true, but it's also true that...

那樣是沒錯，不過……也是事實。

⇒ But on the other hand, ...

不過從另外一方面來看，……。

⇒ But it's more logical to think...

不過，……會更合理。

情境對話

A: Tokyo is the most expensive city in Japan. That is, you have to pay more to live there than in any other part of the country.

B: *That's true, but it is also true that* people in Tokyo, on average, earn more than any other people in Japan.

A：東京是全日本物價最高的城市，換句話說，住在東京的生活費比住在日本其他地方都要高。

B：話是沒錯，不過同樣地，東京人的平均收入也比日本其他地方的人要高。

(8) 否定對方的看法，並說明事實。

⇒ (No.) The truth is that...

（不。）事實上……。

A: The U.S. trade deficit has increased because Japan wouldn't put much effort into creating an open trade system.

B: It's the other way round. *The truth is that* the United States hasn't managed to produce high-quality goods to sell abroad and thereby earn money.

A：美國的貿易赤字之所以會增加，是因為日本沒有致力於設計一個開放的貿易制度。

B：正好相反。事實上是因為美國沒有盡力製造出高品質的產品，所以沒辦法外銷賺錢。

(9) 暗示對方思慮不夠周全。

➟ But have you considered...?

不過你有沒有想過……？

A: The best way to reach the peak is to take the route on the west slope.

B: *But have you considered* the danger of avalanches?

A：最佳的攻頂路線是從西坡進入。

B：不過你有沒有把雪崩的可能性考慮進去？

(10) 要求對方正視事實。

➟ But do you realize that...?

不過，你是否了解……？

➟ But are you aware of [that]...?

不過，你有沒有注意到……？

A: Can't we invest in this exciting venture?

B: *But are you aware of* our difficult financial situation?

A：我們不能投資這項有趣的事業嗎？

B：你沒注意到我們所面臨的財務困難嗎？

(11) 提出對立的看法。

⇒ If you think..., what about...?

如果你覺得……，那……又怎麼說？

情境對話

A: Sumo wrestlers ought to be big in size. A wrestler under 100 kg is out of the question.

B: *If you think* size is that important, *what about* Mainoumi? He is very strong indeed for his size.

A：相撲選手的體型一定要夠份量，體重 100 公斤以下絕對沒辦法。

B：如果你覺得體重那麼重要，那舞之海又怎麼說？他塊頭不大，但十分強壯。

(12) 用自己的話重述對方的意思，藉此提出疑問。

⇒ Are you saying...?

你的意思是……？

情境對話

A: If you have a baby, it will be difficult for you to continue your job.

B: *Are you saying* that a married woman should stay home looking after her child all day long?

A：如果你有了小孩，就很難繼續工作了。

B：你的意思是說，結了婚的女人就應該整天在家帶小孩？

(13) 強調那是對方主觀的看法。

⇒ That's what you think.

那是你個人的看法。

情境對話

A: Professor Wilson is not very approachable. I think he is an authoritarian.

B: *That's what you think.* The fact is that he is willing to talk to students. You will find him quite friendly if you get acquainted with him.

A：威爾森教授不太好相處，我覺得他很獨裁。

B：那是你個人的想法。事實上他很願意和學生討論，如果你和他熟了，會發現他其實很親切。

03

第 3 章
指出錯誤

溝通討論時，進攻和防守是一體
的兩面。進攻的重點在於指出對
方論點上的錯誤，懂得運用第 2
章的反對與本章的指出錯誤的句
型，就學會進攻的基本功了。

Useful English Expressions
for Communication

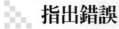 **指出錯誤** ◉MP3 026

■ 你錯了。

1. You're wrong [mistaken].	你錯了。
2. You're wrong [mistaken] in...	關於⋯⋯你是錯的。
3. You're wrong to... [to have...]	⋯⋯是錯的。
4. I'm afraid you've got it wrong.	你恐怕搞錯了。
5. You're completely mistaken!	你完全弄錯了！
6. You've missed the point (of...).	你沒有抓到（⋯⋯的）重點。
7. It's misleading to...	⋯⋯會讓人產生誤解。
8. Your ... is far from the truth.	你的⋯⋯跟事實相去甚遠。

■ 句型解說

1. 簡略的說法。如果要表示對方錯得離譜，可以在 mistaken 前面加上副詞 badly（非常）。

- *If you think you'll change my mind by threatening me, you're badly wrong.*
  如果你以為威脅我就能讓我改變心意，那你就大錯特錯了。

2. 例如：

- *You are wrong in* saying [thinking]...
  你⋯⋯的說法〔想法〕是錯的。

- *You are wrong in* the assertion you made on...
  你主張的⋯⋯是錯的。

3. 例如：

- *You're wrong to have* said that at the meeting.
  你不該在會議上說那些話的。

8. 例如：

* *Your* account *is far from the truth.*
  你的說明和事實相去甚遠。

■ 重點提示

　　上述句型只是用來告訴對方做錯了，沒有著重在細節部分。如果要指出哪裡錯了，請參考下一個句型。

■ 具體指出錯誤為何　　　　　　　　　● MP3 027

■ ……是錯的。

1. The mistake that you've made is in...　　你犯的錯誤是在……。

2. That's where you're wrong.　　那就是你錯的地方。

■ 句型解說

---

1. in 後面要接動名詞，例如 in thinking that...（想……）、in assuming that...（假設……）。

情境對話

A: A computerized system will solve all the problems that we've had.

B: I don't agree. *The mistake that you've made is in overestimating* the capabilities of computers.

A：電腦化系統就能解決我們所有的問題了。

B：我不同意，你的錯誤在於你高估了電腦的功能。

論點有瑕疵

● MP3 028

■ ……的論點有誤。

1. ... doesn't make any sense.	……一點都不合理。
2. The argument that ... is false.	……的論點有誤。
3. That's not a good argument.	那不是很好的論點。
4. The weakness of your argument is...	你論點上的缺陷是……。
5. I'm not (entirely) convinced by your argument.	你的論點沒辦法（完全）說服我。
6. I don't see the relevance of your point.	我看不出你的論點（和討論的內容）有什麼關係。
7. ... cannot be the reason [grounds] for...	……不是……的理由〔根據〕。

■ 句型解說

5. 幾經思考後，還是無法完全認同對方的看法。

6. 認爲對方的論點跟討論主題無關，relevance 是「關聯」的意思。

7. 請看以下對話。

[情境對話]

A: We had an important decision to make, but you weren't in your office yesterday.

B: That *cannot be the grounds for* accusing me of neglecting my duties. I took a day off yesterday, but that was a paid holiday.

A：昨天要進行一項重大的決議，可是你卻沒來上班。

B：不能因此就說我怠忽職守。我昨天雖然休假，但那是特休。

和討論的重點無關

◉MP3 029

■ 那不是重點。

1. That's not the question [problem].	那不是問題所在。
2. That's not the point.	那不是重點。
3. It's not a question [a matter] of...	不是……的問題。
4. ... has nothing [little] to do with...	……和……一點關係也沒有。
5. ... is irrelevant [is not relevant] to...	……和……毫無關聯。
6. That's another matter.	那是另外一個問題了。
7. That's a completely different matter [question].	那是完全不同的問題。
8. The question is not whether...	問題不在於是否……。
9. That shouldn't be a problem.	那不該是問題。
10. ... is not important here.	……不重要。
11. ... is irrelevant here.	跟……毫無關聯。

■ 這和我們的討論內容是兩回事。

12. I'm [We're] here to...	我〔我們〕來這裡的目的是……。
13. (But) We're talking about...	（但）我們正在討論的是……。
14. (But) We're not talking about...	（但）我們並不是在討論……。
15. Just a moment. I never agreed to talk about...	等等，我從沒答應要討論……。

■ ……是另一回事。

| 16. ... is one thing, ... is another. | ……是一回事，……又是另一回事。 |
| 17. But ... is another matter (all together). | 但……（完全）是另一回事。 |

■ 句型解說

1. 指對方的論點並不是問題所在，例如 That's not the question [problem]. The question [problem] is...（那不是問題，問題在於……。）

情境對話

A: I think Mr. Cox is not suitable for the job because he can't speak English.

B: *That's not the question. The question is* whether he is ready to go to a foreign country.

A：我認爲考克斯先生並不適合這個位子，他不會講英文。

B：那不是問題。重點是他是不是做好外派的準備了。

若要提醒對方注意討論的重點，可參考以下說法：

● But please don't forget we are talking about...
　不過別忘了，我們現在討論的是……。

2. 也可以說 That's off [beside] the point.（那不是重點。）

情境對話

A: I think he is suitable for the post.

B: But he is too young.

A: *That's not the point.*

A：我認爲他適合這個位子。

B：但是他太年輕了。

A：那不是重點。

3. 對方的論點並非問題所在，後面可以接著說出眞正的重點爲何。

情境對話　1

A: Don't you think it's the right thing to do?

B: *It's not a question of* right or wrong.

A：你不認爲這樣做是對的嗎？

B：不是對錯的問題。

情境對話 2

A: I have lost confidence in writing the thesis. I think I'm not intelligent enough to complete it.

B: *It's not* really *a matter of* intelligence. It is a matter of patience.

A：我對於寫論文已經失去信心了，我覺得我不夠聰明，沒辦法完成。

B：這其實跟聰不聰明沒關係，重點是耐心。

---

4. 例如：

- That *has nothing to do with* what we're talking about.
  那和我們正在討論的事情一點關係都沒有。

情境對話

A: Poverty is the cause of crime.

B: Poverty *has nothing to do with* crime.

A：犯罪肇因於貧窮。

B：貧窮和犯罪沒有關聯。

也可以用疑問句來反問，例如：

- What's this got to do with our discussion?
  這和我們的討論有什麼關係？

---

5. 例如：

- That *is irrelevant [is not relevant] to* our discussion [main point/the subject].
  那和我們的討論〔重點／主題〕無關。

---

6. 請看以下對話。

情境對話

A: The building needs repairs.

B: What about money? Do you think we can afford the expense?

A: Oh, *that's another matter*.

A：這房子需要整修。

B：錢的問題怎麼辦？你覺得我們負擔得起整修費用嗎？

A：喔，那是另外一回事。

---

7. 對方將兩件事情混爲一談。也可以直接說 Don't mix up the two things.（不要把兩件事混爲一談。）

---

11. 例如：

- Whether you can speak English fluently or not *is irrelevant here*. What is important is whether you have something to say or not.
  你能不能說一口流利的英文不是重點，重點是你是否言之有物。

---

12. 討論的內容和目標不符，也可以用否定形 I'm [We're] not here to...（我〔我們〕來這裡不是要……。）

情境對話 1

A: The management is to blame for our financial difficulties.

B: *We're here to* negotiate an end to the strike, and not to quarrel about the responsibility for the difficulties we are facing now.

A：之所以會發生財務困難，管理階層要負全責。

B：我們來這裡的目的是要商討如何結束罷工，不是來爭論財務困難的責任歸屬問題。

情境對話 2

A: Don't you think Shakespeare was prejudiced against women?

B: Well, *I'm not here to* talk about Shakespeare's attitude towards women.

A：你不覺得莎士比亞對女性有偏見嗎？

B：嗯，我來這裡不是要討論莎士比亞對女性的態度爲何。

13, 14. 指出話題已經偏離主題。

情境對話

A: ... But isn't the pilot to be called into question for causing the passengers' injuries?

B: Just a moment. *We are not talking about* his responsibility. *We are* now *talking about* compensation for the injured passengers.

A：……不過，難道乘客受傷機長不用負責嗎？

B：請等一等。我們現在不是在討論他的責任問題，而是受傷乘客的賠償問題。

---

15. 對方單方面地將事情導向對自己有利的說法，因而必須適時中斷討論時使用。

情境對話

A: So, what about Section Five? Are there any questions about that?

B: *Just a moment. I never agreed to talk about* Section Five at this meeting; and besides, we've not finished Section Four yet.

A：那麼第五項呢？有什麼問題嗎？

B：等一等，我從沒答應這次開會要討論第五項，而且，第四項都還沒討論完呢。

---

16. another 指的是「另一回事」。

情境對話

A: I'm going to vote for Mr. Walton. He is a man of good character.

B: His character *is one thing*, but his political ability *is another*.

A：我打算投給華頓先生，他的品格操守沒話講。

B：品格操守好是一回事，但有沒有從政能力又是另外一回事。

---

17. 請看以下對話。

情境對話

A: You ought to go to the United States if you want to study American literature.

B: I wish I could, but I can't afford to.

A: *But* whether you can afford it *is another matter*. For instance, you could borrow some money from the bank.

A：想研究美國文學的話，你應該去美國。

B：我是想去，但我負擔不起。

A：能不能負擔得起學費是另一回事，比方說你可以跟銀行貸款。

■ **重點提示**

　　對方提出跟話題無關的論點，或將兩件事情混為一談時，就可以利用這部分的句型。

離題或答非所問

⬤MP3 030

■ 你離題了。

1. You are straying from the point.	你偏離重點了。
2. You're wandering from [off] the point.	你偏離重點了。

■ 請說重點。

3. So, what's your [the] point?	所以，你的重點是？
4. Will you come to the point?	可以講重點嗎？

■ 請不要迴避問題。

5. Would you answer my question?	可以回答我的問題嗎？
6. Please give me a direct [straight] answer.	請直接回答我的問題。
7. You haven't...	你還沒有⋯⋯。

◼ 句型解說

----

1. stray from... 的意思是「偏離⋯」。整句話也可以用現在完成式 You have strayed from the point.（你已偏離主題了。）另外，請對方不要離題可以說 Please don't stray from the point.（請不要離題。）除了 the point 之外，stray from 後面還可以接 the main point（重點）、what we were talking about（我們的討論內容）、our discussion（我們的討論）、the main point of our discussion（討論的重點）等等。

----

2. wander from... 也是「偏離⋯」的意思。

----

4. 使用 Could you...? 較爲婉轉，如果強烈要求對方說出重點，用祈使句 Come to the point.（講重點。）更能達到效果。

----

5. 對方遲遲不肯答覆時使用，也可以說 My question was...（我的問題是……。），
重複一次問題。

情境對話

A: Where were you when the fire broke out?

B: I saw a man running out of the building. He jumped in his car and...

A: Mr. Chen, *would you answer my question?* Where were you when the fire
broke out?

A：發生火災的時候你在哪裡？

B：我看見一個男的從大樓衝出來，跳進他的車子裡，然後……。

A：陳先生，你可以回答我的問題嗎？火災發生的時候你人在哪裡？

除了 Would you answer my question? ，也可以使用以下的表達法：

• You didn't answer my question properly.
  你沒有好好回答我的問題。

• You didn't answer the question of...
  你沒回答關於……的問題。

• You still haven't answered my question.
  你還是沒有回答我的問題。

還有更強硬的說法：

• Stop evading my question [the issue].
  不要逃避我的問題〔這個議題〕。

- -

7. 還有許多延伸的用法，用來表達對方尚未達成某個要求，例如：

• *You haven't* clearly stated your opinion on...
  你還沒說清楚你對於……的意見。

• *You haven't* shown...
  你還沒表示……。

• *You haven't* given me your reason for...
  你還沒告訴我……的理由。

• *You haven't* explained...
  你還沒解釋……。

- -

■ 重點提示

上述的句型用來指出對方已經離題或答非所問，另外主詞也可以用第一人稱的 We，提醒自己和其他參與討論的人已偏離主題。

- We've strayed from the main point. Let's get back to what we're talking about.

  我們已經偏離重點了，讓我們回到主題吧。

◆▲ 論點無確切根據　　　　　　　　　　　◉MP3 031

■ 這項論點不夠充分。

1. There is not much point in...	……沒什麼意義。
2. But it's hard to see...	但是很難理解……。
3. ... is not enough.	……還不夠充分。
4. The assumption that ... is wholly without foundation.	……的推論毫無根據。
5. Your opinion is based on the assumption that...	你的看法是根據……的推論而來。
6. You can't assume that ... just because...	你不能只是因為……就假設……。
7. But nobody knows...	但是沒人知道……。

■ 句型解說

- -

2. 請看以下對話。

　情境對話

A: The man killed the shop assistant for money.

B: *But it's hard to see* why he killed her for such a small sum.

A：那個男人爲了錢而殺害店員。

B：但很難理解他爲什麼會爲了這麼一點點錢把她殺了。

---

3. 對方所提的事項（證據或數據等等）不足以支持某個論點。

情境對話

A: The statistics for the last five years clearly show that the educational standard of high school students is going down.

B: But just giving the figures of the last five years *is not enough*. You need to provide more data.

A：過去五年的統計結果清楚顯示，中學生的教育程度一直走下坡。

B：但是只有五年的數據並不足以代表什麼，你必須提供更多數據才行。

---

6. 請看以下對話。

情境對話

A: The computer isn't working. It must be broken. I'll have to send it back.

B: *You can't assume that* it's broken *just because* it isn't working. The trouble must be with the software. You should check the operating system.

A：電腦動也不動，一定是壞了，得送回去維修才行。

B：不能只是因爲無法運作就認定它壞了。我想問題一定出在軟體上，你應該檢查一下作業系統。

---

7. 對方不能一口咬定未知或無法肯定的情況。

情境對話

A: I think Anthony Trollope's main concern was money.

B: *But nobody* really *knows* what was in his mind then.

A：我認爲安東尼‧特洛勒普的主要考量是錢。

B：不過沒人眞的知道他在想些什麼。

類似的說法還有：

• No one can tell what [why]...
   沒人知道是什麼〔爲什麼〕……。

• How would you know?
   你怎麼知道？

● How can you say that?
　你怎能確定？

■ 重點提示

　　認同對方提出的所有根據，等於同意最後的結論。因此，討論過程中有必要進一步確認對方是以什麼樣的根據來支持其論點，並指出不足之處，包括證據或理由不夠充分等情況，這時候就可以使用上述句型。

▨ 扭曲事實　　　　　　　　　　　● MP3 032

■ 說……是扭曲事實。

1. You are stretching the point.	你那樣是扭曲事實。
2. That's stretching it a little [a bit].	那樣有點扭曲事實了。
3. To say ... is stretching the point.	說……是扭曲事實。
4. You're carrying it too far.	你說得太過了。

■ 句型解說

1. stretch 原本的意思是「拉長，伸長」，這裡是指「誇大事實，扭曲事實」。

---

2. bit 比 little 口語。You're stretching the truth.（你那樣是扭曲事實。）幾乎等同於 You're telling a lie.（你說謊。），是很嚴重的指控，所以適度使用較委婉的用詞也是很重要的，例如：

● You seem to be stretching the point.
　你好像扭曲了事實。

● You're stretching it a little.
　你講得有點誇張了。

■ 重點提示

上述句型主要在對方做出太多無謂的解釋、企圖掩飾真相時使用。某種程度而言是在指責對方說謊，所以使用時要特別謹慎。

老調重彈 ● MP3 033

■ 又來了！

| 1. There you go again! | 你又來了！ |
| 2. How many times have I heard... | ……我都聽了好幾遍了。 |

■ 句型解說

1, 2. 表示厭倦對方不停重複同樣的說詞。

情境對話

A: But as Professor Peterson says,...

B: *There you go again!* Just stop quoting the professor.

A：但就如彼特森教授所說的，……。

B：你又來了，不要再說教授說什麼了。

說法不合理 ● MP3 034

■ 這說法並不合理。

| 1. It's too much to say [suggest]... | 說是〔建議〕……太不合理了。 |
| 2. It's unreasonable to say... | 說……並不合理。 |

■ 你說的是⋯⋯嗎？

3. What you are in fact saying is that...	你的說法就等於⋯⋯。
4. That's as much as to say...	那就好像在說⋯⋯。
5. Are you saying that...?	你的意思是⋯⋯嗎？
6. If I understand you correctly, you are saying [telling me/suggesting]...	如果我的理解沒錯的話，你的意思是〔你要告訴我的是／你建議〕⋯⋯。

■ 你不能說⋯⋯。

7. You can't say that...	你不能說⋯⋯。

■ 句型解說

1. too much 是指所說的話太過、太不合理了。

情境對話

A: The director is responsible for the accident, so I think he should resign.

B: I agree he is responsible for the accident, but *it's too much to suggest* he should give up his post.

A：所長必須爲這次的意外負責，因此我認爲他應該辭職。

B：我同意他該爲意外負責，但說是要他辭職又太過頭了。

3. 也可以用 effectively（實際上） 替代 in fact。

情境對話

A: I would suggest that we reduce the budget for the project to a maximum of three million dollars.

B: Are you kidding? *What you are in fact saying is that* we shouldn't continue the project any more.

A：我會建議刪減這項計畫的預算，總額以 300 萬美元爲上限。

B：你在開玩笑嗎？你的說法等於計畫不用繼續下去了。

4. 等於 That's as if to say... 或 That's like saying...。

情境對話

A: Japan is playing by unfair rules. You should stop discriminating against imports. Then the U.S. trade deficit will become smaller.

B: Wait a minute! *That's as much as to say* that Japan is solely responsible for your trade deficit. Look at your own economy, and you'll see you can't necessarily blame Japan for the trade imbalance.

A：日本的作法並不公平。你們不該再歧視進口貨品，這樣美國的貿易赤字就會縮小。

B：等等，你這就好像在說日本要為美國的貿易赤字負全責。請看看貴國的經濟狀況，你就會明白貿易不平衡的責任不全在日本身上。

- -

6. 請看以下對話。

情境對話

A: The sources of your information are from documents of minor importance, and I wonder whether they are reliable or not.

B: *If I understand you correctly, you are saying* that my report is not reliable, aren't you?

A：你的資訊是從一些不重要的文件來的，我懷疑那些文件的可信度有多高。

B：如果我的理解沒錯的話，你的意思是說我的報告不可靠就是了？

- -

7. 對某個看法抱持懷疑的態度。相關用法請參考「邏輯錯誤」的句型 (p. 66)。

情境對話

A: I'm going to ask him to give me English lessons. He is an American, and he will make me a fluent English speaker!

B: But *you can't say that* he is a good English teacher just because he was born and raised in America.

A：我要請他教我英文。他是美國人，可以讓我的英文說得很流利！

B：但你不能因為他在美國土生土長，就認定他會教英文。

- -

◼️ 重點提示

發覺對方的言論有不合理之處，必須要求對方解釋時使用，藉機也讓對方了解哪裡出了問題。

言過其實

◼ 太誇張了。

1. That's exaggerating it a little [a bit].	有點言過其實了。
2. That's oversimplifying it.	太簡化了。
3. That's (a bit of) an exaggeration.	（有點）誇大其詞。
4. It's a gross exaggeration (to say...).	（說是……）實在太誇張了。
5. You're exaggerating [oversimplifying] the truth.	你把事實過度渲染〔簡化〕了。
6. To say ... is exaggerating [oversimplifying] the truth.	說是……是誇大〔簡化〕了事實。

◼️ 句型解說

- -

1, 3. a bit (of) 是「稍微」的意思。exaggerating 也可以用 stretching 取代。

情境對話

A: The project was a complete failure. It was a waste of time and money.

B: *That's an exaggeration.* Our loss is small, and we've learned a lot from our failure. We may make a fresh start with a new plan.

A：這個計畫真是徹底失敗，浪費時間也浪費錢。

B：你說得太誇張了。我們的損失不大，也從失敗中學到教訓了。我們可以擬定新的計畫，有個嶄新的開始。

- -

4. gross 是「嚴重的」的意思，用來形容誇大的言論。此外，受到責難時也可以用 gross 來凸顯自己的立場。

情境對話

A: You cheated me.

B: Cheated? *That's a gross exaggeration.*

A：你欺騙我。

B：欺騙？說是欺騙也太誇張了。

5, 6. oversimplify 是將複雜的情況過於簡單化，忽略了該思考的重點。句型 6 的 to say 後面接被渲染或簡化的事情。

情境對話

A: In his later years, Walter Scott wrote novels for money.

B: Just a moment. *To say* he wrote only for money *is exaggerating the truth.*
The fact is that he went bankrupt because the firm in which he was a partner collapsed, and he was obliged to work hard to pay his debts.

A：到了晚年，華特‧史考特是看在錢的份上寫小說的。

B：等等。說他只爲了錢而寫作未免太誇張了。其實是因爲他和人合開的公司倒閉，他破產了，不得不努力工作賺錢還債。

▌重點提示

　　上述句型主要用來指出對方的言論過於誇大，或與事實相去甚遠。這樣的表現方式其實有指控他人說謊的意味，使用時要特別注意，可視情況加入 I think...,
a little, a bit 等等來緩和語氣。

▒▒ 說詞矛盾　　　　　　　　　　　　　　　⦿MP3 036

■ 你不是說過……？

1. But you said [told me]..., didn't you?　　但你說〔跟我說〕……，不是嗎？

2. But I thought you said [agreed]...　　　但我以為你說〔同意〕……。

3. But you didn't say [tell me]..., did you?　但你沒說〔沒告訴我〕……，
　　　　　　　　　　　　　　　　　　　　　不是嗎？

4. But you ... yourself.　　　　　　　　　但你自己不也……。

■ 句型解說

1. 直接以反問的方式指出對方的矛盾之處，後面接附加問句語氣更強。

情境對話

A: The investigation will continue into the evening.

B: *But you said* I could go home soon, *didn't you?*

A：調查會持續到晚上。

B：但你說過我很快就可以回家的，不是嗎？

只要稍加變化，這個句型也可以用在對方的論點前後不一的情況，例如 But you said earlier that...（可是你剛剛說……。）

2. 加入 I thought 之後，句子的語氣比較和緩。

情境對話

A: I don't think it's a good idea to invest so much money in the venture.

B: *But I thought you agreed* at the last meeting that it was a promising new business.

A：我不認為在那項事業上投入那麼多資金是個好主意。

B：但我以為上次開會時你也認同那是個有前景的事業。

3. 除了 say 和 tell，也可以接 explain（解釋）、oppose（反對）、mention（提及）等動詞。

情境對話　1

A: You shouldn't have increased the dose without my consent. You are now suffering from the side effects.

B: *But you didn't explain to me* exactly what the side effects of the drug would be.

A：你不應該沒經過我的允許就擅自增加藥量，你看現在就出現副作用了。

B：但是你沒有告訴我這藥到底會有哪些副作用啊。

直接用疑問句 But didn't you say...?（但你不是說……？）的語氣沒有直述句加上附加問句來得強。

情境對話 2

A: The investigation will continue into the evening.

B: *But didn't you say* I could go home soon?

A：調查會持續到晚上。

B：但你不是說我很快就可以回家嗎？

---

4. 指出對方的言行不一致。

情境對話

A: Why did you agree to join this meaningless project?

B: *But you* are involved in it as a financial adviser *yourself*.

A：為什麼你會答應參加這個毫無意義的企劃？

B：你自己還不是以財務顧問的名義加入了。

■ **重點提示**

表示對方言行不一，前後矛盾時使用。

▓ 證據不足　　　　　　　　　　　　　◉MP3 037

■ **你能證明嗎？**

1. Can you prove that [that...]?　　　　你能證明〔……〕嗎？

2. There isn't enough evidence to prove [show/support]...　　　沒有足夠的證據可以證明〔顯示／支持〕……。

3. But you haven't offered any figures [data] to prove [show/support]... | 但是你沒有提出任何數據〔資料〕來證明〔顯示／支持〕……。

4. But you haven't looked into it in enough detail to say that... | 但是你看得不夠深入、不能說……。

5. (I'm afraid) Your data is unsatisfactory. | 你的資料（恐怕）不足以令人信服。

■ 句型解說

1. 語氣非常強硬，言下之意是不相信對方能拿出什麼證據。

- *Can you prove that* I'm wrong?
  你能證明我哪裡錯了嗎？

情境對話

A: I have no doubt that Napoleon was killed with poison.

B: But *can you prove that?*

A：拿破崙絕對是被人下藥毒死的。

B：你能證明嗎？

 邏輯錯誤   ● MP3 038

■ 你不能斷定……。

1. You can't conclude from ... that... | 你不能從……就斷定……。

2. Just because..., it doesn't follow that... | 只是因為……，不表示……。

3. You can't say that ... (just) because... | 你不能（只是）因為……就說……。

4. How can you say [conclude] that...? | 你憑什麼說〔斷定〕……？

■ 未必如此。

5. That's not necessarily the case.　　　　未必是那樣。

■ **句型解說**

1. 請看以下對話。

情境對話 1

A: Our statistics show that sales of the old model have been decreasing over the last few months, so I think it's now time to replace it with a new one.

B: But *you can't conclude from* short-term research *that* the model is out of date.

A：我們的統計資料顯示，過去幾個月來舊款的銷售量持續下降。因此我認為該是改款的時候了。

B：但你不能只以短期的調查數字就斷定舊的款式已經退流行了。

如果要指出對方太快下結論，有以下兩種說法。

- You seem to have jumped to a conclusion.
  你好像太快下結論了。

- Don't jump to conclusions.
  別那麼快下結論。

情境對話 2

A: I see your point, and I agree that we should cancel the plan...

B: Just a moment. *Don't jump to conclusions*. I didn't say we should cancel the plan.

A：我了解你要說的了，我也同意應該取消這項計畫……。

B：等等，別那麼快下結論，我沒有說要取消這項計畫。

2. it follows that... 意思是「（由某件事來推斷）結果當然是……」。

情境對話

A: I think the Finance Minister is to blame for the recession because the economy began to decline when he came into office.

B: That's not true. *Just because* someone is in office when something happens, *it doesn't follow that* he is the cause of it.

A：我認為會不景氣都要怪財政部長。他就任之後，經濟就開始衰退了。

B：話不能這樣說。不能因為某個問題發生在某人在職期間，就說是他造成的。

- -

3. 例如：

- *You can't say that* the gas is harmless *just because* it is odorless.
  不能因為瓦斯無臭無味就說它無害。

- -

4. 請看以下對話。

情境對話

A: John doesn't seem to fit the position. He is too young.

B: *How can you say* he isn't suitable simply because he is young?

A：約翰似乎不太適合那個位子，他太年輕了。

B：怎麼可以只是因為他年紀輕就說他不適合？

- -

5. 請看以下對話。

情境對話

A: If the government charges less income tax, the consumers will have more purchasing power.

B: No, *that's not necessarily the case*, especially in such a difficult economic situation as this.

A：如果政府少收一點所得稅，消費者的購買力就會提高。

B：不見得，尤其現在景氣這麼差。

- -

■ 重點提示

不贊同對方的意見時，光說「我不贊成」、「你的看法是錯」不夠具體，如果反對的原因是出自對方的邏輯有誤，這時便可以利用上述句型明確指出問題所在。

說明不夠充分　　　　　　　　　　　　⦿MP3 039

■ 說明不夠充分。

1. That cannot be the explanation.	原因不可能是那樣。
2. Saying that ... is not enough.	只提出……是不夠的。
3. I'm not satisfied with your explanation.	我不滿意你的解釋。
4. I'm not convinced (by your...).	（你的……）沒辦法說服我。
5. That doesn't make sense to me.	那在我看來說不通。

■ 句型解說

1. 請看以下對話。

情境對話

A: It's because Paris was the city of art that so many artists gathered there from all over the world.

B: It's the other way round. It's because artists gathered there that it became the city of art.

A: But *that cannot be the explanation*. Why did they gather there, then? That's the question.

A：正因為巴黎是藝術之都，才會有那麼多來自世界各地的藝術家聚集。

B：正好相反。正因為藝術家聚集，巴黎才會變成藝術之都。

A：但原因不可能是那樣。為什麼藝術家會聚在巴黎呢？那才是問題所在。

4. 無法接受對方的說明或論點，例如：

• *I'm not convinced by your* argument [explanation].
你的論點〔解釋〕沒辦法說服我。

5. 表示他人的論點看似有理，但自己卻無法接受。

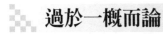

過於一概而論

●MP3 040

■ 不能一概而論。

1. You can't generalize (too much) about...	對……你不能一概而論。
2. You can't generalize from ... that...	你不能從……就一概而論認為是……。
3. It's a big [hasty] generalization.	這麼說太廣泛了。
4. I don't see [understand] why you generalize so much about that.	我不懂〔不能理解〕為什麼你要整個一概而論。

句型解說

1, 2. generalize 的前面也可以改成 I wonder if you can（我不曉得你可不可以）、I don't think you can（我不覺得你可以）和 I don't understand why you（我不了解為什麼你），讓語氣更為婉轉。

• *You can't generalize about* the Tokyo accent from the way people in Tokyo talk because most of them come from different parts of Japan.
  你不能一概而論說住東京的人說的話就是東京腔，因為大部分的東京人來自日本各地。

情境對話

A: The Japanese are all shy; they never express their feelings openly.

B: Well, *you can't generalize too much about* that.

A：日本人都很害羞，從不直接表達出他們的感受。

B：是嗎，也不能一概而論吧。

本句型用不同的例子來反證一般的看法，類似 But some ... are not...（但有些……不是……。），請參考第 9 章「指出例外」的句型 (p. 259)。

意見沒有幫助 ⦿MP3 041

■ ……是沒用的。

1. It [just] won't do.	行不通的。
2. ... is no good. [It's no good...]	……是沒用的。
3. It's meaningless [useless] to...	……是沒有意義的〔沒用的〕。

■句型解說

1. 表示某件事情毫無幫助、無法達成目的，也可以說成 That/This won't do.（那樣 / 這樣是行不通的。）

情境對話

A: Is two thousand dollars enough to repair the damage?

B: No, *that won't do*. I need more.

A：兩千塊美金夠不夠你付修理的費用？

B：不，不夠，我需要更多。

2. 表示某個嘗試或想法沒有用處。

● That idea *is no good*.
　這個主意行不通。

● *It's no good* trying to explain it to him. He will never listen.
　跟他解釋也沒用，他不會聽的。

行動或發言不適切 ⦿MP3 042

■ ……不適合 / 不方便。

1. ... is not suitable [proper/appropriate] 　(for/to...).	……不適合〔不適當 / 不恰當〕。

2. ... is not a suitable [proper/appropriate] ... (for/to...)	……不是個適合的〔適當的 / 恰當的〕……。
3. ... is inconvenient [is not convenient] for...	……對……來說不方便。
4. ... is the wrong... (for/to...).	……不適合……。
5. ... is not enough [sufficient] (for...).	……不足以……。
6. ... is too ... for...	……對……來說過於……。

■ 句型解說

2. 例如：

- This *is not a proper* time *for* joking.
  現在可不是開玩笑的時候。

還有 That's not the suitable [proper] way to...（……不是適當的方式。）、This is not the appropriate occasion to...（……不是個恰當的場合。）等說法。

情境對話

A: Shall we visit him in his office?

B: *That's not the proper way to* approach a man of that status. It's important to phone his secretary first to make an appointment to see him.

A：我們可以到辦公室拜訪他嗎？

B：以他的身分地位來說可能不太適合。請先和他的祕書聯絡，安排見面的時間。

3. 請看以下對話。

情境對話

A: The computers in the language learning room aren't linked to the Information Processing Center.

B: That*'s inconvenient.*

A：語言訓練教室的電腦無法和資訊中心連線。

B：那就很不方便了。

4. wrong 在這裡指的是「不適合」或「與目的不符」。

- I think he *is the wrong* man *for* the post. He knows nothing about that job.
  我認為他不適合這個位子，他對工作內容一無所知。

5. 對方未能達到預期水準，或沒有完成必要的項目時，向對方表達不滿的態度。

- Just writing to him *is not enough*. You must meet him in person.
  光是寫信給他還不夠，你必須親自見他一面。

6. 和句型 5 相反，形容某個行為太過，造成不好的結果。

情境對話

A: We'll have to send someone to negotiate with the dealer.

B: Mr. Hughes *is too* shy *for* that kind of job.

A：我們必須派人去和業者交涉。

B：休斯先生太內向了，不適合去交涉。

也可以用 carry ... too far 來表示「做得太過」，例如：

- You *carried* your joke *too far*. Miss Allen was offended.
  你玩笑開過頭了，愛倫小姐生氣了。

數據或資料有誤　◉MP3 043

■ 你說的和事實不符。

1. You said..., but in fact...	你說……，但事實上是……。
2. I question the truth of...	我質疑……的真實性。

■ 數據有誤。

3. The figure is wrong [inaccurate].	這項數據有誤〔不正確〕。
4. I dispute the figure.	這個數字有問題。

> **5. I'm not sure if the figure is correct.**　我不確定這數字對不對。
> 　　**[Are you sure of the figure?]**　　〔你確定這數字沒錯嗎？〕

■句型解說

1. in fact 用來提示正確的事實。

- *You said* he is a fluent speaker of English, *but in fact* he isn't. I met him yesterday. He couldn't say any more than "hi" and "thank you."
  你說他英文很溜，其實沒有。我昨天和他碰面，他只會說「你好」跟「謝謝」。

情境對話

A: *You said* Abraham Lincoln was the seventeenth President of the United States. I checked it, and he was *in fact* the sixteenth.

B: I'm terribly sorry. I was mistaken.

A：你說亞伯拉罕‧林肯是美國第十七任總統。我查過了，他其實是第十六任。

B：真的很抱歉，我記錯了。

2. question 當動詞用，意思是「質疑」。

4. dispute 是「質疑」的意思。

5. 無法確定對方舉出的數字正不正確，某種程度上這個句型也是一種委婉的說法。

情境對話

A: Thirty-five percent of our students read five to ten books a month; seven percent of them read more than ten.

B: *Are you sure of the figures?*

A：本校學生有 35% 平均一個月讀 5 到 10 本書，其中有 7% 的學生讀 10 本以上。

B：這項數據正確嗎？

■ 重點提示

指出對方陳述的內容有誤時使用。沒有人希望被質疑或指責，所以學會以下委婉的表達方式也很重要。

- May I point out that...?
  容我指出……。
- I'm afraid [Unfortunately] your ... is not correct.
  抱歉，您的……恐怕不正確。

例如：

- You referred to Winston Churchill as having received the Nobel Peace Prize. But *may I point out that* in fact he received the Nobel Prize in literature?
  你說溫斯頓‧邱吉爾曾獲頒諾貝爾和平獎，但請容我說一句，他得到的其實是諾貝爾文學獎。
- It would be perfectly all right if the figure you gave me were correct, but *I'm afraid it's not.*
  如果你給我的數據是對的，那就完全沒有問題，但數據恐怕是不對的。

▦ 資料的正確性令人懷疑　　　　◉ MP3 044

■ 這個數字有點問題。

1. ... don't seem reliable.	……感覺不太可靠。
2. I doubt the reliability of...	我懷疑……的可信度。
3. I have some reservations about (the truth of)...	我對……（的真實性）有所保留。

■ 句型解說

1. 類似的用法如下：

- I wonder how reliable the figures are.
  我懷疑這數字的可信度。

- The figures are not reliable.
  這項數據不太可靠。

3. 猶豫該不該相信。

- *I have some reservations about* the sources.
  我對資料的來源有所保留。

■ 重點提示

　　對他人提出的數據 (data)、數字 (figure)、證據 (evidence)、資料來源 (source of information) 有所懷疑時使用。在這裡，委婉地說會比斷然否定來得妥當，可以用 seem（似乎）或 I wonder if...（我不知道是否……。）

▓ 違反規定　　　　　　　　　　　　　　　● MP3 045

■ ……違反規定。

1. It's against the rules [the terms of our agreement] to...	……違反了規定〔我們的協議〕。
2. It's illegal [against the law] to...	……是違法的。
3. It's not normal (here/in this country) to...	（在這裡／在這個國家），……並非常態。
4. It's against etiquette to...	……有失禮節。

句型解說

2. against the law 和 illegal 意思相同。

- *It's illegal* for citizens *to* have guns in Taiwan.
  在台灣，一般人持有槍械是違法行為。

3. 表示某個行為、標準或習慣在某些場合或國家並非常態，normal 是「正常的，常態的」的意思。

- *It's not normal in* Japan *to* address one's seniors by their first names.
  在日本，通常不會直呼長輩的名字。

4. etiquette 是「日常生活中的禮節和規矩」，medical etiquette 是「醫界的規矩」，diplomatic etiquette 則是「外交禮節」。

04

第4章
責備

沒有人喜歡責備他人，但如果討論時牽涉到利害關係卻沒有妥善處理，除了可能造成自身權益受損，甚至還得承擔所有後果。因此，適時指出對方的責任或過失是非常重要的。雖說是責備，但說話的方式和語氣也得恰到好處才能達到效果。本章將介紹各種場合都用得到的句型。

責任歸屬

◉ MP3 046

■ 那是你的錯。

1. That's your fault.	那是你的錯。
2. You are to blame.	都要怪你。
3. That's your fault, and not mine.	錯不在我，在你。

句型解說

1. 責備他人的最常見的用法。

情境對話

A: Twenty-five dollars, please.

B: It can't be twenty-five!

A: Look at the meter. It shows twenty-five dollars.

B: But you took the wrong way, and drove me around the streets for a few extra miles. *That's your fault.*

A：總共 25 塊美金。

B：怎麼可能是 25 塊！

A：你自己看一下計費表，上面顯示 25 塊。

B：但是你走錯路，繞了好幾圈、多跑了好幾哩，那是你的錯。

類似的說法還有 It's your fault that...（⋯⋯是你的錯。）、It's your inability to...（是因為你無法⋯⋯。）。另外，為了加強語氣，也可以在具體的內容後面加上 Don't say you didn't！（別說你沒有！）。

• You opened my mail. *Don't say you didn't!*
  你拆了我的信，別說你沒有！

2. 如果要指出要對方負責的內容，可以說 You are to blame for...（你應該對⋯⋯負責。）

情境對話

A: I'm sorry that the boy got injured, but it's not our fault.

B: *You are to blame for* the accident because you failed to set up a warning sign by the deep pit.

A：我對那個小男生受傷的事情感到遺憾，但錯不在我們。

B：你們應該要為這件意外負責，因為你們沒有在凹洞旁邊設立警告標誌。

重點提示

　　討論過程中，劃清責任歸屬十分重要。有的人比較客氣，儘管錯在他人，似乎已經習慣先道歉再說。還是表明責任歸屬比較妥當，這時便可以使用上述句型。

行為不合常理　　　　⦿MP3 047

■ ……的意義何在？

1. Why do [did] you...?	你為什麼要……？
2. What's the point of (doing)...?	（做）……的目的何在？
3. What do you mean by (doing)...?	你（做）……是什麼意思？

句型解說

1. Why...?（為什麼……？）是單純詢問原因的問句，但在以下例句中帶有責備意味。

• *Why do you* put so much emphasis on Japan's trade surplus? There are many other issues to be discussed here.

　你為什麼一直強調日本的貿易順差？明明還有很多其他的議題要討論。

2. 例如：

- *What's the point of taking* such a long holiday at the busiest time of the year?
  為什麼要在一年當中最忙的時候請這麼長的假？

---

3. 除了用來表示無法理解對方的想法或做法，進而要求對方進一步說明之外，也可以表達出說話者的不滿。

- *What do you mean by making* such an offensive remark at the press conference?
  你在記者會上那些讓人不悅的發言是怎麼一回事？

情境對話

A: We have to charge you an extra ten dollars.

B: What! An extra ten dollars! *What* on earth *do you mean?*

A：我們要跟您多收 10 塊美金。

B：什麼！多收 10 塊美金？你到底什麼意思啊？

■ 重點提示

上述句型可用於兩種情境，一是詢問對方行為的動機，一是質疑討論的重點。適度運用以上句型，便可達到責備的效果。

沒有做該做的事　　　　　● MP3 048

■ 你應該要⋯⋯，不是嗎？

1. You should [shouldn't] have...	你應該〔不該〕⋯⋯。
2. Why did [didn't] you...?	你為什麼〔為什麼不〕⋯⋯？
3. You failed to...	你沒能⋯⋯。
4. Didn't [Haven't] you...?	你沒有⋯⋯嗎？
5. You might (have)...	你應該⋯⋯。
6. I wish you...	希望你⋯⋯。

7. It's unkind [unreasonable] of you to...   你……（的行為）很不客氣〔不合理〕。

8. I'm surprised you (don't/didn't)...   我很訝異你（沒有）……。

9. I hardly expected to [that]...   我沒有想到……。

■ 句型解說

1. 指出對方該做卻沒有做（或不該做卻做了）某事。表示過去應該做或不該做某事時，可以用〈should [shouldn't] have + 過去分詞〉表示。

情境對話

A: Sorry I'm late. My flight was delayed. It's a pity I couldn't attend the conference.

B: Being late is all right, but *you should have* phoned us to let us know you were delayed.

A：對不起我遲到了，因為飛機誤點。很遺憾沒能出席會議。

B：遲到就算了，但你至少也該打通電話，告訴我們飛機誤點才是。

2. 乍看之下是問句，但真正目的並不在要求對方回答。

情境對話

A: I pressed the button and the machine suddenly stopped!

B: What? *Why did you* touch the red button? You shouldn't have done that.

A: But you didn't tell me I shouldn't.

A：我按下按鈕，結果機器突然停了！

B：什麼？為什麼要碰那個紅色按鈕？你不該那麼做的。

A：但你又沒說不可以按。

3. fail to... 是指該做的沒有做到，其他說法還有 But you didn't..., did you?（你沒有……，對吧？）、But did you...?（不過你是不是……？）（請參考句型 2 的例句）。

4. 請看以下對話。

情境對話

A: Why didn't you tell me that the money was not refundable?

B: *Haven't you* read the contract? Everything is written there.

A：之前爲什麼不告訴我錢是不能退的？

B：你沒有看合約嗎？上面寫得清清楚楚。

---

5. 指責對方該辦到卻沒有辦到，帶有焦慮及遺憾的意味。

情境對話

A: I've been trying very hard to turn the machine on, but it still isn't working.

B: Oh, didn't you know? It is broken. I was just going to have it repaired.

A: *You might have* told me that earlier.

A：我想盡方法打開電源，但這機器還是動也不動。

B：喔，你不知道嗎？這機器壞了，我正準備把它送去修理。

A：你好歹可以早點告訴我吧。

---

6. 希望對方已經做了某件事（但實際上對方還沒做），或沒做某件事（但對方已經做了），帶有指責的意味。如果和現在事實相反，that 子句的時態用過去式，如果和過去事實相反，that 子句用過去完成式。

情境對話

A: I'm looking for the copy of *Time* magazine. It was definitely on my desk last night.

B: Oh, I threw it away.

A: You threw it away! *I wish you* hadn't.

A：我在找一本《時代雜誌》，昨天晚上明明還在我桌上的呀。

B：喔，我把它丟了。

A：你把它丟了？你若沒丟就好了。

---

7. 除了 unreasonable，還可以用其他的形容詞來描述對方的行爲。

- *It's irresponsible of you to* sell computers but refuse to provide technical support.
  你販賣電腦卻不提供技術支援，這樣的行爲很不負責任。

---

8. 對於他人的行為感到意外，並婉轉指責。

　　情境對話

　A: Why didn't you tell me the software doesn't run on my computer?

　B: The instructions on the package tell you all about the compatibility. *I'm surprised you didn't* notice them.

　A：你怎麼沒告訴我這個軟體沒辦法在我的電腦上運作？

　B：關於軟體相容性，包裝上的說明寫得清清楚楚。我很訝異你居然沒有注意到。

---

9. 和期待有所落差。

　　情境對話

　A: *I hardly expected to* find so many mistakes in your typing.

　B: I'm terribly sorry. Let me try again.

　A：我沒有想到你的打字會錯誤百出。

　B：實在很抱歉，請再給我一次機會。

■ 重點提示

　　指出錯誤之處，同時傳達責備的語氣時使用。另外，多數句型使用了「設問法」(rhetorical question)，這是一種帶有詢問口氣但不需要或不期待對方回答的說話方式。這部分句型可以和「責任歸屬」(p. 80) 的 That's your fault. 或 You are to blame. 搭配使用。

無視自己的建議　　　　　　　●MP3 049

■ 就跟你說了吧！

1. I told you (that)!	我就說了吧！
2. I told you that...	早告訴你……。
3. I told you to..., didn't I?	不是跟你說了要……？
4. Didn't I tell you?	我不是跟你說了嗎？

■ 句型解說

1. 非常口語的說法，常見於家人、熟識的朋友之間的對話。

> 情境對話

A: I went to the shop yesterday, but it was closed.

B: The shop is closed on Wednesdays. *I already told you that!*

A：我昨天去了那家店，結果沒開。

B：那家店每週三都休息啊，我早跟你說了。

---

2. 請看以下對話。

> 情境對話

A: Here is the report.

B: *I told you* it must be in by Friday! Why is it so late?

A：這是我的報告。

B：我不是告訴你最慢禮拜五要交，為什麼拖了這麼久？

* be in 是「繳交」的意思。

---

3. 指責他人沒能做到你所交代的事情。tell ... to... 是「叫⋯去做⋯」的意思，「叫⋯不要做⋯」則是 tell ... not to...。

> 情境對話

A: I pressed the button and then the machine suddenly stopped!

B: What? *I told you not to* touch the red button!

A：我按下按鈕，機器突然就停了！

B：什麼？我不是跟你說過不要碰那個紅色按鈕嗎！

---

4. 和句型 1 一樣是很口語的用法，非常直接。

> 情境對話

A: The cost for the sightseeing tour will be added to your hotel bill.

B: *Didn't I tell you* I wanted to cancel the tour?

A: No, you didn't.

B: Yes, I did.

A：觀光的費用會加到你的飯店帳單裡。

B：我不是跟你說要我取消這項行程嗎？

A：你沒有說。

B：有，我有說。

■ 重點提示

　　明明已經告訴對方應該怎麼做或不該做什麼，但對方卻忘得一乾二淨，完全沒放在心上，這個時候就可以用上述句型來表達你的不滿。由於語氣頗為直接，除非真的很生氣，不然多半用於家人或熟識的朋友之間。如果要緩和語氣，I thought I told you about that? 是個不錯的說法，意思是「我以為我告訴過你了」，句尾稍稍上揚。

言行讓人遺憾 　　　　　　　　　　◉MP3 050

■ 真遺憾。

1. It's a great pity...	……真是相當遺憾。
2. It's unfortunate that...	……真是令人遺憾。
3. I feel very disappointed that...	我對……感到非常失望。

■ 句型解說

1. 例如：

- *It's a great pity* you talked like that at the meeting. Mr. Johnson was very hurt.
  我很遺憾你在會議上那樣講話，強森先生覺得很受傷。

情境對話

A: Are you going to expel me?

B: Certainly. *It's a great pity* you broke the school rules.

A：我會被退學嗎？

B：當然，很遺憾你違反了校規。

---

2. 這裡的 unfortunate 是「遺憾的」的意思，用來對某些不好的結果表示惋惜。除了不幸的情況，也可間接指責造成該情況的人。

- *It's unfortunate* this had to happen.
  事情演變成這樣令人遺憾。

---

3. 強調結果不如預期，並責備對方。

- *I feel very disappointed that* you were unable to meet our expectations.
  你沒能達到我們的期望，我覺得非常失望。

■ 重點提示

當他人犯下重大過失的時候，比起直接責備，上述間接責難的句型反而較為常見，且這類句型比較能凸顯說話者的情緒。另外，It's unfortunate this had to happen. 也可用在責任歸屬不明確的情況。

▨ 搞不清楚狀況　　　　　　　　　　　◉MP3 051

■ 你不了解……。

1. You are not aware of...	你沒有意識到……。
2. You don't (seem to) realize...	你（似乎）不了解……。
3. You don't (seem to) understand...	你（似乎）不明白……。

▎句型解說

1. 例如：

* *You are not aware of* the importance of learning how to speak polite English.
  你沒有意識到學會說一口優雅的英文有多重要。

aware 後面也可以接連接詞 that 或疑問詞 how, what 等構成的名詞子句。

2. 加上 seem to（似乎）語氣比較委婉。

* *You don't seem to realize* the main concern of the consumers.
  你似乎不了解消費者主要的考量。

3. 例如：

* *You don't understand* the importance of providing the library with a good selection of classical works.
  你不明白提供圖書館豐富的經典作品有多重要。

▎重點提示

交換意見時如果發現對方無法掌握問題的核心，或者搞不清楚狀況，可以使用上述句型，表達責備的態度。

▎和事實有出入　　　◉MP3 052

■ 你說的話和事實不同。

1. You said [told me]..., but in fact...	你曾說〔告訴我〕……，但事實上……。
2. You didn't tell me...	你並沒有告訴我……。
3. I thought you were going to...	我以為你會……。
4. You said something different.	你不是這樣說的。

▉句型解說

1. 請看以下對話。

情境對話

A: *You said* you would complete the report by Friday, *but in fact* you didn't.

B: I'm very sorry. I tried to, but I couldn't.

A：你說你最慢星期五會把報告做完，但你卻沒做到。

B：眞的很抱歉。我盡力了，但還是沒能做完。

2. 指責對方沒有告知某件事。

情境對話

A: You've spent too much money on your research.

B: But *you didn't tell me* exactly how much I could spend.

A：你花了太多錢在研究上。

B：可是你又沒有明確告訴我可以花多少。

3. 表示自己的認知和對方不同，並責備對方未能履行承諾。

情境對話

A: *I thought you were going to* write to me last month.

B: I'm sorry. I was too busy.

A：我以爲你上個月要寫信給我。

B：對不起，我太忙了。

對話第一句後面也可以加上 Why didn't you?（你爲什麼沒寫？），加強責備的語氣。

4. 請看以下對話。

情境對話

A: I want you to pay five thousand dollars as a deposit.

B: But *you said something different* the other day. You said I had only to pay two thousand dollars.

A：請先付五千塊美金的訂金。

B：但你上次不是這樣說的，你說只要先付兩千塊就好。

■ 重點提示

　　上述句型可用在對方說話不算話的情況。除了能釐清自己和他人的認知有何出入之外，也可以用來化解誤會。不過，如果錯在對方，便可利用這些句型達到婉轉責備的效果。

▓ 態度不佳

◉ MP3 053

■ 你怎麼那麼……？

1. Why are you so...?	你為什麼那麼……？
2. Why do you...?	你為什麼會……？
3. How can you be so...?	你怎麼能這麼……？
4. You might...	你應該……。
5. Can't you...?	你難道不能……？
6. You shouldn't ... like that.	你不應該像那樣……。
7. It's unreasonable [unkind/foolish] of you to...	你……（的行為）很不講理〔不客氣／愚蠢〕。

■ 你以為你是誰啊？

8. Who are you to...?	你以為你是誰，憑什麼……？
9. Who [What] do you think you are!	你以為你是誰啊？

■ 如果你以為……，你就錯了！

10. If you think..., you're wrong [mistaken].	如果你以為……，你就錯了！

■ 句型解說

---

1. 類似的說法還有 I don't know why you're so...（我不懂你為什麼那麼……。）

情境對話

A: What bloody nonsense! What the hell do you mean by...?

B: Be quiet! *Why are you so* rude?

A：簡直是胡扯！你到底在想什麼啊？

B：安靜一點！你怎麼那麼沒禮貌？

---

2. 請看以下對話。

情境對話

A: I'm going to invest in automated animal husbandry because Professor Harris says that it's going to be a promising new line of business.

B: *Why do you* always quote the professor as a reliable source of information?

A：我打算投資自動化管理的畜牧業，因為哈里斯教授說那是極有潛力的新事業。

B：為什麼你對教授的話總是深信不疑呢？

---

3. 請看以下對話。

情境對話

A: There is no need to worry. Things will improve.

B: *How can you be so* optimistic?

A：沒有什麼好擔心的，事情會好轉的。

B：你怎麼能這麼樂觀？

---

4. 用助動詞 might 婉轉請求或責備對方應該要做某事。

- *You might* at least apologize.
  你至少應該道個歉。

- *You might* at least say thank you.
  你好歹說聲謝謝。

---

5. 例如：

- *Can't you* be more cooperative?
  你就不能合作一點嗎？

---

7. 請看以下對話。

情境對話

A: I told him that he should leave here.

B: *It's unreasonable of you to* say that.

A：我跟他說他應該離開這裡。

B：你這麼說有點不講理。

8. 責備對方太過自以爲是。

情境對話

A: You are too young. You can't handle the situation.

B: *Who are you to* tell me I can't?

A：你還太年輕，沒辦法處理這種場面。

B：你以爲你是誰，憑什麼說我處理不了？

9. 除了責備對方自以爲是，也能表現半開玩笑的口氣。另外，Who [What] do you think I am!（你以爲我是誰？）可用來間接表示對方態度有待改善。

情境對話

A: I doubt that you know much about English.

B: *Who do you think I am?* I have been teaching English at high school for thirty years!

A：我懷疑你的英文會有多好。

B：你以爲我是誰？我可是在高中教了 30 年英文！

10. 認爲對方的想法過於天眞。mistaken 前面可以加上副詞 badly（非常）。

- *If you think* you can always impress people by referring to your father, *you're badly mistaken.*

  如果你以爲老是把你爸的名字搬出來就可以讓人對你另眼相看，那你就大錯特錯了。

■ 重點提示

Why do you...? 和 How can you...? 等這類用疑問句構成的句型，不直接挑出個人的態度或性格問題，而用「為什麼……？」的方式，把問題丟回給對方，是一種常見的用法。

把事情看得太簡單　　　　●MP3 054

■ 你說得倒簡單，但是……。

| 1. It's all right (for you) to say that [so], but... | （你）說得倒輕鬆，但是……。 |
| 2. It's easy (for you) to say..., but... | （你）說得倒簡單，但是……。 |

■ 句型解說

----

1. 也可以說 It's all right saying that, but...（可以那樣說，但是……。）

情境對話

A: Just tell the customers we are not responsible for any damage.

B: *It's all right for you to say that, but* have you thought about how hard it will be for us to listen to their complaints?

A：你就告訴客人我們不負責損壞賠償。

B：你說得倒輕鬆，但是你有沒有想過我們接聽客訴電話的難處？

----

2. 類似說法有 It's easy for you to blame...，意思是「要責怪……很容易」。

情境對話

A: Why not invest in the venture?

B: *It's easy to say* that, *but* are you ready to take the risks?

A：投資這項事業怎麼樣？

B：說得簡單，但你做好承擔風險的準備了嗎？

回應對方無理的言論

■ 你到底在說什麼？

1. What do you mean [by...]! 你〔說……〕是什麼意思！

2. How can you say that! 你怎麼能那樣說！

3. How can you say all this, when...? 當……時，你怎能這麼說呢？

4. What are you talking about? 你在說什麼？

5. What are you implying? 你到底想說什麼？

■句型解說

1. What do you mean! 確實如字面上的意思是用來詢問對方的想法。不過，只要稍微改變語調，就可以用來對他人無理的言論做出反應。

情境對話 1

A: You cheated me!

B: *What do you mean!* I didn't cheat you.

A：你欺騙我！

B：你是什麼意思！我沒有騙你。

對方說了令人不悅的話，這時你可以複述對方的話，再補上一句 What do you mean!，強調自己的不滿。

情境對話 2

A: Women are all the same.

B: Women are all the same? *What do you mean!*

A：女人都一樣。

B：女人都一樣！你這話什麼意思！

2. 請看以下對話。

情境對話

A: You were careless. You didn't look where you were going, and that's why you bumped into my car.

B: *How can you say that!* It's your fault.

A：你太不小心了，都沒有在看路，難怪會撞上我的車。

B：你怎麼可以那樣說！明明是你的錯。

▌**重點提示**

　　對他人不合理的言論做出反應時使用。此外，也可以使用帶有制止意味的說法，例如 Now, just a minute!（等等！）、Wait a minute!（等等！）。更簡略且口語的說法則是 Come on!（拜託！）、Hold on!（等一下！）。

▚ 表達不滿　　　　　　　　　　　◉MP3 056

▌我並不滿意……。

1. (I'm afraid) I'm not happy about [with]...	對於……，我（恐怕）無法滿意。
2. ... is not ... enough.	……不夠……。

▌你應該更……。

3. I don't know why you can't ... more...	我不懂你為什麼不能更……。
4. It could be better.	應該可以更好才是。
5. I know how hard you..., but I hope you can ... better [more/earlier]...	我知道你很認真地……，但我希望你能……更好〔更多／更早〕一點。
6. You could have done better.	你應該可以做得更好。

7. It can't go on like this.　　　　　　　　這樣下去是不行的。

句型解說

1. happy 在這裡指的是「滿意的」。

   - *I'm not happy with* your work.
     我不滿意你的表現。

   - *I'm not* very *happy with* the conditions.
     我對這些條件不是很滿意。

   - *I'm not* very *happy about* the way the chairman was elected.
     我對選舉主席的方式不太滿意。

2. 若不滿的原因是因為某種行為過當，可以加上 too（太）。

   - I'm not happy with the machine. Its operating speed *is not* fast *enough*, and it's *too* noisy.
     我對這台機器不滿意。它的運作速度不夠快，而且運轉聲太吵了。

   not enough 的用法如下，主詞用名詞或動名詞。

   - Just apologizing *is not enough*. I'd like you to make up for the loss.
     光道歉還不夠，我要你賠償損失。

3. I don't know why you can't... 其實是暗示「你應該要能⋯⋯」。其他類似的說法有 I want to know when...（我想知道什麼時候⋯⋯。）

   - *I don't know why you can't* get *higher* grades.
     我不懂你為什麼就不能多得一點分數。

   - *I want to know when* you will finish the job.
     我想知道你什麼時候會把工作做完。

6. 利用比較級暗示對方「應該可以做得更好」。

7. 提醒對方「這樣下去是不行的」，要求對方改善。

■ 重點提示

當他人的表現無法令人滿意，或工作成果不如預期時，都可以用上述句型表達你的不滿。然而，無論怎麼說都會令對方難受，所以請多用 I'm sorry to say this, but...（很抱歉這麼說，但是……。）的句型（請參考第 6 章）。

有所偏頗　　　　　　　　　　　　　　　　　　　　● MP3 057

■ 這樣並不公平。

1. That's not fair.	這樣不公平。
2. You do me an injustice.	你這樣對我不公平。
3. That's prejudice.	那是偏見。
4. It's wrong to...	……是錯的。

■ 句型解說

4. wrong 原是「錯誤的」的意思，在這裡是指「不道德的，不對的」。
- *It's wrong to* tell a lie.
  說謊是不對的。

越權　　　　　　　　　　　　　　　　　　　　　● MP3 058

■ 你沒有權利……。

1. You have no right [don't have the right] to...	你沒有權利去……。
2. You have exceeded your authority.	你已經越權了。

3. Who are you to...?　　　　　　　　　　你憑什麼……？

句型解說

1. 例如：
   - *You have no right to* say that.
     你沒有權利那樣說。

3. 請參照「態度不佳」的句型 8 (p. 91)。

言行不一　　　　　　　　　　　　　　　⏺MP3 059

■ 如果是……，為什麼你……？

1. If..., why did [didn't] you...?　　　如果是……，為什麼你會〔你沒有〕……？

句型解說

1. 也可用現在式 If..., why do [don't] you...?。

   情境對話

   A: Sorry I'm late. I missed the bus. I know this is a very important meeting, but...
   B: *If* you really knew it was important, *why didn't you* take a taxi?
   A：對不起我遲到了，因為錯過了公車。我知道這個會議非常重要，但是……。
   B：如果你真的知道這會議很重要，為什麼不搭計程車？

■ 重點提示

責備對方言行不一，並要求解釋。

■ 無法認同對方的看法　　　　　　　　　　⊙MP3 060

■ 你真的這麼想嗎？

1. It can't be true. [Can it be true?]	不可能是真的。〔有可能是真的嗎？〕
2. What makes you so sure?	你怎麼能這麼肯定？
3. How can you say that [that...]?	你怎麼可以那樣說〔說……〕？
4. Do you actually believe that [that...]?	你真的相信那個〔……〕嗎？
5. You are just imagining it!	那只是你的想像！

■ 我從來不記得自己講過這種話。

6. Who said that! [Who said/says that...!]	誰說的！〔誰說……！〕
7. I didn't say that!	我沒有那麼說！
8. I didn't agree to... [I didn't agree with you on that.]	我不同意……。〔關於那點，我並不認同你的看法。〕

■ 句型解說

----

1. 也可以直接說 It can't be.（不可能。）

情境對話

A: I'm sure the treasure is buried here.

B: *It can't be.*

A：我確定寶藏就埋在這裡。

B：不可能。

----

2. 直譯是「是什麼東西（原因）讓你這麼肯定？」，也就是說「你怎麼能這麼肯定？」。What makes you...?（什麼讓你……？）也是很常見的用法。

情境對話

A: Mr. Jones is the criminal!

B: But *what makes you so sure*? There isn't enough evidence to prove that.

A：犯人是瓊斯先生！

B：但你怎麼能這麼肯定？目前還沒有足夠的證據可以證明。

---

6. 對方開始談論和事實不符的事情時加以制止。

情境對話

A: Who do you think is the best candidate for the post after you resign?

B: *Who said* I'm resigning!

A：你辭職之後，你覺得誰最適合接你的位子？

B：誰說我要辭職的！

---

8. 雙方未能達成共識時，制止對方往下進行。

情境對話

A: So please sign here.

B: What's this for?

A: This is to confirm the fact that you will pay two hundred pounds as a deposit.

B: *I didn't agree to* do so.

A：那麼請在這裡簽名。

B：為什麼要簽名？

A：確認您會付兩百英鎊的訂金。

B：我沒有同意要付啊。

▌**重點提示**

　　當對方所理解的和事實有所出入，或無法達成共識時，便可利用上述句型適時予以回應。如果勉強配合，只會讓結果變成半強迫下的認同。

提出警告

● MP3 061

■ 你最好……。

1. You had better (not)..., or you will...	你最好（不要）……，不然你會……。
2. You have to...	你一定要……。
3. Unless..., [If ... not....,] you will...	除非……，不然你會……。
4. I (must) warn you.	我（得）警告你。

句型解說

1. 指出可能會發生的狀況，達到警示的效果。
   - *You had better* try to make everything clear to the employees, *or* your managerial authority *will* be questioned.
   你最好把每件事都跟員工講清楚，不然你的管理權限會被質疑。

2. 例如：
   - She is a sensitive girl, and *you have to* be very careful not to hurt her feelings.
   她是個心思細膩的女孩，你一定要非常小心，不要傷了她的心。

3. 例如：
   - *Unless* you keep attending the class, *you will* not be able to improve your English.
   除非你固定來上課，不然你的英文是沒辦法進步的。

4. 對於緊急的事態提出警告或要求對方注意，用於勸告的情況。也可以說成 I'm warning you.。
   - Do not touch the machine. *I'm warning you*, it's dangerous.
   不要碰那台機器。我可警告你喔，很危險的。

05

第5章
交涉

請求他人的協助也好，回應他人的要求也好，必須透過各式各樣的對話才能進行，而對話的過程中又會使用哪些句型呢？本章從最簡單的「請求協助」開始，一步步擴及「拒絕」、「讓步」等主題，循序漸進介紹各個場景的常用句型。

Useful English Expressions
for Communication

請求協助

◉MP3 062

■ 想請你幫個忙。

1. I need your help.	我需要你的幫忙。
2. Could you help me...?	能不能幫我……？
3. I need some assistance from you.	我需要你的協助。
4. I was wondering if you could help me.	不曉得可不可以請你幫個忙？
5. Is there anything you can do to...?	你有什麼辦法可以幫我……嗎？

句型解說

2. 後面可以先接 with 再接需要幫忙的事情，也可以直接接原形動詞。

- *Could you help me with* my programming?
  能不能幫我一起寫程式？

情境對話

A: *Could you help us* raise funds for the language training center?

B: I'm afraid there is nothing I can do.

A：能不能幫我們籌募成立語言訓練中心所需的資金？

B：很抱歉，我恐怕幫不上忙。

請求許可

◉MP3 063

■ 請讓我……。

1. Can I...?	我可不可以……？
2. Do you think I could...?	你覺得我可以……嗎？

3. Is it all right if I...?　　　　如果我……可以嗎？

4. I wonder if I could...　　　　不曉得我能不能……？

5. May I have your permission to...?　　能不能讓我……？

6. Do you have any objection to my...?　你對我的……有任何異議嗎？

■ 句型解說

2. 請看以下對話。

情境對話

A: *Do you think I could* take two weeks holiday in April?

B: Well, I don't think you can. You know April is one of our busiest months of the year.

A：你覺得我四月可以休兩個禮拜的假嗎？

B：恐怕不行，你也知道四月是我們一年當中最忙碌的月份之一。

3. 請看以下對話。

情境對話

A: *Is it all right if I* borrow this book?

B: Sure.

A：我可以借這本書嗎？

B：當然可以。

6. 例如：

• *Do you have any objection to my* exceeding the budget just this once?
我就這麼一次超出預算，對此你有什麼異議嗎？

強烈要求

◉MP3 064

■ 我要求你……。

1. I demand...	我要求……。
2. I insist you...	我堅持你要……。
3. I will claim... [I think I can claim...]	我要求……〔我認為我可以要求……〕。
4. I want [I want you to]...	我要〔我要你去〕……。
5. I must have...	我一定要……。

句型解說

1. demand 通常用在單方面要求對方的情況，是一種制式的說法。I demand 後面可以接名詞、that 子句或〈to + 原形動詞〉。

- *I demand* an explanation [apology/a recount].
  我要求你給我一個解釋〔道歉／說法〕。

- *We demand that* all the facts about the incident be made public.
  我們要求關於那個事件的真相必須公諸於世。

- It's a waste of time talking to you. *I demand to* speak to the manager.
  跟你說話簡直浪費我的時間，我要跟你們經理談。

2. insist 是遭到拒絕時，反過來堅持到底的說法。

情境對話

A: Is the number correct? I doubt it.

B: It's correct.

A: Could you check it?

B: I've already checked it.

A: *I insist you* check it again!

A：這號碼是對的嗎？我很懷疑。

B：是對的沒錯。

A：能不能再確認一次？

B：我已經確認過了。

A：我堅持你再確認一次！

3. claim 是「要求」，包括對應得的權利或費用等方面的要求，後面可直接接要求的內容，例如 money（金錢）、expenses（費用）、compensation（賠償金）、the right of...（…的權利）、the ownership of...（…的所有權）等等。而 claim for damages/loss 則是「要求損害賠償金」的意思。

情境對話 1

A: *I think I can claim* travel expenses.

B: Yes of course.

A：我想我可以要求旅費吧。

B：當然可以。

情境對話 2

A: *I will claim for* damages.

B: That's for the court to decide.

A：我要求損害賠償金。

B：那得看法院怎麼判。

4. want 是「希望，想要」的意思，I want you to... 則稍微帶有要求的語氣。

- *I want* twenty thousand dollars in compensation.
  我要二萬美金的賠償。

- *I want* an apology from you.
  我要你道歉。

5. must have 和 want 意思幾乎相同，但語氣更強硬一點。

- *I must have* a three year guarantee.
  我要求要有三年保固。

▎重點提示

　　權益受損時，一味保持沈默實在不是明智之舉。應該直接說出心裡的想法，該要求的時候就要據理力爭，上述句型便可以派上用場。

抱怨   ◉ MP3 065

■ 我要抱怨一下。

1. I'm afraid I have to make a complaint.	抱歉，我想要抱怨一下。
2. I'd like to complain about...	我想要抱怨一下……。
3. I have a complaint to make.	我要抱怨。
4. I really must complain.	我一定要抱怨一下。

▎重點提示

　　想要抱怨時，可以使用上述句型，但要注意的是，一開始就怒氣沖沖可不是聰明的作法，得讓接收抱怨的一方做好心理準備。名詞 complaint 就是抱怨的內容。此外，抱怨的對象最好是能負起責任、位居某個地位的人。找錯對象抱怨，往往不能讓事情得到解決。以下是兩個例句。

- Please let me speak to the manager.
  請讓我和經理說話。
- I'd like to speak to your boss.
  請你的老闆出來。

緩和主張

■ 我的意見就說到這裡了。

1. I won't press the point any more [any further].　　　我的意見就說到這裡了。

句型解說

1. 不再強烈主張論點。

提出條件 (I)

■ 如果……，我會……。

1. I'll ... if...　　　如果……，我會……。

2. I can..., if...　　　如果……，我可以……。

3. I'm willing to ... if...　　　如果……，我會很樂意……。

4. I'm prepared to ... if...　　　如果……，我就可以……。

5. I will [can] ... as long as...　　　我會〔可以〕……，只要……。

6. I'll..., but first ... has to... [but first I'd like ... to...]　　　我會……，前提是……必須要……〔但首先我希望……〕。

7. I'll ... on (the) condition(s) that...　　　在……的條件下，我可以……。

8. I'll ... on the understanding that...　　　在……的共識下，我可以……。

9. I'll ... on one condition. (That is...)　　　這個條件成立的話，我就會……。（條件就是……。）

10. One of the conditions [points] to be specified in ... is that...　　　……標明的條件〔要點〕之一就是……。

11. My conditions for ... are that...	對於……，我的條件是……。
12. My ... is conditional on...	對我而言，條件是……。
13. ... must..., or I'm not interested.	……必須……，不然我沒有興趣。

■ 句型解說

2. 例如：

- *I can* lend you ten thousand dollars *if* you promise to pay me 6% interest.
  假如你答應付我 6% 的利息，我可以借你一萬美金。

3. 例如：

- *I'm willing to* join the project *if* you give me full financial support.
  如果你給我全額經費贊助，我就願意加入這項計畫。

4. 也可以說 I'd be prepared to think about [consider] ... if...（如果……，我就會好好考慮……）。向對方透漏會依照條件來決定接下來的行動，是交涉中常用的說法。

5. as long as... 就跟上述 if... 用法相同。

情境對話

A: I must ask you to work overtime this week.

B: I don't mind *as long as* I'm paid.

A：這禮拜得請你加班了。

B：我無所謂，有加班費就好。

6. 例如：

- I'd be prepared to consider introducing your language training system to the university, *but first I'd like* you *to* agree to one thing. Please offer us free maintenance service for three years. Is that all right?

我打算將你們的語言訓練系統引進學校，但首先想要請你們答應一件事。請提供我們三年免費的維修服務，不知道可不可行？

---

7. 例如：

- *I'll* sign the contract *on condition that* I take no responsibility for any loss you may suffer.

  只要不必負擔你的任何損失，我願意簽這份合約。

---

9. on one condition 表示「在某個條件之下」。

<u>情境對話 1</u>

A: *I'll* let you use my computer *on one condition*.

B: What's that?

A: You let me use your video-player in return.

A：我可以讓你用我的電腦，但是有個條件。

B：什麼條件？

A：讓我用你的放影機。

如果想要強調這項條件，可以參考以下的對話。

<u>情境對話 2</u>

A: We may close the shop down, because it's been operating in the red for so long.

B: Right, *I'll* take care of the shop; *but on one condition*, I'll do it my way.

A：我們可能會把店收起來，因為長期以來入不敷出。

B：好，我可以接手，但有個條件，我要用自己的方式經營。

---

11. 例如：

- *My condition for* joining the project *is that* we divide all the profit among us.

  要我加入這項企劃的條件就是利益要均分。

---

12. be conditional on...（以⋯為條件）是固定說法。

- *My* agreement to take the position in London *is conditional on* your assurance that I can come back in three years' time.

  我可以接受調職到倫敦去，條件是你要保證三年內把我調回來。

■ 重點提示

談條件是交涉過程中重要的一環，條件談不攏，也就沒有繼續討論的必要了。上述的句型都用第一人稱的 I 或第三人稱的 My... 當主詞，其實用第二人稱的 You 當主詞也可以達到類似效果：

- *You* can take the book on condition that you return it within a month.
  你可以借這本書，前提是要在一個月之內歸還。

如果要討論條件的具體內容，可以用以下句型：

- Let's talk over the terms of...
  我們來討論一下……的條件吧。
- What's the ... you'll offer?
  你願意提供什麼……？
- What's the ... you'll accept [agree to] ?
  什麼樣的……你才接受〔同意〕？
- What are the terms you'll agree to?
  什麼樣的條件你才會同意？

情境對話 1

A: *Let's talk over the terms of* our agreement. What would you say if I paid a deposit of fifty thousand dollars?

B: Fifty thousand dollars? That's a great amount of money.

A：我們來談談合約的條件吧。如果我說我可以付五萬美元的保證金呢？

B：五萬美元？那可是一大筆錢。

情境對話 2

A: *What's the* maximum *you'll offer?*

B: I can't pay more than three thousand pounds.

A：你最多可以拿出多少？

B：三千英鎊。再多就沒有了。

提出條件 (II) ⦿MP3 068

■ 在……的條件下才要……。

1. I'll ... only if...	只有……我才會……。
2. I'll..., but only if...	我會……，但只有在……（的條件下）。
3. I'll never ... unless... [if ... not...]	除非……，不然我不會……。

■ 句型解說

1. 提出條件並告知接下來可能的行為。如果不用 will，則表示說話者的原則或方針不輕易更動。
   - *We* refund the money *only if* you bring your receipt with you.
     唯有帶著收據過來，我們才會退錢。

3. 例如：
   - *We will never* reply *if* you *don't* send a self-addressed envelope along with your letter.
     如果沒有附上回郵信封，我們將不予回覆。

提出條件 (III) ⦿MP3 069

■ 儘管……我也……。

1. I'll ... even if...	儘管……我也會……。
2. I'll never ... even if...	就算……我也不會……。

■句型解說

1. 例如：

- *I'll* vote for him *even if* I know he'll lose the election.
  就算知道他會輸掉這次選舉，我也會投給他。

2. 例如：

- *I'll never* work overtime *even if* I'm paid a lot of money.
  就算付我再多薪水，我也絕不加班。

無法接受提議或要求

⦿ MP3 070

■ 我無法接受……。

1. I can't accept...	我無法接受……。
2. I'm afraid I don't accept that.	我恐怕不會接受。
3. I find that [this] difficult to accept.	那〔這〕讓我難以接受。
4. It's difficult for me to accept...	我很難接受……。
5. That's completely unacceptable.	那是完全無法接受的。

■ 我沒辦法……。

6. I am afraid I find that [this] difficult to do.	我恐怕沒辦法做那件事〔這件事〕。
7. That's just not possible.	那是不可能的。

■句型解說

1. 請看以下對話。

情境對話

A: We propose that the raise for this year should be 3%.

B: *I can't accept* that.

A：我們提議今年的調薪幅度為 3%。

B：恕難接受。

類似的用法還有：

- I can hardly accept that.
  我簡直沒辦法接受那件事。

- I find that rather hard to accept.
  我覺得那讓人有點難接受。

- That would be unacceptable.
  那是讓人無法接受的。

4. 若非全盤拒絕，而是想保留一些討論的空間，可以說 It would be difficult for me to accept...（要我接受……有點困難。）

7. 用於無法接受請託或指示的情況。

情境對話

A: Would you type all the pages by 5 o'clock?

B: *That's just not possible.*

A：可以在五點以前把這幾頁都打完嗎？

B：那是不可能的。

拒絕請託或要求

◉MP3 071

■ 抱歉，我沒有辦法……。

1. I don't think I can.	我不認為我辦得到。
2. I'm sorry. I would if I could, but I'm afraid...	抱歉，可以的話我一定會盡力，但我恐怕……。
3. I'm afraid I can't help you.	抱歉，我恐怕沒辦法幫你。
4. I'm afraid I can't [I'm not interested].	抱歉，我恐怕沒辦法〔不太有興趣〕。
5. I'm sorry, (but) I can't.	抱歉，（但）我沒辦法。
6. It would be difficult.	會有點困難。
7. Unfortunately...	可惜的是……。

■ 句型解說

2. I'm afraid 後面接沒辦法幫忙的理由。

情境對話

A: Would you like to come with me to the International Conference on Multimedia this weekend?

B: *I would if I could, but I'm afraid* I have other plans.

A：想跟我一起參加週末舉行的國際多媒體會議嗎？

B：可以的話我也想去，但我已經有其他計畫了。

4. 請看以下對話。

情境對話

A: Could you help me in carrying out the research?

B: *I'm afraid I can't.*

A：能不能幫我完成這項調查？

B：抱歉，恐怕不行。

5. 類似的說法還有：

- I'm sorry, I can't do that.
  抱歉，我辦不到。

---

7. 請看以下對話。

情境對話

A: Could you lend me your copy of *A Brief History of Time*?

B: *Unfortunately* I gave it to one of my students yesterday.

A：能不能借我《時間簡史》這本書？

B：真可惜，昨天剛好拿給我一個學生了。

■ 重點提示

　　拒絕請託的時候，除非對方的要求十分不合理，不然態度要婉轉一點，並搭配使用 I'm afraid..., I'm sorry..., Unfortunately... 等字詞。禮貌雖然重要，但要是真的無能為力，也要清楚表達自己的立場，用 I can't... 明白地告訴對方吧。

斷然拒絕　　　　　　　　　　●MP3 072

■ 不行。

1. Certainly not.	當然不行。
2. No I won't.	不，我拒絕。
3. I absolutely refuse.	我絕對拒絕。
4. There is nothing I can do (to help you).	我無能為力。
5. It's too much to ask of me.	這對我來說根本不可能。
6. That's impossible.	那是不可能的。
7. That's just not possible.	不可能就是不可能。

8. I can't do it.　　　　　　　　　　我辦不到。

9. I can't possibly do it.　　　　　　我不可能辦到。

■ 句型解說

1. 請看以下對話。

情境對話 1

A: Will you lend me ten thousand dollars?

B: *Certainly not.*

A：可不可以借我一萬塊美金？

B：當然不行。

拒絕的時候，No way! 比 Certainly not. 更口語，意思是「想都別想！」，不過 No way! 只用在熟人之間，要特別留意。

情境對話 2

A: Will you help me with my work?

B: *No way!*

A：你可以幫我做我的工作嗎？

B：想都別想！

---

4. 也可以說 There is nothing I can do about...（關於……，我幫不上忙。）

情境對話

A: It's too late. In fact, you're two days late in submitting the paper.

B: Is there any possibility of getting my application accepted?

A: No, the time's over. *There's nothing I can do about* it.

A：太遲了。事實上報名時間已經過了兩天。

B：有沒有可能讓我完成報名手續？

A：不可能，已經截止了。我無能為力。

---

6. 除了代名詞 that，也可以用疑問詞 what 引導的名詞子句當主詞。

- *What* you are asking me to do *is impossible*.
  你的要求我無法辦到。

■ 重點提示

　　上述句型主要是斷然拒絕他人的要求、請託時使用。如果還有轉寰的餘地，就可以說 What you are asking me to do is impossible. What I can do, however, is to...（你的要求我無法辦到，但我可以……。）

語帶保留、不直接答應要求　　◉MP3 073

■ 讓我想想。

1. I'll see.	我想一下。
2. I'll see what I can (do).	我看看我能做些什麼。
3. I'll see if there is anything I can do.	我看看我能幫上什麼忙。
4. I'll do what I can.	我會做我能做的。
5. I'll manage to..., somehow.	總之我會設法去……。
6. I'll try to...	我會試著……。

■ 句型解說

1. 不想立刻給對方答覆，意思是要對方給自己一些考慮的時間。答案可能是肯定也可能是否定的。

[情境對話]

A: Can you spare a couple of hours to help me with my English composition this weekend?

B: *I'll see.*

A：這個週末能不能撥出幾個小時幫我看一下英文作文？

B：我想一下。

---

2. 用來表示幫得上忙的話一定會去做，但實際上又不一定的情況。類似的用法有 I'll see what can be done.（我看看能做些什麼。）

---

4. 雖然不見得幫得上忙，但表示會盡一份心力。

[情境對話]

A: I'm looking for a flat in London, and I was wondering if you could help me.

B: All right, *I'll do what I can* to help you find suitable accommodation.

A: I'd appreciate it.

A：我在找倫敦的公寓，想說能不能請你幫忙。

B：好啊，我看看有沒有辦法幫你找到合適的公寓。

A：謝謝。

■ 重點提示

無法確定自己能提供什麼幫助時使用，上述句型給人肯定、正面的感覺。

▨ 請對方考慮　　　　　　　　　　　●MP3 074

■ **請考慮一下。**

1. Please think about it.　　　　　　　　　請考慮一下。

■ 句型解說

1. think about... 是「考慮…」。

• There are a few positions available for you at the moment. You can go to Egypt to be director of our language institute, but I wouldn't recommend you to apply for that. I would suggest you take a post in London. It's a teaching position at one of our schools. *Please think about it.*
目前有幾個適合你的位子。你可以去埃及擔任語言機構的主任,但我個人並不推薦。我比較建議你接下倫敦的工作,是到我們某一所學校教書。請考慮看看吧。

■ 重點提示

請對方考慮自己所提出的建議或要求時使用。這個句型很普遍,除了從旁出主意的時候可用,也常見於討論的對話中。

請對方重新考慮 ● MP3 075

■ 能不能重新考慮一下?

1. Could you please think it over?	可不可以請你重新考慮一下?
2. Won't you change your mind?	難道不能改變心意?
3. Shouldn't you think twice [again]?	你不再考慮一下嗎?
4. Let me ask you to think it over.	請你再想想。
5. Would you reconsider your decision to...?	能不能重新考慮……?
6. Let me know if you change your mind.	如果你改變心意了,請告訴我。
7. You'll have to think very carefully about...	關於……,你一定要想清楚。

■ 句型解說

----

3. think twice [again] 是一種要別人打消念頭或重新考慮的說法。

- *Shouldn't you think twice* before you decide?
  在你做決定之前，難道不再考慮一下？

----

5. reconsider 是「重新考慮」的意思，有推翻原決定的意味。

情境對話

A: *Would you reconsider your decision to* resign?

B: No, I wouldn't.

A：辭職的事能不能再考慮一下？

B：不行。

■ 重點提示

希望對方重新思考已經做了的決定時使用。

▨ 表示還需要進一步討論　　　◉ MP3 076

■ 需要進一步討論。

1. We have to talk a little more to...	我們還需要再談談才能……。
2. We have to talk it over before...	在……之前，我們需要再討論一下。

■ 句型解說

1. 例如：

- *We have to talk a little more to* see if we can get [come] closer together on...
  我們還需要再談談，看看是否能在……上達成共識。

2. 例如：

- *We have to talk it over before* we finally make our decision.
  做出最後的決定之前，我們需要再討論一下。

■ 重點提示

交涉陷入膠著時急著做決定是很冒險的事，這時候可以利用上述句型，請大家進一步討論，找出最佳的解決方案。

▨ 進行交涉

◉MP3 077

■ 如果……，你會怎麼做？

1. If you..., what do you...?	如果……，那你會怎麼做？
2. If you don't agree to [with]..., what is your...?	如果你不同意……，那麼你的……是什麼？

■ ……可以／不可以。

3. If you..., then we can [can't]...	如果你……，那我們就可以〔不可以〕……。
4. If you insist on..., then we can't...	如果你堅持……，那我們就沒辦法……。

■ 如果⋯⋯，我們就可以讓步。

5. We're prepared to compromise on this if...	如果⋯⋯，我們就可以讓步。
6. We could reconsider this if...	如果⋯⋯，我們就願意重新考慮。

■ 最後的條件是⋯⋯。

7. If we can't..., our final option would be...	如果我們沒辦法⋯⋯，最後的選擇就是⋯⋯。
8. We want..., but we'll have to settle for ... instead.	我們想要⋯⋯，但我們得接受⋯⋯。

■句型解說

2. 例如：

- *If you don't agree to* our offer of eight million dollars, *what is your* proposal?
  如果你不同意我方提出的八百萬美元，那麼你的提案是？

4. 例如：

- *If you insist on* ten million dollars, *then we can't* make an agreement with you.
  如果您堅持要一千萬美元，那我們就沒辦法和您簽約。

7. 例如：

- *If we can't* agree on these terms, *our final option would be* to review the contract and try to find out some ways of making concessions.
  如果我們無法同意這些條件，最後只好重新審閱契約內容，看看有沒有讓步的可能性。

8. settle for...（勉強接受⋯）是指雖然不符合期望，但願意接受。

■ 重點提示

　　以上句型是在了解對方接下來的提案之後，一邊觀察對方的態度一邊做出決定。請參考「提出條件」的部分 (pp. 109 ~ 114)。

▦ 請對方給予考慮的時間 (I)　　　⊙MP3 078

■ 讓我考慮一下。

1. Let me think about it.	讓我考慮一下。
2. I'll give it some thought.	我會想一想。
3. Let me [I need to] think it over.	讓我〔我需要〕想一想。

■ 請給我一點時間考慮。

4. Please give me time to consider [to think about it].	請給我一點時間考慮。
5. Could you give me some time [a few days] to think about it?	能不能給我一點時間〔幾天〕考慮一下？
6. Could you give me more time to think about it?	能不能多給我一點時間考慮？
7. Let me give some [more] thought to that before...	在⋯⋯之前，讓我多花點時間想想。
8. I'm trying to..., but I need more time.	我試著要⋯⋯，但我需要更多時間。
9. I'd like to have more time to think it over.	我需要更多時間想一想。
10. I think I should have some time to consider that.	我想我應該要多一點時間考慮一下。

■ 句型解說

1. 類似的說法還有 I'll think about it.（我考慮一下。）

- *I'll think about it* and let you know tomorrow.
  我考慮一下，明天再回覆你。

3. think over... 是「仔細考慮…」的意思。

- *Let me think it over* before making my decision.
  做出決定前請先讓我好好想一想。

4. 例如：

- *Please give me time to think about it.* I can let you know my decision by this weekend.
  請給我時間想一想，週末前就可以告訴你我的決定。

  也可以把 consider 換成其他動詞，例如 Please give me time to make a choice.（請給我時間做出選擇。）

■ 重點提示

面對他人提出的請求無法當下回應，或是根本沒有興趣了解時，上述句型就能派上用場。

■ 請對方給予考慮的時間 (II)　　　◉ MP3 079

■ 我想和上司談談。

1. I'll have to talk to my boss (to discuss the point).	（關於這點）我必須和上司討論一下。
2. I'll have to discuss this with...	我必須和……商量一下。

3. I'll have to refer this to my boss.　我必須讓上司知道這件事。

4. I'll have to check this with...　我必須和……確認這件事。

5. Let me phone my boss to see what he says.　讓我打通電話問問上司的意見。

6. Can I come back to you on this?　能不能之後再跟你討論這件事？

7. I'll have to win [get] the approval of...　我必須獲得……的許可。

■ 句型解說

1 ~ 4, 7. I'll have to 也可以改成 I need to（我需要）、I'd like to（我想要）和 I must（我必須）。

2. 例如：

  • *I'll have to discuss this with* my wife.
    這件事我必須跟我太太商量一下。

4. 例如：

  • *I'll have to check this with* my boss.
    我必須跟我的老闆確認一下這件事。

■ 重點提示

　　代表公司和他人交涉，或討論中遇到無法自行判斷的問題時，經常需要上司或同事的建議，這時候便可利用上述句型，告訴對方必須和他人討論之後才能告知結果。

對意見或答覆持保留態度

● MP3 080

■ 目前還不能確定。／尚未決定。

1. I can't say anything today [now].	今天〔目前〕還說不準。
2. I'm afraid I can't give you any answer now.	我現在恐怕還不能給你任何答案。
3. I can't agree to anything now.	我現在還不能同意任何事。
4. I'm not sure if I can ... now.	我不確定現在是否能……。
5. I can't tell you any more than that at the moment.	目前只能告訴你這麼多。
6. I'm afraid I don't have any ready answer.	現在恐怕還沒有確切的答案。
7. I haven't given it much thought yet.	我還沒有仔細想過。
8. I'd rather not decide anything now.	現階段我還不想做出任何決定。
9. I can't make a promise.	我無法做出承諾。
10. I haven't decided yet.	我還沒決定。
11. At this point, I'm not sure if it's a good idea or not.	目前我還不確定這想法是好是壞。

■ 我想暫時保留意見。

12. I'd like to keep [leave] my options open for a moment.	我暫時還不想做任何選擇。
13. I'd like to suspend judgment on this ... until...	直到……之前，我想暫時保留對……的判斷。
14. Can I give you my answer later [tomorrow/next week]?	能不能改天〔明天／下禮拜〕再給你答案？
15. I'll give you my answer by... [by this weekend/in a few days.]	……之前〔這個禮拜以內／這幾天〕我會給你答案。

16. I'll (have to) see. 我（得）考慮一下。

17. I'll decide later. 我之後再決定。

18. I'll think about it later. 我之後再想想。

句型解說

4. 猶豫該不該表明態度。

- *I'm not sure if I can* give you a straight answer *now*.
  我不確定現在能不能直接給你答案。

13. 問題尚未解決或疑點尚未釐清，直到弄清楚狀況才表態。

情境對話

A: What do you think would be the best solution to this problem?

B: *I'd like to suspend judgment on this* issue *until* I've looked into it in more detail.

A：你覺得這個問題最好的解決辦法是？

B：直到知道更多細節之前，對這個問題我暫時不做任何判斷。

16. 對事情不太關心，是一種很模稜兩可的回答。

18. 表示稍後再考慮，可見對討論的內容不感興趣。

重點提示

　　面對他人詢問自己的意見或答案時，總會碰到無法立刻回答的情況，需要更多討論、蒐集資料，深思熟慮後才能提出見解，這時除了上述句型外，還有以下說法：

- I'm afraid I can't ... now.
  目前我恐怕無法……。

- Can I ... later?
  我能不能之後再……？
- I can't ... until...
  直到……前，我不能……。

請對方再給一次機會　　　　　　　　　◉MP3 081

■ 再給我一次機會。

| 1. Will you give me another chance? | 能不能再給我一次機會？ |
| 2. Please let me try again. | 請讓我再試一次。 |

■句型解說

----

1. 請看以下對話。

情境對話

A: You failed in your attempt to discover the treasure, and we can't give you any
   more financial support.

B: *Will you give me another chance?*

A：你沒能找到寶藏，所以我們無法再給你任何金錢上的援助了。

B：能不能再給我一次機會？

提出原則或方針　　　　　　　　　　　◉MP3 082

■ 原則上……。

| 1. I [We] (don't) usually... | 我〔我們〕通常（不）……。 |

2. I [We] never... (even if...)	我〔我們〕從不……（即使……）。
3. As a rule...	原則上……。
4. My [Our] policy [principle] is that...	我〔我們〕的政策〔原則〕是……。
5. We're [I'm] working on the basis [assumption/theory] that...	我們〔我〕是在……的基準〔假設／理論〕下工作。
6. It's against our [my] principles [rules/policy] to...	……違反我們〔我〕的原則〔政策／方針〕。
7. As a matter of principle...	依據原則……。

■ 句型解說

1. 可以用 normally 取代 usually，意指某種原則或標準下的行為。

情境對話

A: When shall I pay the bill?
B: *Normally we* ask our guests to pay in advance.
A：什麼時候付款？
B：通常我們會請客人先付款。

2. never 是「從未，從不」的意思，在這裡表示不允許有任何例外。另外，整個句型前面接 I'm afraid...（我恐怕……。），語氣比較婉轉。
   • *We never* return tuition once it is paid.
   學費一旦繳了我們就不會退還。

4. 例如：
   • *Our principle is that* if we have a complaint from customers, we just listen and tell them we will consider it.
   我們的原則是如果有顧客抱怨，我們就傾聽並告訴顧客我們會檢討。

類似的說法還有 My [Our] policy/principle is to... 和 It's my [our] policy/principle to...。

- *It's my policy* not *to* promise anything at this stage of the negotiation.
  談判在這個階段時不承諾任何事情是我的原則。

---

5. basis 是「基礎，基準」的意思，後面除了接 that 子句，也可以直接接〈of + 名詞〉。

- *I'm working on the basis that* even if I'm unsuccessful, I'll be rewarded.
  我的原則是，即使不成功，我也會得到我應得的。

請對方通融 ⊙MP3 083

■ 能不能通融一下？

1. Can't you stretch [bend] the rules [your principles] just this once and...	一次就好，不能改變一下規則〔放寬你的原則〕而…… 嗎？
2. Could you relax the rule [law] in this [my] case?	這次能不能通融一下？

句型解說

1. stretch 原是「曲解」的意思，這裡指的是放寬規則或原則。bend 的原意是「彎曲」，這裡也是放寬原則、通融的意思。and... 後面接讓步的內容。類似的例子還有 stretch the deadline（延期）。

情境對話

A: It's against my principles to get involved in political activities.

B: I know that, but *can't you bend your principles just this once and* join our election campaign?

A：參與政治活動違反我的原則。

B：我知道，但這次可不可以放寬原則，來參加我們的選舉活動？

2. relax 是指放寬嚴格的規範或原則。

情境對話

A: We are obliged to fine you $50 for the parking violation.

B: *Couldn't you relax the law in my case?* The thing was that I left my car just for a moment to get some medicine.

A：你違反停車規定，我們必須罰你 50 塊美金。

B：難道不能通融一下嗎？我只不過是下車買個藥而已。

* be obliged to... 是「依法必須…」的意思。

請對方讓步 ●MP3 084

■ 能不能退一步呢？

1. Could you be more flexible over... 關於……，能不能有點彈性呢？

2. Could you make a little concession? 可以請你稍微退讓一點嗎？

句型解說

1. 例如 be flexible over the terms（放寬條件）。

表示願意讓步

⦿MP3 085

■ 這次就放寬規則吧。 / 僅此一次下不為例。

1. I will [may] stretch the rules just this once.	我就不管什麼規則了，但就這麼一次。
2. I will stretch a point, and let you...	我就稍微放寬規則，讓你……。
3. I'm not supposed to ... but I'll make an exception in your case.	我不應該……的，不過這次就為你破個例。
4. Normally [Usually] I..., but I can [will] ... this time [this once].	通常來講我應該……，但這次〔就這麼一次〕我可以〔會〕……。

句型解說

1. 請看以下對話。

情境對話

A: Can we play music after 9 o'clock in the dormitory just for tonight's party?

B: You are not allowed to do that, but *we may stretch the rules just this once.*

A：能不能看在派對的份上，讓我們今晚 9 點以後在宿舍裡玩音樂呢？

B：平常是禁止的，不過今天就例外吧。

4. 例如：

• *We* don't *usually* do this, *but* to speed up the flow of the traffic, *we'll* let you in here.

通常我們不會這樣做的，但為了讓交通更順暢，就讓你通過吧。

有條件讓步 ◉MP3 086

■ 如果你……，我願意……。

1. I might yield on ... if...　　　　　　如果……，我願意就……讓步。

2. If you accept..., then I can...　　　如果你接受……，那我就可以
　　　　　　　　　　　　　　　　　　……。

3. I will consider ... if...　　　　　　　我會考慮……，如果……。

4. I would be prepared to reconsider　　如果……，我就可以重新考慮。
　 it [to think it over] if...

5. If..., I can reach an agreement.　　　如果……，我就可以達成協議。

▪句型解說

1. 也可以說 yield the point（對這點做出讓步）。

4. reconsider 的結果可能推翻已經做出的決定。think ... over 則是下結論前再三考慮。

提出最後方案 ◉MP3 087

■ 這是最後的提案。

1. This is my final offer [request].　　　這是我最後的提案〔要求〕。

2. I'll make you a final offer [proposal].　我將提出最後的提案。

3. If we can't agree on this,...　　　　如果我們無法就這點達成共識
　　　　　　　　　　　　　　　　　　的話，……。

4. My decision is final.　　　　　　　　這是我最後的決定。

■ 句型解說

2. 例如：

- *I'll make you a final offer*, fifty thousand dollars, what do you say?
  我出最後一次價，五萬美金，如何？

---

3. 暗示 this 已經是最後的提案或選擇。

- *If we can't agree on this,* our final option is to...
  如果無法就這點達成共識的話，最後的選擇就是……。

情境對話

A: I still hesitate to take route Y to get back to the tent.

B: *If we can't agree on this,* our final option would be to divide the party into two groups and take two different routes.

A：對於沿著 Y 路線走回營地我還是有疑慮。

B：如果我們沒辦法達成共識的話，最後的選擇就是兵分兩路、走不同的路線試試看了。

另外，這個句型也可以用來暗示討論破局，沒有繼續的必要。

- *If we can't agree on this,* it's a waste of time negotiating.
  如果無法就這點達成共識，再談也只是浪費時間而已。

▨ 拍板定案 ● MP3 088

■ 好，就這麼決定。 / 就這樣吧。

1. That settles it.	就這樣決定了。
2. Fine, that's settled [fixed] then.	好，那就這麼決定了。
3. Let's fix [settle] on...	就決定是……。
4. Fine, that will fix [settle] everything.	好，這樣一切都沒問題了。
5. That's that.	就這樣了。

■句型解說

1. 也可以說 That settles the matter.，指的是出現某個決定性的條件，而決定了所有的事。

2. settle 不只當「解決（問題）」解釋，也有「決定（日期）」的意思，例如 to settle the date。fix 也當「決定」解釋，決定的內容可以是日期、地點、場所或價格。

   情境對話

   A: Let's fix the time for the meeting.
   B: What about ten o'clock on Monday morning?
   A: *Fine, that's fixed then.*
   A：來決定開會的時間吧。
   B：星期一早上 10 點如何？
   A：好，那就這麼決定了。

3. 表示從若干選項中擇一。

   情境對話

   A: I recommend James.
   B: I agree. He will be the right person for the position.
   A: Fine. *Let's settle on* James.
   A：我推薦詹姆士。
   B：我贊成，他很適合這個位子。
   A：好，那就是詹姆士了。

5. 比較口語的表現方式。

對提案表示贊同

◉MP3 089

■ 那是不錯的辦法。

1. That's a good idea.	那是個好辦法。
2. ... would be fine.	……應該沒問題。
3. That seems [sounds] reasonable.	那似乎〔聽起來〕蠻合理的。
4. That's acceptable.	我可以接受。

句型解說

1. 日常生活中常用，表示認同對方的看法。

2. 例如：

- That *would be fine*.
  那應該沒問題。

情境對話

A: Could we meet again on Tuesday?

B: That's not suitable.

A: Then, what about Friday?

B: Yes, Friday *would be fine*.

A：星期二可以再見個面嗎？

B：那天不太方便。

A：那星期五呢？

B：好，星期五沒問題。

4. 並不是打從心底認同，只是表示大致上可以接受。

對提案感到為難　　　　　　　　　◉ MP3 090

■ ……不是好辦法。

1. I don't think it's a good idea to...　　　　我不認為……是個好辦法。

2. That doesn't sound like a very
   good idea.　　　　　　　　　　　　　聽起來不是個太好的辦法。

3. That may be a good idea, but...　　　　　那辦法或許不錯，但是……。

句型解說

3. 用來表示對方所提的方法不錯，但因為某些因素仍無法接受。
   • *That may be a good idea, but* it's impractical in this case.
   那辦法或許不錯，但就目前的狀況來看有點不切實際。

不同意對方提出的條件　　　　　　　◉ MP3 091

■ 無法接受這個條件。

1. That's not exactly what I want
   [expected].　　　　　　　　　　　　那不是我想要〔期待〕的。

2. That's not exactly what I have
   [had] in mind.　　　　　　　　　　　那不是我心裡所想的。

3. That's not suitable.　　　　　　　　　那不適合。

4. That will be a little difficult.　　　　　那會有點難度。

5. That's out of the question.　　　　　　那是不可能的。

6. I can't agree to these terms.　　　　　我無法同意這些條件。

7. I can't accept the terms of...	我無法接受……的條件。
8. I can't accept ... on any terms.	不管在什麼樣的條件下我都無法接受……。

■ 句型解說

6, 7. 通常用複數形 terms。也有 the terms of this agreement 的說法，意思是「本協議的條款規定」。

◆◆ 確認意見是否一致　　　　　　　　　◉ MP3 092

■ 我們對這件事的看法一致，對吧？

1. Is that all right?	這樣可以嗎？
2. Does that sound all right?	聽起來沒問題嗎？
3. (Are there) Any objections?	有任何反對意見嗎？
4. Can we all agree on this?	大家都同意這點嗎？
5. Can we now agree on the question [issue] of...?	針對……這問題〔議題〕，大家能達成共識了嗎？
6. Are we all agreed on that point?	大家都能同意那一點嗎？
7. Does that meet with everybody's approval?	大家是否都同意呢？
8. We must now agree on....	我們必須就……達成共識。

■ 來看看我們達成了哪些共識。

9. Now let's see what we've agreed on so far.	讓我們來看看到目前為止達成了哪些共識。

10. Let me summarize what we have agreed on so far.	讓我簡單整理一下目前達成了哪些共識。
11. We agreed upon ... earlier.	稍早我們都同意……。

■ 句型解說

11. 提醒對方已經就某件事達成共識，也可以說 We've already agreed that...（我們已經同意……。）

■ 重點提示

句型 1 到 8 主要用在發表意見後、統整結論的部分。句型 9 到 11 則用來確認彼此的認知是否一致。開會或交涉時如果忽略了確認的步驟，難保之後不會有一方跳出來推翻結論。

▨ 請對方換一個角度看　　　　　　　　　◉MP3 093

■ 從這個角度來看。

1. Look at it this way.	從這個角度切入。
2. Try to see it from ...'s point of view.	試著從……的觀點來看。

■ 句型解說

1. 帶有「從這個角度看也可以」的意味，想把某個觀點或意見傳達給對方時使用，類似的說法有 Can't we look at it this way?（不能從這個角度看嗎？）。

2. 例如：

- *Try to see it from my point of view.*
  請試著站在我的角度來看看。

請對方理解

■ 你難道不明白……？

1. Can't you see...?	你難道不明白……？
2. Don't you understand...?	你難道不了解……？

句型解說

1. 請看以下對話。

情境對話

A: We should invest in this exciting new venture.

B: But *can't you see* we are now in financial difficulty?

A：我們應該投資這項有趣的新事業。

B：可是我們正面臨財務危機，你難道不了解嗎？

要求對方採取行動

■ 務必……。

1. I must insist (that) you...	我堅持你一定要……。
2. Can't you...?	難道你不能……？

3. You must...　　　　　　　　　　你一定要……。

4. I strongly suggest that you...　　我強烈建議你……。

■ 句型解說

3. 說的時候強調 must，就能帶出「非這麼做不可」的語氣，是一種強烈要求對方的態度。

4. 強烈要求對方或提出忠告。
- You look very tired. I'm sure you need to have a rest. *I strongly suggest that you* take a week off.
  你看起來非常疲倦，需要好好休息一下，我強烈建議你放一個禮拜的假。

■■ 要求對方放棄　　　　　　　　　　◉ MP3 096

■ 你必須打消……的念頭。

1. You must give up all thoughts of...　　你必須打消所有……的念頭。

2. You've got no choice.　　　　　　　你沒有選擇的餘地。

■ 句型解說

1. 也可以用祈使句 Give up all thoughts of...（打消所有……的念頭。）
- We are now in financial difficulty, and you realize that. So, *give up all thoughts of* continuing the research.
  各位都很清楚，我們現在面臨了財務困難，所以，請打消繼續進行研究的念頭。

2. 沒有其他選擇的意思。請參考「提出方法選項」的說法 (p. 240)。

請對方注意

◉MP3 097

■ 我想說的是……。／請注意……。

1. I'd like to point out that...	我想指出……。
2. We shouldn't [Let's not] forget that...	我們不能〔我們不要〕忘記……。
3. We have to recognize that...	我們必須了解……。
4. We have to bear [keep] in mind that...	我們必須牢記在心……。

■ 要把……放在心上。

5. It is important to remember...	記住……很重要。
6. It is important to bear [keep] ... in mind.	牢牢記住……是很重要的。

■ 請看……。

7. Just look at...	光看……就好。
8. We must look at...	我們必須注意……。
9. Are you aware that...?	你有注意到……嗎？

句型解說

3. recognize 指的是看清楚現實、了解實際情況。

• *We have to recognize* the situation we are in.
我們必須認清目前的處境。

7. 例如：

- We shouldn't be content with our position as the world's second largest economic power. Some nations in Asia are trying to catch up with us. *Just look at* Singapore. They're doing very well.

  我們不能因為是世界第二大經濟體就感到自滿。亞洲有些國家正迎頭趕上，就看新加坡好了，他們表現得很不錯。

---

8. 請看以下對話。

情境對話

A: I think what we have now is all right, and I don't see why we have to introduce new computers into our office.

B: *We must look at* what's happening in the real world. We'll be left behind if we stick to the old facilities.

A：我認為現在的設備就已經夠用了，我不了解為什麼還要引進新的電腦設備。

B：我們必須看看現實世界的動態，只用過時的老舊設備只會讓我們落於時代之後。

明確表達權限或立場　◉MP3 098

■ ……的責任是……。

1. ...'s responsibility is to... [It's ...'s responsibility to...]	……的責任是……。〔……是……的責任。〕
2. ... has the responsibility to...	……有……的責任。
3. ... is responsible for...	……必須負責……。

■ ……有……的立場。

4. ... is in a [the] position to...	……有……的立場。
5. ... in one's capacity as...	……有資格去……。

■ ……有……的權力。

6. ... has the authority to...	……有……的權力。
7. ... has a say [voice] in...	……擁有……的決定權。
8. ... is authorized to... [... is given the authority to...]	……被賦予……的權力。
9. ... has the power to...	……有……的權力。

■ 句型解說

1, 2. responsibility 可以換成 duty。若要說「不是……的責任」，則用 ... is not ...'s responsibility.。

情境對話

A: What have you got to say about the loss of the top-secret documents from the file? Wasn't it your job to take care of them?

B: Well, actually *it's not my responsibility*. I'm only in charge of the legal documents concerning the contract.

A：檔案中的機密文件遺失一事，你有什麼話要說？保管文件不是你的工作嗎？

B：其實不是我的責任，我只負責保管和合約有關的法律文件而已。

3. 例如：

• As the head of the language training center, I'*m responsible for* all activities concerning language learning and teaching.
身為語言訓練中心的負責人，我負責所有和語言學習及語言教學相關的活動。

4. 說明責任和立場。

情境對話

A: I want you to promise to compensate me for all the damage caused by this accident.

B: I'm afraid I'*m* not *in a position to* do that. Could you talk to Mr. Taylor? He is the head of our office and holds all responsibility for the accident.

A：對於這次意外造成的損失，我要你承諾全部賠償。

B：抱歉，我恐怕沒有立場給您承諾。麻煩您向泰勒先生反應好嗎？他是公司的負責人，會負起意外的所有責任。

此外，如果希望對方了解自己的立場，可以說 Let me explain my position.（容我說明一下我的立場。）或是 You must understand my position.（請了解我的立場。）

5. 請看以下對話。

情境對話

A: Are you a representative of the Student Union?

B: Yes, I'm talking to you *in my capacity as* its president.

A：請問你是學生會的代表嗎？

B：是的，我是以學生會會長的身分來跟您見面。

6. authority 指的是權威、規則或以法律為根據的權限或職權。

• I don't *have the authority to* sign the document [make the decision].
我沒有權力簽署這份文件〔做決定〕。

7. say 當名詞使用，意思是「發言權，決定權」。關於主張發言權的說法，請參考第 6 章。類似的說法還有 ... doesn't have much say in...（……沒有……的發言權。）

9. 如果要說沒有能力或立場做某事，可以用 It's not in ...'s power to...（……沒有權力去做……。）或 ... is beyond ...'s power.（……超出……的權限。）

■重點提示

　　了解自己的權限、被賦予的工作及責任範圍為何是很重要的。如果沒有先弄清楚，可能會越權侵犯到他人的領域，或干涉他人的行為。請多加利用這部分的句型，表現各種情況下的責任或能力。

明確指出職權範圍　　　　　　　⦿MP3 099

■ ……的工作是……。

1. ...'s job is (not) to...	……的工作（不）是……。
2. It's (not) ...'s job to...	……（不）是……的工作。
3. ... is doing the job.	工作由……負責。
4. ... is in charge of...	……負責……。
5. ... take care of...	……負責……。
6. As..., ... can... [What I can do as ... is to...]	身為……，……能夠……。〔身為……，我可以做的是……。〕
7. It's (not) for ... to...	……要做（不用做）……。

▪ 句型解說

1, 2. job 在這裡指的是「職務」而非「職業」，可以用 responsibility 取代。

情境對話

A: You are responsible for the loss of packages in the stores.

B: No, I'm not. *My job is* just *to* lock the door, and I did so yesterday. *It's not my job to* keep an eye on the stores all night.

A：倉庫裡的包裹不見了，你得負責。

B：不是我的責任。我只負責鎖門，而且昨天我確實鎖上了。整晚守著倉庫可不是我的工作。

2. 例如：

• *It's my job to* listen to complaints from customers.
傾聽顧客的抱怨是我的工作。

4. in charge of 後面接負責的內容，用來凸顯責任範圍。

情境對話

A: Can I talk to someone *in charge of* foreign students?

B: I'm afraid this is the accounting office. The foreign students section is in the next room.

A：我要找負責留學生事務的人。

B：抱歉，這裡是會計室，留學生事務的辦公室在隔壁。

---

5. take care of... 原來是「照顧…」的意思，這裡是指「負責…，處理…」。

情境對話

A: What's my job here going to be?

B: You will file all the legal documents concerning the contract. But don't touch the confidential documents. I'll *take care of* them.

A：請問我在這裡要做些什麼工作？

B：你的工作是將所有和合約相關的法律文件歸檔。但不要碰機密文件，我來處理就好。

---

6. 描述職務範圍內的事項。

情境對話

A: The two presidents are trying to find an opportunity to discuss the matter. What can you do to help them?

B: *As* ambassador, I *can* arrange a meeting place for them, and I will do my best to help them reach an agreement.

A：兩位總統正努力找機會討論這件事，你可以提供什麼樣的協助？

B：身為大使，我可以為他們安排見面的場所，我也會盡全力協助雙方達成共識。

---

7. 例如：

- *It's not for* the managers *to* discuss the problem.
  管理者不需要討論這個問題。

▍**重點提示**

清楚說明某人的身分或職稱，進一步了解其職務內容或負責事務時使用。

06

第6章
表達意見

表達意見有許多方式，包括猜測、肯定、提案等等。討論的對象若為多數，也要懂得學習如何要求發言，以表達自己的看法。本章要介紹的就是和表達意見有關的各種句型。

Useful English Expressions
for Communication

陳述意見的基本動詞　　　◉MP3 100

I think... ——

「我想……」或「我認為……」的意思，是非常普遍的說法，帶有判斷、推測的意味。除了單純表達個人看法，一般而言，也包含說話者的主觀印象在內。

- *I think* scientists are right in their view that the greenhouse effect will cause some serious problems.
  我認為科學家對於溫室效應將導致嚴重問題的看法是對的。

情境對話

A: Can you swim to the other side of the river?
B: *I think* I can.
A：你能游到河的另一頭嗎？
B：我想我可以。

I suppose... ——

「我猜……」的意思，帶有推測的意味。

- You speak English, *I suppose?*
  我猜你會講英文吧？

I believe... ——

「我相信……」或「我認為……」的意思，用來表示「相信」某個沒有確切根據或無法說明白的事實，著重的是理念上的想法。

- *I believe* he is innocent.
  我相信他是清白的。
- *I believe* China should do something in international affairs that generates trust.
  我認為中國在國際事務方面應該採取一些能讓人產生信賴感的舉措。

I hope... ─────────────

「我希望……」的意思，後面要接 that 子句。否定的「我不希望……」
是 I hope not. 或 I hope that ... not...，不要說成 I don't hope that...。

* *I hope* that I will be able to succeed next time.
  我希望下次能成功。

情境對話

A: There will be some objections to our proposal.

B: *I hope not.*

A：關於我們的提案，應該會出現一些反對意見吧。

B：希望不會。

I imagine... ─────────────

「我猜想……」的意思，表示推測。

* I think the school rules are a bit too strict and *I imagine* most students
  feel the same.
  我認為校規太嚴格了點，而且我猜大部分的學生也是這麼想。

I feel... ─────────────

「我覺得……」的意思，表達對某件事的感想。

* *I feel* things have gone wrong since we adopted the new method.
  我覺得自從我們採用新方法之後，事情就開始變得不順利了。

I assume... ─────────────

「我假定……」或「我以為……」的意思，表示假設或假定，特別是
沒有根據的情況。

* I'm going to talk about Shakespeare, and *I assume* everyone attending
  this lecture has read all of his works.
  我要來談談莎士比亞，我就當做來上這門課的同學都讀過他全部的作品了。

I suspect...

「我猜想……」的意思，表示猜測，後面接 that 子句時，帶有「不就是這樣嗎」的語氣。

- *I suspect* that the missing boy is dead now.

  我猜那個失蹤的男孩應該是凶多吉少了。

I doubt...

「我懷疑……」的意思，對某件事的真偽感到懷疑。

- *I doubt* whether he is telling the truth.

  我懷疑他說的話是不是真的。

表達意見 (I)

◉MP3 101

■ 我的意見是……。

1. I think...	我認為……。
2. In my opinion [view],...	在我看來，……。
3. My opinion [view] is that...	我的意見〔看法〕是……。
4. I would say...	我會說……。

■ 句型解說

---

1. 請看前述的「陳述意見的基本動詞」(p. 152)，還有很多動詞可以取代 think。

---

2. 請看以下對話。

> 情境對話

A: I wonder why we failed in the experiment.

B: *In my opinion*, it's because we didn't keep the correct temperature.

A：實驗會什麼會失敗呢，實在想不通。

B：在我看來，是因為我們沒有維持在正確的溫度。

---

3. 如果要強調這就是自己的見解，可以加入 own 而變成 My own opinion [view] is that...，有加強語氣的效果。另外，也可以在陳述完自己的意見後補上一句 That's my view.（這就是我的看法。）作結。

---

4. 較為婉轉的說法。

表達意見 (II)　　　　　　　　　　　　● MP3 102

■ 我的看法是……。

1. The way I see it,... [The way I look at it is...]	在我看來，……。
2. It seems to me...	我覺得好像……。
3. From my point of view,...	在我看來，……。
4. ..., as I see it,...	……，在我看來，……。
5. I take a different view from...	我和……看法不同。
6. As far as I can see [I see it],...	在我看來，……。
7. ... That's my view.	……。這就是我的看法。
8. At least, that's the way I see it.	至少我是這樣覺得的。

■ 句型解說

----

1. 例如：

- *The way I see it*, the situation is becoming worse.
  在我看來，情況是愈來愈糟了。

----

5. 例如：

- *I take a different view from* other members of the committee.
  我和委員會其他成員看法不同。

----

7. 如果把重音放在 my，可以用來強調是「我的」意見，不是其他人的。請參考「表達意見 (I)」的句型 3 (p. 155)。

從某個角度來看　　　　　　　　　◉MP3 103

■ 有一種看法是……。

1. There are several ways of looking at it.　這個問題可以從很多方面來看。

2. One way to look at ... is...　關於……，其中一個看法
　　　　　　　　　　　　　　　是……。

3. Looking at it from ... point of view,...　從……的觀點來看，……。

4. ...ly speaking, ...　從……上來說，……。

句型解說

2. 類似的用法有 Another way to look at ... is...（關於……，另一個看法是……。）

3. 例如：
- *Looking at it from* another *point of view,...*
  從另一個觀點來看，……。
- *Looking at it from* a financial *point of view,...*
  從財務的觀點來看，……。

4. 以〈副詞 + speaking〉的形式表示，例如 historically speaking（從歷史上來說）、economically speaking（從經濟上來說）。

從其他角度來看　　　　　　　　　◉MP3 104

■ 有必要從不同的角度切入。

1. But there is another side to...　但……還有另外一面。

2. We have to look at two other things.	我們還要注意其他兩點。
3. The other side of ... is...	……的另外一面是……。
4. ... is ... in some ways, but ... in other ways.	……就某些方面來說是……，但就其他方面來說是……。
5. But there are other considerations.	不過還有其他考慮因素。
6. But that's only one aspect of...	但那只是……其中一個面向。

■ 不能單單討論……。

7. You can't just talk about...	不能單單討論……。

■ 句型解說

1. 提出和他人不同的看法。

- *There is another side to* the question.
  這問題可以從另一個角度來看。

- *There is another side to* what you have been saying.
  你所說的還有另一個面向。

4. 強調某件事就某個角度來看是對的，但從其他角度來看則否。

- Economic sanctions against the country *are* beneficial *in some ways, but* not *in others*.
  對該國實施經濟制裁就某方面來說是有利的，但其他方面則否。

7. 如果要解決問題，不能單就某個面向來討論的意思。

解釋意思

■ ……可以解釋成……。

1. You [We] can see ... as...　　　　你〔我們〕可以把……看成是
　　　　　　　　　　　　　　　　……。

2. My reading of ... is that...　　　　我對……的解讀是……。

3. My understanding of ... is that...　我對……的理解是……。

4. My [One] interpretation of ... is　　對於……，我的〔有一個〕解
　　that...　　　　　　　　　　　　釋是……。

■ ……的意思是……。

5. What is meant [implied] by this is...　這個意味著〔暗示著〕……。

6. The meaning of this is that...　　　這個的意思是……。

7. ... suggests...　　　　　　　　　……意思是……。

句型解說

1. 請看以下對話。

　情境對話

　A: Do you think Mozart received ideal training in music?
　B: *You can see* his case *as* a typical example of an ideal education given to a
　　　gifted child.
　A：你認為莫札特受過理想的音樂訓練嗎？
　B：你可以把莫札特的例子看成是天才兒童接受理想音樂訓練的典型。

要表示自己所看到的情形為何時，可以用下面的句型：

● ... That is how it appears to me.
　……。在我看來是這樣。

● ..., as I see it,...
　……，在我看來，……。

2. reading 在這裡是指「解讀，解釋」，等於 interpretation，尤其是在解釋某種狀況時使用。

- *My reading of* the situation *is that* everything is uncertain.
  我對情況的解讀是，一切都還不確定。

---

5. 也可以說 This means [implies]...（這意味著〔暗示著〕……。）

---

7. 例如：

- Our investigation into the new drug has shown that it is effective for 95 percent of the patients suffering from the disease. But, it has caused serious side effects on three patients. That *suggests* two things: One is that we have to look into the cause of the side effects. The other is that we must continue our examination of the effectiveness of the drug.
  根據我們的調查，新藥對於 95% 罹患該疾病的病患有效，但其中有三名病患出現嚴重的副作用。這意味著兩件事：一是我們要找出引發副作用的原因，一是我們必須持續對新藥的療效進行研究。

一般而言　　　　　　　　　　　　　◉MP3 106

■ 大致上來說，……。

1. On the whole,...	整體來說，……。
2. In general,...	一般來說，……。
3. Generally (speaking),...	一般來說，……。
4. ... more or less...	……或多或少……。
5. We can generalize about ... (to some extent) and say that...	關於……，我們（大致上）可以說……。

■句型解說

1. 看事物的整體。

- *On the whole*, the exhibition was a success.
  整體來說，這次展覽是成功的。

4. 雖然不嚴重，但仍有一定程度。

- He is *more or less* a moody person.
  他多少有點陰晴不定。

5. 例如：

- *We can generalize about* chimpanzees *and say that* they are gentle animals.
  我們大致上可以說黑猩猩是一種溫和的動物。

類似說法有 I may generalize from ... and say...（從……我大致上可以說……）。

- *I may generalize from* the mistakes he made *and say* that he is unreliable.
  從他所犯的錯誤來看，我大概可以說他是個不能信賴的人。

■重點提示

表示自己的意見適用大多數的情況，或用於概括性的討論。

表示印象

◉MP3 107

■ 有……的印象。

1. I have the impression that...	我的印象是……。
2. My (general) impression is that...	我（大概）的印象是……。
3. The impression that I obtained from ... is that...	我對於……的印象是……。

4. I have a feeling that...　　　　　　　　我有個感覺，就是……。

5. My feeling is that...　　　　　　　　　　我的感覺是……。

6. My own instinctive feeling is that...　　我自己的直覺是……。

■ 句型解說

2. 請看以下對話。

情境對話

A: Do you think that the library needs improvement?

B: Absolutely! I went there last week and *my impression was that* the librarians didn't really know the users' needs.

A：你認為圖書館需要改善嗎？

B：當然要！我上禮拜去了一趟，感覺館員不太了解使用者有哪些需求。

4. 請看以下對話。

情境對話

A: Do you really believe that this project is going to be profitable? Last time we had a similar project, and it wasn't very successful, was it?

B: No, but *I have a feeling that* we will be successful this time.

A：你真的相信這個企劃會賺錢嗎？上次我們有過一個類似的計畫，不太成功對吧？

B：嗯，不過我感覺這次會成功。

■ 重點提示

　　feeling 偏向毫無根據的推測和感覺，用來表達某種直覺。impression 則是一種印象，未經過縝密思考的感想或見解。

表示臆測

■ 我猜會不會是……？

1. I would say...	我會說……。
2. I [would] guess...	我〔會〕猜……。
3. My guess is that...	我的推測是……。
4. It's just a guess, but I think...	這只是個猜測，不過我認為……。
5. ... That's my guess.	……。那是我的猜測。
6. If I had to venture a guess, I would say...	如果要我猜的話，我會說……。
7. It seems to me that...	我覺得好像……。

■ 句型解說

1. 不直接斷言，而是用推測的方式陳述意見。

情境對話

A: How much would you say it costs to study in London for a year?

B: Oh, *I would say* ten thousand pounds, or perhaps more.

A：你覺得去倫敦留學一年要花多少錢？

B：喔，我想要一萬英鎊，或許更多吧。

2~6. guess 是一種憑空臆測的說法。

* *If I had to venture a guess, I would say* the economy won't recover until the end of this year.

　如果要我猜的話，我會說整個經濟要到年底之後才會好轉。

情境對話　1

A: How many people will apply for the grant?

B: *I guess* there will be about one hundred.

163

A：有多少人會申請補助？

B：我猜一百個人左右吧。

情境對話 2

A: How old is she?

B: She could be about thirty, but *that's* just *my guess.*

A：她幾歲？

B：可能 30 左右吧，不過那只是我的猜測而已。

■ 重點提示

　　爲了說服對方，陳述正確的事實確實是必要的。不過，某些情況下單用臆測的說法也可以，只是臆測的內容不能過於誇大，才能達成目的。這種情況下便可以使用上述句型。

❚ 表達個人看法　　　　　　　　　　　　⦿ MP3 109

■ 我的看法是……。

1. Personally I think...	我個人認為……。
2. My (own) personal opinion [view] is that...	我（個人）的意見〔看法〕是……。
3. As far as I am concerned,...	在我看來，……。

■ 句型解說

1. I think... 的用法請參考「陳述意見的基本動詞」(p. 152) 的部分。

2. 例如：

- When I said that children should work harder on their subjects, I was speaking as a teacher. *My own personal opinion is that* they should spend more time on extracurricular activities.

  當我說孩子應該更努力學習各科目時，我是站在一個老師的立場發言的。至於我個人的意見，我認為他們應該花多一點時間從事課外活動。

■ 重點提示

站在個人而非客觀的立場發表意見時使用。

站在特定的立場表示意見　　●MP3 110

■ 就……的立場來說，……。

1. I'm speaking as...	我是站在……的立場發言的。
2. Speaking as..., I (would) think [suggest]...	就……的立場而言，我（會）認為〔建議〕……。
3. As..., I think...	身為……，我認為……。
4. From a ...'s point of view, I think...	從……的觀點來看，我認為……。
5. When I ..., I am [was] speaking as...	當我……，我是站在……的立場發言的。

■ 句型解說

---

1. as 後面可以接各種代表身分的名詞，例如 as a friend（身為朋友）、as a member of...（身為…的成員）、as a representative of...（身為…的代表）、as an expert on...（身為…的專家）。

情境對話

A: Are you suggesting that Mr. Davis should resign? I'm surprised. He is your close friend, isn't he?

B: Yes, he is one of my close friends. But, *I'm speaking as* a representative of the committee, and I think he should give up his post.

A：你的意思是說戴維斯先生應該辭職嗎？我真是驚訝，他不是你的好朋友嗎？

B：是，他是我的好朋友，但我現在是站在委員會代表的立場來發言的，而我認為他應該辭職。

2. 請看以下對話。

情境對話

A: What is your opinion on the new models?

B: I'm quite interested in model A because of its user-friendly gears. But, *speaking as* a consumer, *I would* buy model B because it is more affordable than model A.

A：你對這些新車款有什麼看法？

B：我對 A 款蠻有興趣的，因為它的排檔非常好操作。不過，從消費者的立場來看，我會買 B 款，因為價格上比較負擔得起。

4. 例如：

- *From a* reformist's *point of view*, the plan seems a little disappointing to me.
  從一個改革派的角度來看，這項計畫讓我有點失望。

5. 例如：

- *When I* suggest that we should withdraw from the project as soon as possible, *I am speaking as* an accountant.
  當我建議我們應該盡早從這項計畫中抽手，我是站在一位會計師的立場來發言的。

■ 重點提示

不是從個人的角度，而是站在公司、團體或是某個特定職務的立場來發言時使用。

沒有意見

● MP3 111

■ 對……沒有意見。

1. I don't have any opinion on [about]...　　我對……沒有任何意見。

2. I don't have anything to say on [about]...　我對……沒有什麼要說的。

■ 想不出答案。

3. I don't know what to think of [about]...　　對……我不知道該怎麼想才好。

4. I don't have any easy answer.　　　　　　我沒有任何簡單的答案。

5. I'm afraid I don't know the answer to　　　對於那件事我恐怕沒有答案。
　 that.

6. I have no idea.　　　　　　　　　　　　我不知道。

■ 我對……不清楚。

7. I don't know much about...　　　　　　對於……我知道的並不多。

8. I know nothing of...　　　　　　　　　我對……一無所知。

9. You'll have to ask ... about that.　　　那件事你得去問……才知道。

句型解說

1. 對事情不表示意見，類似的用法還有 I don't have any opinion to offer.（我沒有什麼意見要說的。）

情境對話

A: What do you think of the education system in Britain?

B: I'm afraid *I don't have any opinion on* that. I'm not particularly interested in education.

A：你對英國的教育體制有什麼看法？

B：我恐怕沒有什麼看法，我對教育並不特別感興趣。

167

6. 對他人提出的問題毫無頭緒，不知道該怎麼回答。

情境對話

A: How old is she?

B: Oh, *I have no idea.* Well, perhaps twenty five ... um ... or thirty.

A：她幾歲？

B：喔，我不知道。嗯，可能 25，呃，或者 30 吧。

---

9. 與其自己回答，不如請對方去請教更適合的人。

情境對話

A: The patient was suffering from sudden attacks of vertigo. Are they a symptom of diabetes?

B: I'm not sure. *You'll have to ask* Dr. Smith *about that.* He is an expert on diabetes.

A：患者突然感到暈眩，這是糖尿病的徵兆嗎？

B：我不確定。你得去問史密斯博士，他是研究糖尿病的專家。

■ 重點提示

　　積極表達意見是討論事情的基本態度。不過，如果真的沒有什麼意見，與其敷衍了事，不如主動表示自己沒有意見，這時，上述句型便可派上用場。

表示確定　　　　　　　　　　　　　　　◉MP3 112

■ 我確定……。

1. I'm (absolutely) sure that [about/of]...	我（非常）確定……。
2. I have no doubt about... [I don't doubt that...]	對於……，我不懷疑。〔我不懷疑……。〕
3. I'm convinced that [of]...	我相信……。

4. There is no question about...   對於……，我沒有任何問題。

5. I can say with certainty that...   我可以肯定地說……。

▪句型解說

1. 也可以用 certain 代替 sure。
   - *I'm sure of* his success.
     我相信他會成功。

   情境對話

   A: I saw a man in a white shirt dashing out of the room.

   B: Are you sure about his clothes?

   A: Yes, *I'm absolutely sure that* the man was wearing a white shirt and that he's
      the thief.

   A：我看見一個穿白襯衫的男人衝出房間。

   B：你確定他穿白襯衫？

   A：對，我非常確定他穿白襯衫，而且他就是小偷。

---

2. 類似的說法是 There is [can be] no doubt that...（……是毫無疑問的。）

---

3. convinced 比 sure 或 certain 更確定。

---

5. 稍微誇張的表現方式。

▦ 表示不確定   ●MP3 113

■ 我不確定……。

1. I'm not sure about [that/what]...   我不確定……。

2. I'm not sure, but I think...	我不確定，但我認為……。
3. I'm not so sure about...	對於……我不是很確定。
4. We can't really be sure about ... until...	……之前，我們不太能確定……。

■ 句型解說

1. 表示不確定，將前項「表示確定」的句型 1 改為否定即可。

- Mr. Scott will win the election, but *I'm not sure about* Mr. Thomas.
  史考特先生會當選，但湯瑪斯先生我就不確定了。

- I think the yen will go higher for the next few days, but *I'm not* quite *sure what* will happen after that.
  我認為接下來幾天日圓會走升，但那之後會怎麼樣我就不太確定了。

2. 在不確定的情況下表達意見。

情境對話

A: Could you tell me how long it takes to fly from Taoyuan to San Francisco?

B: *I'm not sure, but I think* it's about twelve hours non-stop.

A：你知道從桃園機場飛舊金山要多久嗎？

B：我不確定，但我想直飛大概要 12 小時吧。

3. 對於對方提出的意見感到懷疑時，可以用副詞 so 來加強語氣。

情境對話

A: The best location for our new factory is surely Thailand.

B: *I'm not so sure about* that.

A：新工廠的最佳地點絕對是泰國。

B：我可不是那麼確定。

4. until...（直到…）表示條件，也就是說在…之前都不能確定。

情境對話

A: I heard the new medicine is very good for treating cancer.

B: *We can't be sure about* that *until* we receive the findings of the committee.

A：我聽說新藥對於癌症的治療非常有效。

B：收到委員會的結果前我們都還不能確定。

要求發言　　　　　　　　　　　●MP3 114

■ 可以說句話嗎？

1. Can I say a few words?	我可以說幾句話嗎？
2. Can [May] I just say,...	我可以說一下嗎？……。
3. Could I say something about...?	關於……，我可以說句話嗎？
4. Let me just say,...	讓我說一下，……。
5. I'd just like to say a few words as to...	關於……，我只是想說句話。
6. Can [May] I just comment on...?	我可以針對……發表一下意見嗎？
7. Just a brief word [comment].	只要一句話就好。

■ 我想補充一下。

8. Can I make just one point?	可以讓我只補充一點嗎？
9. I have a point to make here.	關於這個，我有一點要補充。
10. Can I make one other point?	可以讓我補充另外一點嗎？
11. If I could just make a point here,...	如果能讓我補充一點的話，……。
12. Let me give [voice] my opinion.	讓我說說我的看法。

▌句型解說

---

2. Can [May] I...? 雖然有尋求對方同意的意味，但有時只是一種客氣的表現。換句話說，不用得到他人的允許即可發言。

情境對話

A: I love Japanese kimonos. They are beautiful. Yukatas are also beautiful. I'd like to have a yukata to wear for a party.

B: *Can I just say*, the yukata is not formal dress. It's just casual wear suitable after taking a bath on a hot summer's day.

A: Oh, I was mistaken.

A：我喜歡日本和服，和服漂亮，浴衣也是。我想穿浴衣去參加派對。

B：我可以說一下嗎？浴衣不是正式服裝，只是夏天洗完澡後穿的居家服。

A：喔，我搞錯了。

---

4. 以 Let me... 開頭，表示不尋求他人的允許，直接發表言論。

情境對話

A: The sales of model X have dropped sharply over the last few months, and I've been wondering whether it is due to the lack of morale on the part of the sales department. We've spent a lot of money on...

B: *Let me just say,* I'm not here to represent my people or to make excuses, but the fact is that we haven't had enough money for advertising.

A：X 款的銷售量在過去幾個月掉了很多，我一直在想是不是業務部缺乏士氣的關係。我們花了很多錢在……。

B：讓我說句話，我今天來這裡不是代表我們部門說話，也不是要找藉口，但現實的狀況是我們一直沒有足夠的宣傳經費。

---

8 ~ 11. point 是「意見，論點」的意思。

---

12. voice 當動詞用，意思是「發聲，表達，表示」，是比較強烈的表現。

重點提示

　　遇到人多的場合，適時發言能夠讓大家了解自己的看法。開會時，除了向主席提出發言的要求，也有自己主動發言的情況，這時便可使用 Can I...? 或 May I...? 等句型，表面上帶有請求他人允許的意味，實際上只是一種禮貌的表現。

中途加入意見 ● MP3 115

■ 請讓我插句話。

1. Can [May] I come in here?　　　　　可以讓我插句話嗎？
2. Can [May] I come in to say,...　　　可以讓我插句話嗎？……。

句型解說

2. to say 後面接要說的話。

情境對話

A: I appreciate the idea Mr. Stewart presented, because...

B: *May I come in to say*, it's not exactly Mr. Stewart's idea. The idea originally came from some of his colleagues.

A：我很感謝史都華先生的提議，因為……。

B：請讓我插句話，那其實不是史都華先生的提議，是他一些同事想出來的。

重點提示

　　討論進行到一半想要補充意見時使用。參與討論的人數較多時，上述的表達方式不但較為得體，也能讓討論順利進行。

主張自己的發言權 ◉MP3 116

■ **輪到我說了。**

1. It's now my say.	現在輪到我說了。
2. Let me have my say.	讓我說一下我的看法。
3. I haven't had my say yet.	我還沒發表意見。

句型解說

1. 對方已經說過了，現在輪到自己表達意見，給人一種對立的感覺。say 當名詞用，指「發言權」。

2, 3. 表示自己有權發言。若要主張自己在某件事情上有發言權，可以說 I want a say in... 或 I must have a voice in...，兩者都是「關於……，我有話要說」的意思。
   • *I want a say in* this matter.
     關於這件事我想說句話。

靈光一閃 ◉MP3 117

■ **我突然想到，……。**

1. I've just had a thought.	我突然有個想法。
2. I hit on [got] a good idea.	我想到了個好點子。
3. It has just occurred to me that...	我突然想到，……。
4. An idea has just come to me.	剛剛浮現一個想法。
5. Oh, I know.	啊，我知道了。

■ 句型解說

---

1. 用現在完成式來表示剛剛想到的點子，也可以用現在式，例如 I have an idea for...（關於……，我有個想法。）

---

3. it 指的是接下來提出的看法。

情境對話

A: We must send someone to Paris as soon as possible.

B: *It has just occurred to me that* Mr. Mitchell can speak French. Why don't we send him to Paris?

A: That's a good idea.

A：我們得盡快派人去巴黎。

B：我突然想到，米契爾先生會說法文，不如派他去吧。

A：好點子。

---

5. 腦中突然浮現某個念頭。

情境對話

A: We must send someone to France to carry out market research. Mr. Harris may be an appropriate person to go, but he can't speak French.

B: That will be a problem. Well, ... *oh, I know*, we've got Mr. Robinson of the Sales Department. I believe he has a good command of French because he majored in French literature at university. Why don't we have him go with Mr. Harris?

A：我們得派人去法國進行市場調查。哈里斯先生還蠻適合的，不過他不會說法文。

B：那確實是個問題。嗯，喔，我知道了，還有業務部的羅賓森先生啊。他大學主修法國文學，法文應該不錯。不如讓他跟著哈里斯先生一起去？

提議

● MP3 118

■ 就……吧！

1. Let's...	就……吧。
2. (I think) We should...	（我認為）我們應該……。
3. Why don't we...?	我們何不……？
4. What about...?	……如何？
5. I (would) suggest...	我（會）建議……。
6. I've a suggestion to make. [I'd like to make a suggestion.]	我有個建議。
7. May I suggest...?	我可不可以建議……？
8. Can't [Could] we...?	我們不能〔我們可以〕……嗎？
9. I have a brilliant idea to propose.	我有個很棒的提議。
10. I say we...	我說我們就……。

句型解說

1. 帶有強烈建議的語氣，也可以加上附加問句而成為 Let's..., shall we?。如果要建議什麼都不要做，可以用 Let's not...（我們不要……。）

   • *Let's* turn to the next question.
     我們接著看下一個問題。

   • *Let's not* talk about it any more.
     我們就不要再討論這件事了。

2. 比較強勢的說法。

3. 雖然是以問句徵詢對方意見，但所表達的意思是「我們應該要……」。其他請參考句型 8 的解說。

情境對話

A: This is a complicated question.

B: Yes, indeed. Well, I'm a little tired. *Why don't we* have a break?

A：這是個複雜的問題。

B：確實是。嗯，我有點累了，不如我們休息一下？

---

4. What about 後面接名詞或動名詞。

情境對話 1

A: Could we meet again on Tuesday?

B: That's not suitable.

A: Then, *what about* Friday?

B: Yes, Friday would be fine.

A：星期二能再見個面嗎？

B：星期二不太方便。

A：那，星期五如何？

B：好，星期五沒問題。

情境對話 2

A: The engine has stopped suddenly. What shall I do?

B: Have you tried pulling the lever?

A: Yes, but it didn't work.

B: *What about* pushing it?

A：發動機突然不動了，該怎麼辦才好？

B：你有試著拉控制桿嗎？

A：有，但沒用。

B：那推一下看看呢？

---

7. 婉轉地給他人建議的說法，也可以說 Could I suggest...?。

---

8. Can't we...? 帶有「沒有不能的道理吧，既然這樣的話，就……吧」的暗示。

情境對話

A: We must take decisive action as soon as possible.

B: But *can't we* wait for a couple of days to see what will happen?

A：我們必須盡快採取果斷的行動。

B：但不能多等個幾天、看看之後的情況嗎？

---

10. I say 是比較強勢的說法，I say we... 是一種強烈建議的表現。

情境對話

A: Let's get back.

B: Do we really have to return?

A: Yes, there's a danger of avalanches.

B: Well.

A: *I say we* get back!

A：我們回頭吧。

B：眞的得掉頭回去嗎？

A：對，因爲有雪崩的危險。

B：是嗎？

A：我說掉頭！

■重點提示

　　表示提議的句型可用於正式場合（例如會議上針對某項議題提出檢討），也可以用於日常生活中，有「一起……吧」的勸告意味。另外，也要視情況和場合決定使用婉轉或強勢的說法。

▨ 提出解決方法　　　　　　　　　　　　● MP3 119

■ 我有一個方法。

1. It would be an idea [a good idea] to...	……是個方法〔好方法〕。
2. ... would be an idea [a good idea].	……會是個方法〔好方法〕。
3. One idea is to...	有個方法是……。
4. We [You] could...	我們〔你〕可以……。

5. ... is at least worthy of consideration.　　……至少有考慮的價值吧。

6. ..., say,...　　……，比如說，……。

7. I know what.　　我有辦法了。

■句型解說

1. 也可以改用疑問句，即 Wouldn't it be a good idea to...?。

---

2. would 的前面可以填入名詞、動名詞或不定詞。

情境對話

A: We have to send someone to Paris to carry out market research. The question is, who is to go? I think Mr. Mitchell or Mr. Thomas would be suitable for the job.

B: To send Mr. Mitchell *would be a good idea*. He has a good command of French.

A：我們得派人去巴黎進行市場調查。問題是派誰去？我認爲米契爾先生或湯瑪斯先生都蠻適合的。

B：派米契爾先生去不錯，他的法文說得很好。

---

3. 請看以下對話。

情境對話

A: I tried to approach Mr. Parker several times, but I was turned away at the door.

B: *One idea is to* talk to his friend Mr. Collins first, and obtain a letter of reference.

A：我有好幾次想和派克先生碰個面，但都吃了閉門羹。

B：有個方法是先和他的朋友柯林斯先生聯絡，請柯林斯先生幫忙寫封推薦信。

---

4. could（可以，能）不是表示過去，是讓語氣變得婉轉的表現方式。

---

6. say（比如說，例如）是插入語，用來提示具體的選項，是一種簡略的說法。

• Would you come to my office, *say*, at 1:30?
  你可以來我的研究室嗎，比如說一點半的時候？

7. 簡略說法。

■ 重點提示

就某個提案進行討論而提出單一方法時使用。

▦ 提出替代方案 　　　　　　　　　　　　　⦿MP3 120

■ ……比較好吧？

1. Wouldn't ... be better [more...]?	……不會比較好〔比較……〕嗎？
2. I have a better idea.	我有個更好的辦法。
3. It might be better [more...] to...	……可能會比較好〔比較……〕。
4. But can't we..., instead?	但難道我們不能……？
5. Would it be all right if ... instead?	如果改成……可以嗎？
6. Instead of..., what about...?	不要……，改成……你覺得如何？
7. It would be an idea not to..., but to...	不要……，而是……，或許是個方法也說不定。

■ 句型解說

1, 3. 表示替代方案優於原先的提案，重點在於使用比較級，如 quicker（較快）、cheaper（較便宜）、more convenient（較方便）、more practical（較實用）。

----

3. might（可能）不是表示過去，是讓語氣變得婉轉的表現方式。

情境對話

A: Shall we fly to Kaohsiung?

B: *It might be cheaper to* go by train.

A: Let me check.

A：該搭飛機去高雄嗎？

B：搭火車可能比較便宜。

A：我查一下。

---

5. 請看以下對話。

情境對話

A: Could you come to my office tomorrow to discuss the matter?

B: *Would it be all right if* you came to my office *instead*?

A：你明天能不能來我辦公室討論一下這件事？

B：方不方便改成你過來一趟？

---

6. 請看以下對話。

情境對話

A: I'm planning to go to the United States.

B: *Instead of* the United States, *what about* Canada?

A：我打算去美國。

B：不要去美國，改去加拿大如何？

■ 重點提示

提出更好的提案使對方打消原來的念頭時使用。

有話直說

⦿ MP3 121

■ 坦白說，……。

1. Frankly (speaking),...	說真的，……。
2. To tell you the truth,...	老實說，……。
3. Let me tell you straight.	我就直說了。

■ 我必須說……。

4. I (really) must say...	我（真的）必須說……。
5. I really must point out that...	我真的必須指出……。
6. If you ask me, (I think)...	如果你問我的話，（我覺得）……。

■ 我心裡真正的想法是……。

7. Let me speak my mind.	我就說出心裡真正的想法吧。

■ 句型解說

1, 2. 說出來的話可能會讓對方覺得刺耳。類似的用法還有 Let me be frank and tell you that...（我老實跟你說……。）

• *Frankly speaking*, you are not suitable for the position.
老實說，你不適合這份工作。

----

3. 也可以說 Let me be straight.。

情境對話

A: Frankly, your party is unfit for government.

B: Thank you for telling me straight. *Let me be* equally *straight*. You just argue against the government and that's all you can do.

A：說真的，貴黨不適合執政。

B：謝謝你的直言。那我也直說了，你們只會跟政府唱反調，除此之外沒有任何建樹。

5. 對方不講理時，可用這個句型提出反論。比較婉轉的說法是 May I point out that...?（我可以指出……嗎？）。

6. If you ask me 只是用來強調自己的意見，和對方有沒有提問無關。

情境對話

A: The management went so far as to say that the employees were overpaid. What's your reaction to that?

B: *If you ask me*, that's just nonsense.

A：資方竟然說付給勞方的薪水太多了。關於這點，你的看法是？

B：如果你問我的話，我認為那根本是胡說八道。

7. 直率地說出內心的想法。

■ 重點提示

有話想說而且用較直接的口吻說出來時使用。

語帶保留　　　　　　　　　　　　◉MP3 122

■ 無論好壞……。

1. Rightly or wrongly,...	不論是對是錯，……。
2. ... has [offers] both advantages and disadvantages.	……有好有壞。
3. The answer is both yes and no.	答案既是肯定的也是否定的。
4. It's true that..., but it's also true that...	……沒錯，但……也是事實。

■ 句型解說

1. 不下判斷，單純陳述事實。

- *Rightly or wrongly*, he told us what he saw.
  不論是對是錯，他把他看見的告訴我們了。

2. 請見以下對話。

情境對話

A: Do you welcome the strong yen?

B: Well, the strong yen *offers both advantages and disadvantages*, and we can't look at it only in terms of good or bad.

A：日圓走強，你樂觀其成嗎？

B：怎麼說呢，日圓走強有優點也有缺點，不能單純說是好還是壞。

3. 表示答案有肯定與否定兩種面向，進而從內容中加以說明。

情境對話

A: Do you think English education in Taiwan is working well?

B: *The answer is both yes and no.* Yes, in the sense that students are taught to have quite a wide vocabulary, and they know a lot about grammar. No, in the sense that students never learn to speak the language proficiently.

A：你覺得台灣的英語教育成功嗎？

B：一方面成功一方面不成功。成功的地方是學生學到很多單字，也很熟悉文法。不成功的地方在於學生沒辦法說一口流利的英語。

■ 重點提示

在現實生活中，很多事情都沒有絕對的標準答案，不表達明確立場反而有利。因此，可以同時提出正反兩面的意見，不要妄下判斷，這時便可以使用上述句型。

無可奉告

■ 我無法表示意見。

1. I'm afraid I can't comment on that at the moment.	目前我恐怕無法針對那件事表示意見。
2. I can't say anything of...	關於……，我什麼都不能說。
3. I'm not in a position to say anything about...	關於……，我沒有立場表示任何意見。
4. I'd rather not say (anything about it).	（關於那件事）我什麼都不想說。
5. I'd prefer not to say anything about it.	關於那件事我不想表示任何意見。
6. I decline to comment on...	我拒絕對……表示意見。

■ 句型解說

1. 類似的說法還有 I'd rather not pass comment on that at the moment.（目前我不想針對那件事表示意見。）另外，我們常說的「無可奉告」，英文要說 no comment，面對他人不禮貌的質問時，可用來拒絕回答。

6. decline 是「婉拒，婉謝」的意思。
   - *I decline to* answer your question.
     我拒絕回答你的問題。
   - *I decline to* say any more about...
     關於……，我拒絕再表示任何意見。

■ 重點提示

　　面對他人太過直接的提問，有時基於職務不便表示意見，有時則因涉及隱私而不願回應，這時便可以利用上述句型，婉轉而堅定地表明自己的立場。

收回意見　　　　　　　　　◉MP3 124

1. I want [would like] to withdraw a statement I made earlier.	我想收回剛才所說的話。

■ 句型解說

請參考第 7 章「要求對方收回所說的話」(p. 200)。

附帶說明　　　　　　　　　◉MP3 125

■ 再者，……。

1. Added to that [this],...	除了那個〔這個〕之外，……。
2. In addition,...	此外，……。
3. On top of that [this],...	在那個〔這個〕之外，……。
4. Besides,...	此外，……。
5. What's more,...	另外，……。
6. More importantly,...	更重要的是，……。

■ 還有一點。

7. There is something to add to this [that].	關於這個〔那個〕還有一點要補充。
8. And there is another thing.	還有一件事。
9. Another thing [problem/question] is...	另外一件事〔一個問題〕是……。

10. ... (but) not only that. There is a (further)...

……，（但）不只如此，還有一個（更）……。

■ 附帶說明的是，……。

11. Let me [Allow me to] add that...

讓我補充說明……。

12. I'd (just) like to add that...

我（只是）想補充說明……。

13. Let me (just) say one other...

讓我再多說一點……就好。

14. I might add that...

我想補充說明……。

15. If I could just add...

如果可以讓我再補充……。

16. There is one more thing I wanted to say.

我還有一件事想說。

17. Uh, just one other [more] thing.

對了，還有一件事。

18. I hasten to add...

我還得說……。

19. That's not the end of the story.

我的話還沒說完。

■ 句型解說

1. 例如：

- The demand for that type of car is decreasing. *Added to that,* there are pressures from shareholders for a greater return on investments.
  那種車款的需求量一直在減少，除此之外，還有來自股東要求更多投資收益的壓力。

4. 當副詞使用，也可以說成 And besides,...，表示追加的意見。

- I find nothing particularly interesting about the job. *Besides,* it doesn't pay well.
  我找不出這份工作哪裡有趣，而且薪水也不高。

5. What's more, 後面的內容是重點，用來補充說明前述內容，給人「不僅如此，還……」的感覺。

- He passed the entrance examination, and, *what's more,* he won a scholarship.
  他通過入學考試，而且還拿到了獎學金。

另外，也可以用類似的結構來表示更糟的情況，例如 What's worse,... （更糟的是，……。），也可以說成 To make matters worse,...。

---

10. 例如：

- He came late. And *not only that,* he didn't apologize.
  他遲到了。而且不只那樣，他連個道歉也沒有。

---

11. 例如：

- The theory was propounded by a Japanese scientist, Professor Tanaka, and *let me add that* it deserves a Nobel Prize in chemistry.
  該理論是由日本的田中教授所提出，而且，容我補充一句，該理論絕對足以爲田中教授贏得諾貝爾化學獎。

---

11 ~ 19. 補充說明。

---

18. 補充說明剛說過的事項。

- Our offer is two thousand pounds, tax-free, *I hasten to add.*
  我們的條件是 2,000 英鎊，而且免稅。

難以啓齒　　　　　　　　　　　◉MP3 126

■ 很抱歉我得這麼說，但……。

1. I'm sorry to have to tell you this [say this], but...	很抱歉我必須告訴你這件事〔這麼說〕，但……。
2. I hate to tell you [say this], but...	我不想告訴你〔這麼說〕，但……。

3. I don't know how to tell you this, but...

我不知道該怎麼跟你說這件事，但……。

4. I hope you don't mind my mentioning this, but...

希望你不要介意我提這件事，但……。

5. I'm sorry, but I have to say...

抱歉，但我必須說……。

6. I don't mean to hurt your feelings, but...

我不是故意要讓你難過，但……。

7. I'm afraid it isn't very good news, but...

這恐怕不是件好消息，但……。

8. I don't know whether I should ask you this, but...

我不知道該不該問你這件事，但……。

9. Perhaps I shouldn't tell you this, but...

或許我不該告訴你這件事，但……。

■句型解說

1. 請看以下對話。

情境對話

A: *I'm sorry to have to tell you this*, *but* we've decided to cut the budget for your research.

B: How disappointing!

A：很抱歉必須告訴你，但我們決定要刪減你的研究預算了。

B：太令人失望了！

2. 請看以下對話。

情境對話

A: I'd like to ask for a raise of 20%.

B: *I hate to tell you*, *but* I think you are asking too much.

A：我希望能加薪 20%。

B：我不想這麼說，但我覺得你要求太多了。

■ 重點提示

說出的話也許會傷人或不如對方預期的時候，可以使用上述句型。

猶豫該不該說　　　　　　　　　　　　●MP3 127

■ 這真的很難開口，但……。

1. I'm a little reluctant to say this, but...	我不太想說這件事，但……。
2. I hesitate to say this, but...	我很猶豫要不要講這件事，但……。
3. I find it hard to say what I feel, but...	很難說出我的感受，但……。
4. It's very difficult to say, but...	這很難開口，但……。

■ 重點提示

由於某種狀況、立場或問題太過複雜而難以啓齒，但卻又不得不說時，可以利用上述句型。but 後面接要說的話。

直言不諱　　　　　　　　　　　　　　●MP3 128

■ 我必須說……。

1. I must tell you...	我必須告訴你……。
2. I venture to say...	恕我冒昧，……。
3. If I may venture an opinion [a suggestion/comment], I would say...	如果可以讓我發表拙見〔建議／意見〕的話，我會說……。
4. I don't have any hesitation in saying that...	我毫不猶豫地說……。

5. At the risk of..., I must say [point out]...

即使冒著……的危險，我也要說〔指出〕……。

■ 句型解說

1. 對對方感到生氣時使用。

3. 也可以說 May I venture an opinion [a suggestion/comment]?（能否冒昧提出拙見〔建議／意見〕？）。

5. at the risk of... 是指「冒著…的風險」，表示已經知道可能會導致哪些不利的結果，但仍決定做某一件事，例如 at the risk of sounding critical（冒著被人家說太挑剔的風險）、at the risk of seeming rude（冒著被人家以為很沒禮貌的風險）。

- *At the risk of* offending some members of the committee, *I must say* I disapprove of the budget plan.
  冒著得罪部分委員會成員的風險，我必須說我不贊成這個預算案。

可能有錯的情況下表達意見　◉MP3 129

■ 我也許是錯的，但……。

1. I could [may] be wrong, but...　我可能是錯的，但……。
2. (Please) Correct me if I am wrong.　如果我說錯了請糾正我。
3. If I remember rightly [correctly],...　如果我沒記錯的話，……。

■ 重點提示

對自己所說的內容不太有信心，擔心可能有錯時所使用。

▨ 回答問題 　　　　　　　　　　　　　　　　　⊙MP3 130

■ 答案是……。

1. The answer (to your question) is...	（對於你的問題）答案是……。
2. My answer is...	我的答案是……。
3. In answer to your question,...	對於你的問題，我的答案是……。
4. If you ask me..., I would say...	如果你問我……，我會說……。
5. That's a simple question to answer.	這問題很好回答。

■ 我無法回答。

6. I'm afraid I don't know the answer to your question.	我恐怕不知道問題的答案。
7. That's a very difficult question to answer.	這個問題很難回答。
8. That's not an easy question to answer.	這不是個容易回答的問題。

■ 句型解說

1. 例如：

* *The answer is* yes.
  答案是肯定的。

3. 先提其他的事情，再回過頭來回答問題時可以使用。

情境對話

A: English education in Taiwan is not working well. What is the solution? Could you give me your opinion as an English teacher?

B: Can I first comment on what you've said just now? I don't think English education in Taiwan is totally ineffective. Students are in fact taught to have quite a wide vocabulary, and they know a lot about grammar. In that respect, English education is working quite well in this country. The problem is with the lack of training in speaking the language. Now, *in answer to your question*, I would suggest that...

A：台灣的英語教育成效不彰，有什麼解決方法呢？身為一位英文老師，你有什麼看法呢？

B：我可以先就你剛剛說的表達一下意見嗎？我不認為台灣的英語教育完全沒效果，事實上，學生學到很多單字，也學了不少文法。就那方面來看，台灣的英語教育算是相當成功的。問題在於缺少口語訓練。回到你剛剛的問題，我會建議⋯⋯。

如果問題有兩個以上，還可以說 In answer to your second question,... （對於你第二個問題，我的答案是⋯⋯）、In answer to your last question,... （對於你最後一個問題，我的答案是⋯⋯）。

還有一種說法也很常見：

• Let me begin with your last question.
  我先從你最後一個問題開始回答。

▪重點提示

　　討論經常可見問題和答案的交鋒，雙方有來有往、一問一答。因此怎麼回答顯得格外重要，這時，上述句型便可派上用場。

詢問意見時的說法　　　　　　◉MP3 131

用以下的疑問句引導對方表示意見。

What do you...?

- *What do you* think about that?
  你對那件事有什麼想法？

What's your ... of [about/on]...?

- *What's your* view *on* that?
  你對那件事的看法是？

Could you tell me...?

- *Could you tell me* how you see the whole process?
  可不可以告訴我你怎麼看待這整個過程？

Can I have your ... of...?

- *Can I have your* opinion *of* his character?
  能不能告訴我你對他的個性有什麼看法？

Do you have any...?

- *Do you have any* comments on the plan?
  你對這項計畫有任何意見嗎？

07

第 7 章
有技巧地討論

與人討論時，難免遇到被對方強
勢的說詞弄得張皇失措，以致於
最後不得不讓步的狀況。如何表
現自身看法固然要緊，更重要的
是在你來我往的討論中說服對方
認同自己的意見。本章的重點即
有技巧地表達意見，達到說服對
方的目的。

Useful English Expressions
for Communication

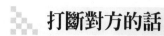 **打斷對方的話**　　　　　　　　　　　　　◉MP3 132

■ 可以打個岔嗎？

1. Excuse me, but...	不好意思，但……。
2. I'm sorry to interrupt, but...	抱歉打斷你的話，但……。
3. Excuse me for interrupting,...	不好意思打斷你的話，……。
4. May I interrupt you for a moment?	能不能稍微打個岔？
5. If I may just interrupt you,...	請讓我打個岔，……。

■ 等等。

6. Wait [Just] a minute.	等等。
7. Hold on (a minute)!	等一下！
8. I really must interrupt you there.	我真的得打斷你一下。
9. Stop there a moment [second].	先暫停一下。
10. Would you stop for a moment?	能不能請你先暫停一下？
11. May I just stop you there?	可以先講到那就好嗎？

▪句型解說

---

2. 更簡潔的說法是 Sorry to interrupt.。

---

7. Hold on! 是非常直接的說法，帶點生氣、不耐的語氣。如果對方的說法毫無道理，或者對方誤解了自己的意思，可以用來打斷對方的話。

• *Hold on.* That's not what I meant at all.
　等等，我的意思完全不是那樣。

情境對話

A: ... Then you bumped into my car.
B: *Hold on!* I didn't bump into your car. You bumped into my car.

A：……然後你就撞上我的車子。

B：等等！我沒有撞你的車子，是你撞我的車子。

這裡的 Hold on! 也可以改成 Come on!，表示對方說出意料之外的話。

---

8. 帶有「被你說成這樣，我也不能沈默以對了」的意味。

---

11. 特別常見於會議中、主席請發言者停止發言的情況。

■ 重點提示

　　打斷說話者的發言時使用。如果討論時發現對方使用了自己不清楚的詞彙，或者對內容有疑問，必須順勢發問或提出自己的看法，這時可以先用 excuse me 打斷對方的話，接著提出自己的問題或意見，例如：

- *Excuse me,* but I have a few questions.
  不好意思，我有幾個問題。

- *Excuse me,* but did you say...?
  不好意思，你剛剛是說……嗎？

- *Excuse me,* but could you speak a little more slowly?
  不好意思，可不可以請你說慢一點？

- *Excuse me,* but I'd just like to say...
  不好意思，我只是想說……。

　　上述的 excuse me 都可以用句型 2 的 I'm sorry to interrupt 代替。此外，句型 4 和 5 使用了讓語氣較婉轉的 may，不過，討論進行地如火如荼時，實在沒時間一一徵詢對方同意後才發表意見，更何況對方也不見得很客氣，這時，用制止對方發言的 Wait a minute!/Hold on!/Come on! 或對他人不合理的發言表示意見的 What do you mean by that? 等說法更為恰當。這些表現多半帶有驚訝或憤怒的語氣，用來制止對方脫韁野馬般的言論。

　　以上句型除了用來打斷對方的話，也能用來表明自己的疑慮或反對。關於表示反對的句型，請參考第 2 章「表示反對」(p. 20) 的部分。

要求對方閉嘴

■ 閉嘴！

1. Shut up (and listen)!	閉嘴（給我聽好）！
2. You've made your point!	你說得夠清楚了！
3. Say no more!	不要再說了！
4. That's enough! [Enough of that!]	夠了！
5. (That's) None of your business! [Mind your own business!]	（那）不關你的事！〔管好你自己就好！〕
6. (All right!) There's no need to say anything else.	（夠了！）不用再說了。

■ 句型解說

1. 看好萊塢電影時經常可以聽到 Shut up!，是非常直接的說法。如果很生氣，不想聽對方任何辯解而只想表達自己的看法時用 Shut up and listen!。

2, 4. 暗示「我已經知道你要說的，再講下去沒有意義」或是「我不想再聽了」，也是要對方閉嘴的意思。

5. 當對方說了不必要的話，或想要介入時，可用這個句型要求對方不要再多說、不要多管閒事。

要求對方讓自己把話說完　　　◉MP3 134

■ 讓我說完。

1. (Wait!) Let me finish!	（等等！）讓我把話說完！
2. (Wait!) I'm just finishing.	（等一下！）我快說完了。
3. Sorry. Could I just finish?	抱歉，讓我把話說完好嗎？
4. Just one moment, please.	請再給我一點時間。
5. Just one more second, if you don't mind.	可以的話，再給我一點時間就好。
6. Don't interrupt me.	不要打斷我的話。

■ 句型解說

3. 婉轉的說法。

5. 婉轉的說法，例如會議上有人提醒主席時間差不多了，這時候主席就可以使用這個句型，表示「我還有一點話要說」。

■ 重點提示

　　表達意見的時候，常會有中途被打斷的情況。除了用 Let me finish. 請對方把話聽完，也可以先加一句 Wait! 或 Stop a moment!，制止對方打斷你的話。如果遇到難纏的對手，則可以用句型 6 的 Don't interrupt me.，甚至是前面提到的 Shut up and listen!，語氣更強硬。

要求對方收回所說的話　　⦿MP3 135

■ 請收回你的話。

1. I'd like you to withdraw the charges you made against me.	請收回你對我的指控。
2. I demand [insist] that you withdraw your remarks on...	我要求〔堅持〕你收回對…… 的發言。

■句型解說

1. I'd like you to... 除了請對方幫忙外，也有強烈要求對方一定要做某件事的意思。另外，withdraw（收回，撤銷）後面可以接 charge（指控）、remark（發言，評論）、statement（言論）、allegation（毫無根據的指控）等名詞。

■重點提示

要求對方收回所說的話，尤其當對方的發言是一些無理的責難時。

在某個前提下表達意見　　⦿MP3 136

■ 回答你的問題之前，請讓我……。

1. Before answering your [the] question, let me...	回答你的〔這個〕問題前，請讓我……。
2. Can I first...?	能不能先讓我……？
3. Well, I don't know much about..., but...	嗯，關於……我不太清楚，但……。

■句型解說

1. 請看以下對話。

情境對話

A: The problem of the greenhouse effect has been raised by scientists over the last few years. What do you think about it?

B: Well, *before answering the question*, *let me* make clear that I'm not an expert on the subject. My understanding of the problem is based on the knowledge provided by newspapers. Now, I would think...

A：這幾年來科學家不斷提起溫室效應的問題，你怎麼看？

B：嗯，回答這個問題之前，先聲明我不是這方面的專家，對這個問題的了解是從報紙上來的。我會覺得……。

2. 例如：

- *Can I first* comment on... [mention/check...]?
  我可以先針對……發表意見〔說／確認……〕嗎？

情境對話

A: English education in Taiwan is not working well. What is the solution? Could you give me your opinion as an English teacher?

B: *Can I first* comment on what you've said just now? I don't think English education in Taiwan is totally ineffective. Students are in fact taught to have quite a wide vocabulary, and they know a lot about grammar. In that respect, English education is working quite well in this country. The problem is with the lack of training in speaking the language. Now, in answer to your question, I would suggest that...

A：台灣的英語教育成效不彰，有什麼解決方法呢？身為英文老師，你有什麼看法？

B：我可以先就你剛剛說的表達一下意見嗎？我不認為台灣的英語教育完全沒效果，事實上，學生學到很多單字，也學了不少文法。就那方面來看，台灣的英語教育算是相當成功的。問題在於缺少口語訓練。回到你剛剛的問題，我會建議……。

■ 重點提示

　　被要求表示意見的時候，不一定得立刻說出來，如果沒想清楚就隨便發言，反而讓對方有機可乘。爭取時間、從對方口中得知必要資訊，是討論時非常重要的技巧。不正面表明意見，守住自己的立場。此外，如果對對方的提問感到疑惑，也必須提出來。基本上，切入正題之前先從相關的話題著手，待態勢明確，再進入正題。

▨ 表示是眾所周知的事實　　　　　　　　　　　⦿MP3 137

■ 如你所知，……。

1. As you know,...	如你所知，……。
2. As you may [probably] know,...	你或許知道，……。
3. You may be aware of the fact that...	你可能知道……。
4. Everyone knows that...	大家都知道……。

■ 你應該明白。

5. You know what I mean.	你了解我的意思。
6. I think [hope] you understand...	我想〔希望〕你了解……。
7. You see,...	你知道，……。

■ 句型解說

1 ~ 4. 暗示是眾所皆知的事實，藉以說服對方。

情境對話

A: How did he become vice-president so soon?

B: *As you know,* he is the president's son. The reason is simple.

A: I know that, but there are more able and more dedicated executives in our company.

A：他怎麼這麼快就當上副董事長？

B：你也知道，他是董事長的兒子，理由就是這麼簡單。

A：我知道，但是公司裡還有很多能力更強、更有企圖心的經理人。

5 ~ 7. 主要讓對方認同說明的內容，尤其句型 7 的 you see 帶有「事情會這樣是理所當然的」的意味。

情境對話

A: I found that the goods were damaged. Can I claim my money back?

B: You can't, I'm afraid.

A: Why not?

B: Well, *you see*, you were late in reporting the damage. It's been two months since we delivered them.

A：我發現商品有瑕疵，可以要求退錢嗎？

B：恐怕不行。

A：為什麼？

B：嗯，你知道，你太晚告知商品有瑕疵了。出貨到現在都兩個月了。

表示強調　◉MP3 138

■ 我要強調的是……。

1. I must [would like to] emphasize that...	我必須〔想要〕強調……。
2. I must [would like to] stress that...	我必須〔想要〕強調……。
3. We cannot be too...	我們……也不為過。

句型解說

1. must 有加強語氣的意味，意思是「一定要」。emphasize 後面除了接 that 子句，也可以直接接名詞片語。

- *I must emphasize that* I am prepared to pay taxes if I fully understand how they will be spent.
  我必須強調，如果能全盤了解稅金的用途，我是很願意繳稅的。
- *I would like to emphasize* the need for a detailed instruction manual in English.
  我想強調的是，的確需要一本詳盡的英文操作手冊。

---

3. 強調某件事的重要性，主詞通常為 we 或 you。

- *We cannot be too* cautious.
  我們得特別小心。

▦ 要求對方注意某個事實　　　　　　　◉ MP3 139

■ 你有注意到……嗎？

1. Are you aware that...?	你知不知道……？
2. Do you know...?	你知不知道……？
3. (Just) Look at...	（只要）看看……。
4. It's important to see [notice]...	了解〔注意〕……是很重要的。
5. Please note that...	請注意……。

■ 句型解說

1~3. 暗示對方忽略了某事。

情境對話 1

A: Can I buy a computer for the new research?

B: *Are you aware that* we're having financial difficulties?

A：為了新的研究，我可以買一台電腦嗎？

B：你知不知道我們有財務困難？

情境對話 2

A: *Do you know* this is private property and you're trespassing?

B: Oh, I'm terribly sorry. I didn't know that.

A：你知道你正闖入私人土地嗎？

B：喔，真的很抱歉，我不知道。

情境對話 3

A: Limiting the size of a class is essential to improving the educational conditions in Britain. We should reduce the size, and we will have to spend more money on employing more teachers.

B: I don't think I agree with you. *Just look at* Japan. The average size of a class at elementary schools is forty, and yet they achieve a high educational standard.

A：限制班級人數是改善英國教育現狀的重點，我們應該減少班級人數，還得增加聘僱教師的經費。

B：我不同意你的看法。只要看看日本就好了，日本的小學平均每班 40 個人，不過他們的教育水準仍然很高。

問題無關緊要

⦿MP3 140

■ 那不是問題。

1. That doesn't matter.	那不影響。
2. That's not a [the] problem. [That's not a cause for concern.]	那不是問題。〔不用擔心那個。〕
3. That's not important here.	那不重要。
4. That's a small point.	那只是個小問題。
5. So, what seems to be the problem [matter/trouble]?	所以，有什麼問題呢？
6. So what?	那又如何？
7. ... counts, but it's not everything.	……雖然重要，但不是全部。

▪ 句型解說

1. 表示「不重要，不影響」的一般說法。

情境對話

A: I'm afraid the manager is out now and won't be back until eleven.

B: *That doesn't matter.* I'll wait.

A：經理目前外出，恐怕要到 11 點才會回來。

B：沒關係。我可以等。

3. 看輕對方的見解，凸顯自己的看法，常用句型包括：

- But that's not important. The real problem is...
  但那不重要，真正的問題在於……。

- I don't think it's important whether ... or not. What is much more important is that...
  是不是……不重要，更重要的是……。

5. 當自己怎麼也不清楚或不了解問題的癥結時，這個句型便可以派上用場。類似的說法還有 Is anything the matter?（有什麼問題嗎？）、Is anything wrong?（有什麼不對勁嗎？）。

6. 非常口語的用法。

7. count 當動詞用，意思是「有其重要性」。否定的說法是 ... does not count for much.（……沒什麼重要的。）

- Money *counts, but it's not everything.*
  錢很重要，但不是一切。

▪ 重點提示

　　強調某個事實或論點並不重要時使用。此外，當對方提出無關緊要的論點，或對某事給予過度評價時，上述句型也可以派上用場。類似的說法還有：

- That's not much of a problem.
  那不是多大的問題。
- I don't think ... is as important as you think.
  我不認為……有你想的那麼重要。
- (But) Why is that so important?
  （但是）為什麼那很重要呢？
- I don't think it really matters.
  我不覺得這真的會有什麼影響。
- I don't see why you raised the point.
  我不明白你為什麼要提出這一點。
- Let's ignore these little details.
  我們直接跳過這些細節吧。
- You shouldn't take too much account of...
  你不該把焦點都放在……。

要求對方仔細聽　◉MP3 141

■ 你聽好了。

1. Listen!	聽著！
2. Look!	你看！
3. Mind you.	好好聽著！
4. Don't forget.	別忘了。

句型解說

1. 請對方不要講個不聽，仔細聽你要講的話。

2. 喚起對方注意。

3. 請對方留意某事、不要弄錯了。

---

4. 用來告誡或提醒對方，是一種強調的表現方式。

- *Don't forget!* I am your boss.
  別忘了，我可是你的老闆。

- Please *don't forget.* I am always available, if you need help.
  請不要忘了，如果你需要幫忙，我隨時都有空。

▋重點提示

　　上述句型主要是提醒對方多加注意。因爲較爲口語，大多用在和關係親近的人的對話上。

▰▰ 向對方確認

◉ MP3 142

■ 真的嗎？

1. ... really...?	……真的……嗎？
2. Are you sure...?	你確定……嗎？

▋句型解說

---

1. 請看以下對話。

情境對話

A: He said you were a liar.

B: Did he *really* say that?

A: He definitely did.

A：他說你是騙子。

B：他真的那樣說？

A：真的。

---

2. 再次確認對方所說的內容，例如 Are you sure you want to...?（你確定你要……嗎？）。

情境對話

A: *Are you sure* you want to resign your post here?

B: I'm sure. I was offered a job in Hong Kong, and I'm more interested in that.

A：你確定要辭掉這裡的工作？

B：是的。有個香港的工作機會，而且是我更感興趣的工作。

提醒對方注意自己說過的話 ●MP3 143

■ 就像我之前所說的，……。

1. As I said [mentioned] before,...　　　　就像我之前所說〔提到〕的，
　　　　　　　　　　　　　　　　　　　　　　……。

2. As I said [mentioned] earlier,...　　　　就像我剛剛所說〔提到〕的，
　　　　　　　　　　　　　　　　　　　　　　……。

3. As I was saying,...　　　　　　　　　就像我之前說的，……。

句型解說

1. before 可能是剛才，也可能是昨天，是指不是當下、而是之前的事情。

---

2. earlier 指的是剛結束不久，和 before 的時間點不同。另外，也可以明確指出說話的時間點，例如 yesterday（昨天）或 a few days ago（幾天前）。

■ 重點提示

對話時，如果要提醒對方先前的討論內容便可以用 As I said,...（就像我說過的，……。），主詞也可以改爲第二人稱 As you said,...（如你所說，……。），表示同意對方之前的說法。

重述對方的話　　　　　◉ MP3 144

■ ……，你是這麼說的吧。

1. You said [mentioned]...	你說〔提〕過……。
2. You said [mentioned] earlier...	剛剛你說〔提〕到……。
3. ..., as you said,...	……，就像你說的，……。
4. To take up the point that you made,...	說起你之前提過的看法，……。
5. I'm interested in what you said about...	我對你說的……很感興趣。

■ 句型解說

1. mention 是稍微帶過，或不經意提起的意思。
   - *You mentioned* the importance of teaching English in Taiwan. Could you tell me a little more about that?
     你提到教英文在台灣的重要性。能否請你進一步說明呢？
   - If I remember correctly, *you said* you were going to accept my offer.
     如果我沒記錯的話，你說過你會接受我的提案。

   類似的說法還有 You said something about... 和 You talked about...，都是「你說過……」的意思。

2. earlier 指的是不久前的事。

- *You said earlier* that there should be a radical change in the position of women in society. Do you mean that more women should have full-time jobs?

  你剛剛提到，女性在社會中的地位應該有更劇烈的變動。你的意思是說，要有更多的女性從事全職工作嗎？

---

3. 用 as you said 來同意對方說過的話，但最終目的在於陳述自己的看法。

情境對話

A: Japan is good at hardware development, but it is behind in software. It's a pity because software development will certainly be the key to creating the advanced technologies of the future.

B: *As you said,* the Japanese are, in general, not very good at software development, but there are in fact some companies that are doing well in this field.

A：日本在硬體方面的技術十分卓越，但在軟體方面卻落後了。有點可惜，因為軟體開發勢必會成為未來發展尖端科技的關鍵。

B：正如你所說，整體來說日本人的確不擅長軟體開發，不過確實有一些企業在軟體開發方面表現得相當不錯。

■ 重點提示

上述句型用來重述對方先前提過的看法，藉此進一步了解重點所在，或審視有何不妥之處，激發其他討論的可能性。

▓ 對他人的意見表示歡迎　　◉ MP3 145

■ 很高興你這麼說。

| 1. I'm glad you mentioned... [you said that.] | 很高興你提到⋯⋯〔你這麼說〕。 |

211

2. I'm glad you raised the point.   很高興你提到那一點。

3. That's a very important point.   那是很重要的一點。

4. That's a good question.   那是個好問題。

■ 句型解說

1, 2. mention 是「提及」的意思，為及物動詞，後面要接所提及的內容為受詞。
raise 則是在對話或會議中提出某個論點。類似的說法還有：

- I'm glad you brought that up.
  很高興你提出那一點。

- I'm glad you pointed it out.
  很高興你指出這一點。

3, 4. 對方提到重點或值得討論的問題。

■ 請對方繼續說   ◉ MP3 146

■ **請繼續說**。

1. (Please) Go ahead.   （請）繼續。

2. (Please) Tell me (more) about it.   （請）說得更詳細一點。

3. What is it?   是什麼呢？

4. So then?   然後呢？

5. And?   所以呢？

▪句型解說

1. 對方的話被打斷或有所停頓時，請對方繼續說下去。

3. 直接提出疑問。

情境對話

A: I have a problem.

B: *What is it?*

A：我有個問題。

B：什麼問題？

5. 語尾上揚的 And? 多用來詢問對方接下來要說些什麼，中文可以理解成「然後呢？」。

情境對話

A: I saw you last night in front of the station.

B: Oh?

A: You were with a pretty girl.

B: *And?*

A: Who was she?

B: That's none of your business!

A：我昨天晚上在車站前面看到你。

B：喔？

A：你和一個漂亮的女生走在一起。

B：所以呢？

A：她是誰？

B：不關你的事！

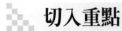 切入重點 　　　　　　　　　　　　　◉MP3 147

■ 我們打開天窗說亮話。

1. Let's talk this over.	我們好好談談這件事吧。
2. Let's be open here.	我們就直話直說吧。
3. Please tell me [say] outright (what you think about...).	請直接告訴我〔直接說〕（你對……有什麼想法）。
4. Let me know your mind [your feelings] on this matter.	請告訴我你對這件事的感想〔感覺〕。
5. I'd like to have a heart-to-heart talk with you.	我們開誠布公地說吧。

■ 請直說。

6. Please say what you think. [Don't be afraid to say what you think.]	請告訴我你在想什麼。〔不用顧慮太多，儘管說出你的想法。〕
7. Please speak your mind (plainly).	請（直接）說出你內心的想法。
8. Please come straight to the point.	請說重點。

■ 句型解說

---

2. open 是「率直的」的意思，指毫不保留地說出看法。
* *Let's be open* with each other.
  我們就有話直說吧。

---

3. 類似的說法是 Please tell me straight.（請直接告訴我。）
* *Please say outright what you think about* my idea.
  對於我的提議，請直接了當說出你的看法吧。

4, 7. mind 是指「內心真正的想法」。

8. 對方支吾其詞時，用來要求對方有話直說。

切入問題點 ◉MP3 148

■ 我們從……開始討論吧。

1. Let's [Let me] start with...　　　　　　我們〔讓我〕從……開始。

2. It's a good idea to begin with...　　　從……開始是個不錯的點子。

3. Let me begin by...　　　　　　　　　讓我從……開始。

■ 我們來討論……吧。

4. Let's talk about...　　　　　　　　　我們來談談……吧。

5. Let's discuss...　　　　　　　　　　我們來討論……吧。

6. Now, let's look at...　　　　　　　　那麼，我們來看一下……。

■ 把焦點放在……吧。

7. Let's focus on...　　　　　　　　　　把焦點放在……吧。

句型解說

1. 除了 Let's... 或 Let me...，也可以用 I'd like to... 或 Can I...?，後面再接動詞。

討論下一個議題

■ 接著來討論⋯⋯吧。

1. Let's move on to...	我們繼續討論⋯⋯吧。
2. Let's turn to...	接著我們來討論⋯⋯吧。
3. Next, we come to...	接著，我們要討論⋯⋯。
4. The next point is...	下一個重點是⋯⋯。
5. This brings us [me] to the question of...	這就把我們〔我〕帶到⋯⋯的問題。
6. This leads us [me] to...	這就把我們〔我〕帶到⋯⋯。
7. Can I move this discussion to the question [issue] of...?	可不可以把討論轉向⋯⋯的問題〔議題〕上呢？
8. Can I turn to [get to]...?	可不可以討論⋯⋯呢？

■句型解說

- -

1. 也可以用比較簡短的 Let's move on.（我們繼續吧。）
   - *Let's move on to* the next point.
     我們繼續討論下一個重點吧。
   - *Let's move on to* the next issue on the agenda.
     我們繼續討論議程的下一個議題吧。

   單純引導對方到下一個話題，可用 Now, let's...（那麼，我們來⋯⋯。）
   - *Now, let's* look at what's happening in the market.
     那麼，我們來看一下目前市場的狀況。

- -

2. 例如：
   - *Let's turn to* the next point.
     接著我們來討論下一個重點。

- -

6. 例如：

- *This leads us* directly *to* the second point.
  這就直接把我們帶到第二點。

7, 8. 討論到一半，想要轉移話題時使用。

- *Can I move this discussion to the* wider *issue of* the natural environment?
  可不可以把討論轉向自然環境這個較大的議題上呢？
- *Can I turn to* more specific points?
  可不可以討論比較具體的點呢？

■ 重點提示

討論中想繼續下一個議題時，可以利用上述的句型。如果認為目前的議題已經不需要再討論、可以繼續進行下一個議題時，可以說：

- I think we have spent enough time on this point [topic/subject].
  我認為我們已經花夠多的時間在這一點〔這個主題〕上了。
- I think sufficient discussion has been made on...
  我想關於……的討論已經很充分了。

依序說明　　　　　　　　　◉MP3 150

■ 首先，……。

1. First [Second/Third],...	首先〔其次／接著〕，……。
2. Then,...	然後，……。
3. After that...	之後……。
4. Next,...	接著，……。
5. Lastly,...	最後，……。

■█ 句型解說

除了用 First, Second, Third 依序表示「首先、其次、接下來」之外，Second 之後也可以用 Next,...（接著，……。）例如 Next, I'd like to talk about...（接著，我想要談談……。），這樣的說法比較簡單。另外，前面提到的 Let me begin by... 意思和 First,... 相同。

▓▒ 改變話題   ◉ MP3 151

■ 換個話題吧。

1. Can we [I] change the subject?	我們〔我〕可以換個話題嗎？
2. To change the subject slightly,...	稍微改變話題，……。
3. To change the subject,...	換個話題，……。
4. Not to change the subject, but...	我並不是要換話題，不過……。

■█ 句型解說

1. 換話題前先徵求對方同意，較為委婉。

----

3. 單方面轉換話題。

----

4. 避免換話題時給人唐突的印象。

話題告一段落　　　　　　　　　　　　◉MP3 152

■ 這個話題到此為止吧！

    1. Let's drop the subject.　　　　　　　這個話題到此為止。

    2. Let's leave ... aside.　　　　　　　　先把……放在一邊吧。

    3. But that's another story.　　　　　　但那是另一回事。

    4. Let's forget it.　　　　　　　　　　忘了這件事吧。

■ 這個話題就別再繼續了。

    5. Let's not discuss [talk about]... (any more).　　我們不要（再）討論〔談〕……了。

    6. Let's not argue about... (any more).　　我們不要（再）爭論……了。

    7. Let's stop talking about...　　　　　不要再討論……了。

    8. This discussion isn't getting us anywhere.　　這樣的討論不會有什麼結果的。

    9. Discussing [Talking about] ... gets us nowhere.　　討論〔談〕……沒有什麼結果的。

   10. I don't want to talk about ... any more.　　我不想再談……了。

   11. I don't want to get into...　　　　我不想討論……。

   12. I don't want to be drawn into this discussion on...　　我不想被扯進這個關於……的討論。

   13. Discussing [Talking about] ... any more seems a waste of time.　　再討論〔談〕……感覺只是浪費時間而已。

句型解說

1. drop 是「丟，扔」，drop the subject 直譯是「丟掉話題」，也就是「話題到此為止」的意思。

2. 不直接打斷討論，而是暫時把話題放在一邊。
   - *Let's leave* this difficult problem *aside* for a moment.
     我們暫時把這個難題放一邊吧。

4. 再怎麼討論下去也沒有意義，不如直接放棄。

6. argue 是「爭論」的意思。

8, 9. not get ... anywhere 和 get ... nowhere 是指不會有結果，換句話說，討論不會有任何進展。此外，句型 8 用進行式來表現怎麼討論也沒有結果。如果要將話題帶回其他更重要的點，可以接著說 Let's get back to the important issue/ point.（我們回到主要的議題 / 重點上吧。）

情境對話

A: I'm not responsible for the accident. It's the director who is to blame.

B: *Talking about* responsibilities *gets us nowhere.* What we have to do now is to face the consequences and think about what we can do to deal with what has happened.

A：這場意外的責任不在我，主任要負責。

B：討論誰該負責不會有什麼結果的，現在我們該做的是面對現實，想想該怎麼處理後續事宜。

重點提示

上述句型主要用在討論中發現怎麼樣也不會有結果，或是把難題先擱在一旁的狀況。

停止討論特定話題

●MP3 153

■ 現在不是討論⋯⋯的時候。

1. Let's not talk about [discuss]...	我們不要談〔討論〕⋯⋯了。
2. We are not here to talk about [discuss]...	我們不是來這裡談〔討論〕⋯⋯的。
3. This is not the time to bring up the subject.	現在不是提起這件事的時候。
4. I think this is not the best moment to talk about [discuss]...	我認為現在不是談〔討論〕⋯⋯的好時機。
5. This is not the appropriate occasion to talk about [discuss]...	現在不是談〔討論〕⋯⋯的好時機。
6. Let's not get drawn into the details of...	我們不要討論⋯⋯的細節了。

句型解說

1. 如果要刻意避開某個話題，可以用 keep off...（避開⋯）。
   - We had better *keep off* politics at the meeting.
     開會時最好避開政治話題。

6. 當討論逐漸失去重點，變得愈來愈吹毛求疵、挑剔細節時，用這個句型讓討論回到正題。

 有機會再討論　　　　　　　　　　　● MP3 154

■ 留待下次討論吧！

1. Let's leave it open. 　　　　　　　　　這件事先保留吧。

2. We can [may] discuss the issue on another occasion. 　　　　　　我們可以下次再討論這個問題。

3. Let's bring the matter up at the next meeting. 　　　　　　下次開會時再提出這件事吧。

4. I'll come back to this (point) later. 　　　我待會會再回來談這一點。

■ 改天再討論吧。

5. We will [can] talk again. 　　　　　　我們下次再討論。

6. Let's discuss it further tomorrow [next week]. 　　　　　　明天〔下禮拜〕再深入討論這件事吧。

7. Let's discuss the details tomorrow [next week]. 　　　　　　明天〔下禮拜〕再來討論細節吧。

8. Can we meet again next week to talk about...? 　　　　　　下禮拜能不能再碰個面、談一談……？

句型解說

---

1. open 是「未決定的」，表示不急著現在決定，等時候到了再討論。

---

2. 類似的例子還有 We can discuss it later.（我們可以等一下再討論。）

---

3. bring ... up 是指「提出…」，也可以用動詞 raise，例如 raise the question（提出問題）。

---

4. 暗示待會再討論某個議題。

■ 重點提示

上述句型可以視情況填入之後討論的時間，如 later（待會）、tomorrow（明天）、next week（下禮拜）等等，例如 We'll talk tomorrow.（明天再說吧。）

轉移話題 ◉MP3 155

■ 先跳去別的話題吧！

1. Let's skip to ... on the agenda.	先跳到議程的……吧。
2. We'll leave the question for the moment and move on to...	我們暫時把問題擱在一邊，先來討論……。
3. I included ... on the agenda, but can I skip it?	我將……列入議程了，但可以跳過嗎？

■ 句型解說

1. 例如：
   • *Let's skip to* the last item *on the agenda.*
   我們跳到議程的最後一個項目。

3. 會議主席常用的說法。

順帶一提 ◉MP3 156

■ 順帶一提，……。

1. Let me mention in passing...	我順便提一下……。

2. I'd just like to digress here for a moment.   在這邊我想稍微離題一下。

3. If I may digress for a moment, I have something to say on [about]...   如果可以稍微離題一下，我想談一談……。

■ 句型解說

1. 也可以說 I'd like to mention in passing...（我想順便提一下……。）

2. 也可以說 Can I just digress here for a moment?（在這裡我可以稍微離題一下嗎？）。

提起不相關的話題   ●MP3 157

■ 對了，……。

1. By the way,...   對了，……。

2. Incidentally,...   對了，……。

3. Before I forget,...   趁我還沒忘記，……。

4. That reminds me,... [That reminds me of...]   那倒提醒了我……。

5. Speaking of...   說到……。

■ 句型解說

1, 2. by the way 和 incidentally 都可帶起不相關的話題，有「順道一提」的意味。

情境對話 1

A: Shall we go out for lunch?

B: That's a good idea. Oh, *by the way*, there was a visitor this morning.

A: A visitor? Who?

B: John Bryant.

A：要一起去吃中飯嗎？

B：好啊。啊，對了，早上有訪客。

A：訪客？誰啊？

B：約翰‧布萊恩。

情境對話 2

A: I don't think the computerized teaching system is that important, Mr. Anderson. First of all, the cost is enormous. Not every school can afford it. Secondly, many students really hate computers.

B: I don't think so. Young people today are very interested in having computers in their class. *Incidentally*, it's Emerson, not Anderson.

A: Oh, I'm terribly sorry.

A：安德森先生，我不認為電腦教學系統有那麼重要。首先，費用實在太驚人了，不是每所學校都負擔得起。再者，很多學生真的很痛恨電腦。

B：我不這麼認為。現在的年輕人對於在教室裡使用電腦非常感興趣。順便一提，我姓艾默生，不是安德森。

A：喔，真是抱歉。

---

3. 忽然想到什麼事情要提醒對方，和正在討論的話題不見得相關。

• Oh, *before I forget*, the library will be closed tomorrow.
  喔，趁我還沒忘記先告訴你，圖書館明天休館。

深入討論

●MP3 158

■ 我們進一步討論……。

1. Let's go a step further.	我們進一步討論吧。
2. Let's take this ... one step further.	我們進一步討論……吧。
3. I would like to develop this point and consider...	我想就這一點擴大討論，並考慮……。
4. I have to stop with this ... now to see how [what]...	我現在必須停在……上，看看可以怎麼做〔做些什麼〕。

重點提示

進一步深入討論問題時的說法。

言歸正傳

●MP3 159

■ 回到……。

1. Can I [we] go back [return] to...?	我〔我們〕可以回到……嗎？
2. Can I [we] look at ... again?	我〔我們〕能不能再看一下……？
3. That brings me [us] back to...	那就把我〔我們〕帶回……。
4. To return to...	回到……。
5. Can I take up [pick up] an earlier point?	我可以回到剛剛講的一個點嗎？
6. It leads us back to what I said earlier.	那就把我們帶回到我剛剛說的。

■ 句型解說

1, 2. go back 和 look at 的前面也可以用 Let's... 或 I'd like to...。

---

3. That 指現在提到的點,藉著這個點回到剛才的話題。

---

4. 也可以說 To get back to... 或 To come back to...。

---

5. take up 的前面也可以用 Let's... 或 I'd like to...。take up... 和 pick up... 是指接下去說(剛剛中斷的話)。

■ 重點提示

　　討論時,有時候會再次提及某個話題,或者正在討論的話題和先前的話題相關,這時就可以利用上述句型回到先前的話題。以句型 Can I go back to...? 為例,可以說:

- *Can I go back to* what I was saying?
  可以回到我剛剛說的嗎?
- *Can I go back to* the question of...?
  可以回到……的問題嗎?
- *Can I go back to* our first issue?
  可以回到第一個議題嗎?
- *Can I go back to* the point you made about...?
  可以回到你對……所提出的看法嗎?
- *Can I go back to* something you said about...?
  可以回到你對……所提出的看法嗎?
- *Can I go back to* something you said at the beginning?
  可以回到你一開始提到的嗎?

 討論時一邊參考資料　　　◉MP3 160

■ 我看一下。

1. Let's have [take] a look at...	我們來看一下……。
2. Let me check.	我看一下。

■ 句型解說

1. 例如：

- *Let's have a look at* the file.
  我們來看一下這份文件。

---

2. 確認計畫表、行事曆等資料時的說法。如果要跟某人確認某件事是否正確，可以說 check with ... to see ...。

- I'll *check with* the accountant *to see* if the figure is correct.
  我會跟會計確認一下這數字對不對。

討論時一邊記下重點　　　◉MP3 161

■ 請讓我記一下重點。

1. Would you mind my taking notes?	介意我做一下筆記嗎？
2. Let me write down... (to be sure...)	讓我記一下……（以確保……）。
3. Just a moment, I'll get a pad and pencil.	等等，我拿一下紙筆。

■ 句型解說

2. 例如：

• *Let me write down* exactly what you're saying.
讓我一字不漏寫下你說的話。

類似的說法還有：

• I'd like to write everything down.
我想把全部的內容寫下來。

• Let me write the outline down on paper.
讓我在紙上列一下重點。

■ 重點提示

認為對方言之有理而想要寫下來參考，或者記下時間和名字時使用。這時候可先請對方稍等（可說 Just a moment.），再寫下想記的重點。

表現出願意討論的態度　　　　　　●MP3 162

■ 我可以和你討論，但是……。

1. I'm ready to talk (, but...).　　　　　我可以和你討論（，但是……）。

■ 句型解說

1. 請看以下對話。

情境對話

A: I was wondering if you had decided to take up our offer of the position in New York. Can we talk about that this afternoon?

B: *I'm ready to talk, but* I haven't decided anything yet and can't give you my answer today.

A：不曉得你是不是已經決定要接受我們的提議、調到紐約去。今天下午可以討論一下嗎？

B：我可以和你討論，但我還沒決定去不去，今天沒辦法給你任何答案。

■重點提示

有時候對方會突然提出新的議題，又或者雖然是舊的議題，但因為自己收集的資料不足，還沒有辦法繼續討論。這種情況下，貿然給出答案或毫無根據的資訊和意見，只會衍生更多問題。因此必須中斷討論，確認資料的正確性或者先和其他人商量後才能和對方繼續討論，這時便可以使用上述句型。

如何表示強調？ ◉MP3 163

(1) 使用強調的句型 It's ... that [who/when/where]...。

- It's *John who* said that.
  是約翰說的。

(2) 使用助動詞 do/does/did。

- I *do* value your contribution, but I'm afraid the result wasn't as good as we expected.
  我確實肯定您的貢獻，但結果恐怕不如我們所預期的好。

情境對話

A: Why didn't you pay?

B: I *did* pay.

A：你為什麼沒付錢？

B：我有付。

(3) 使用簡短的句子。

情境對話

A: Get out!

B: No, I won't.

A: Get out of here!

B: I *will not*.

A：滾出去！

B：我不要。

A：給我離開這裡！

B：辦不到。

(4) 說話時把重音放在想要強調的單字上面（書寫時可用底線或斜體字表示）。

情境對話

A: Thomas Mann's novel *The Magic Mountain* is boring. It's full of philosophical ideas which seem to mean little to me.

B: That's what *you* think.

A：湯瑪斯·曼的小說《魔山》無聊透頂。整本書都在講哲學概念，對我來說沒什麼意義。

B：那是你這麼覺得。

* 說話時重點放在 you 上面。

第 8 章
問題探討

遇到難題時，總會思考該如何解決才好，而其中最迫切需要解決的部分就成為討論的開端。從確認問題、提出解決方法一直到分析各方法的利弊得失，這一連串解決問題的過程會用到哪些句型呢？本章將一一介紹。

Useful English Expressions
for Communication

提出問題 (I)

■ 問題是……。

1. The question is...	問題是……。
2. The problem is...	問題在於……。
3. The problem we [I] have is...	我們〔我〕的問題是……。
4. ... That is the question [problem].	……。那是問題所在。
5. We'll [I'll] have to solve the question of...	我們〔我〕必須解決……的問題。
6. There is the question of...	有……的問題。
7. There is another question [problem].	還有另一個問題。
8. That's not the only problem [trouble/ question].	問題〔麻煩〕不只一個。

■ 麻煩的是……。

9. The trouble with ... is...	……的問題是……。
10. The problem we are facing is...	我們面臨的問題是……。
11. We are confronted with...	我們面臨……。
12. Something has to be done to... [done about...]	必須做些什麼來……〔必須針對……做些什麼〕。

■ 句型解說

----

1. question 指的是「需要討論、考慮或解決的問題」。The question is 後面接疑問詞所構成的名詞子句，例如 The question is what/why/how/who/whether/where...（問題在於什麼 / 為什麼 / 如何 / 誰 / 是否 / 哪裡……。）

   • *The question is whether* we should take the last step.
   問題在於我們是不是該採取最後一個步驟。

此外，也可以直接在 is 後面接代名詞 this，結束句子，之後再以新的句子提示問題為何。

- *The question is this.* If we take a further step to reduce our expenditure, what will happen to the efficiency of the whole plant's operations?
  問題在於，如果我們進一步減少開支，對整座工廠的運作效率會有什麼影響？

---

2. problem 指的是現階段要解決的問題，The problem is 後面可以接連接詞 that 所引導的名詞子句，提示問題為何。

情境對話

A: Mr. Scott seems the right person to be the head of our European branch in Paris. But *the problem is that* he is not good at French.

B: Yes, indeed. That'll be a problem.

A：史考特先生感覺很適合擔任我們在巴黎的歐洲分公司負責人，但問題是他的法文不太好。

B：確實，那會是個問題。

另外，也可以用 problem with... 點出是哪方面的問題。

- *The problem with* the fertilizer is that it smells bad.
  肥料的問題在於味道太臭了。

---

4. 先提出具體的內容，再強調那是問題所在。question 和 problem 前面要接定冠詞 the，表示是前面提到的問題。

- How can we avoid the hard choices? *That's the question.*
  如何才能避開困難的選擇？那才是問題所在。

---

7. 問題不只一個。也可以直接指出還有幾個問題，例如 There are three other questions.（還有三個問題。）

---

9. trouble 是指麻煩的問題或阻礙，後面先接 with 再接問題。

情境對話

A: The best way to reach the peak is to take the route on the west slope.

B: So it seems, but *the trouble with* that side of the mountain *is* that there is a danger of avalanches.

A：攻頂的最佳路徑是沿著西坡攀登。

B：好像是這樣沒錯，但西坡的問題是有雪崩的危險。

----

12. 強調解決問題的必要性。

* *Something has to be done to* find out what went wrong.
  必須做些什麼、找出問題所在。

■ 重點提示

討論問題該如何解決時，會遇到許多需要處理的課題。這時候，確立應該解決的課題為何十分重要，免得討論到最後失去焦點、不知道問題所在。

提出問題 (II)

● MP3 165

■ 必須討論……。

1. We have to talk about [discuss/ consider]...	我們必須談一談〔討論／考慮〕……。
2. The problem we have to discuss [to deal with] is...	我們必須討論〔處理〕的問題是……。
3. The question we have to answer is...	我們必須回答的問題是……。
4. I think there are two issues here. One is..., the other is...	我認為有兩個問題，一是……，一是……。
5. There is an important point that I want to raise.	我想提出一個重點。
6. There are a couple of important points to cover.	有幾個重要的問題必須討論。
7. We have to decide [settle]...	我們必須決定……。

句型解說

7. 跟這個句型有關的是 we haven't decided...（我們還沒決定……。），藉由這個說法來凸顯尚未決定的事項，也可以有效區分已解決和未解決的問題。

- We've decided that we will launch a campaign to raise money for the reconstruction, but *we haven't decided* when we should start it.
  我們已經決定舉辦活動來籌措重建資金，但還沒決定活動的時間。

提出重點

◉MP3 166

■ 重點是……。

1. The point is...　　　　　　　重點是……。

句型解說

1. 請看以下對話。

情境對話

A: I think he is suitable for the post.

B: But he is too young.

A: That's not the point. *The point is* whether he is able to do his job well, and I'm sure he is.

A：我認為他適合這個位子。

B：但他太年輕了。

A：那不是重點。重點是他能不能做好分內的工作，我相信他可以。

⊞ 提出解決方案 ◉MP3 167

■ 其中一個方法是⋯⋯。

1. One way to ... is to...	解決⋯⋯的其中一個方法是⋯⋯。
2. Another way to ... is to...	另一個解決⋯⋯的方法是⋯⋯。
3. It would be a good idea to...	⋯⋯會是個不錯的方法。

■ 唯一的方法是⋯⋯。

4. The only way [solution] is...	唯一的方法是⋯⋯。

■ 最好的方法是⋯⋯。

5. The best way to ... is...	解決⋯⋯最好的方法是⋯⋯。
6. The best solution is to...	最好的解決方法是⋯⋯。
7. It would be simplest [best] to...	⋯⋯最簡單〔最好〕。

■ 找不出辦法。

8. There is no way we...	我們沒辦法⋯⋯。
9. There is nothing we can do about...	對於⋯⋯我們無計可施。

⊞ 句型解說

1. 例如：

- *One way to* make fire *is to* strike stones against each other to produce sparks.
  生火的其中一個方法就是讓石頭和石頭相互碰撞、擦出火花。

2. 提出另一個解決方法。如果還要再提出其他的方法，可以說 Still another way to ... is to...（還有另一個解決……的方法是……。）

4. 例如：

- If that doesn't work, *the only solution is...*
  如果那沒用的話，唯一的方法就是……。

- If all else fails, *the only solution is...*
  如果一切都失敗了，唯一的方法就是……。

5. 例如：

- We could simply continue to give the patient medication. Or, his condition would probably be improved for a while by radioactive surgery. And, a gastrectomy could be the most effective solution, but it has its risks. Considering the patient's poor condition, I believe *the best way to* save him *would be* to perform an operation.
  我們也可以就這樣繼續讓病人服藥，或者，放射線療法也許能暫時改善他的病況。另外，胃切除手術是最有效的方法，不過有其風險。考量到病人的狀況不好，我認為保住一命最好的辦法就是進行手術。

7. 請看以下對話。

情境對話

A: Could you tell me how to get to your office?

B: *It would be simplest to* take a taxi.

A：可以告訴我怎麼去你公司嗎？

B：搭計程車會最簡單。

■ 重點提示

　　幫他人出主意或是提出解決方法時，都可以使用上述的句型。如果不太確定是不是唯一或最佳的解決方法，可以視情況使用 seem (to) 和 would（如句型 3 和 7），避免語氣太過肯定。

提出方法選項

■ 你有幾個選擇。

1. You have two [three] options.	你有兩〔三〕個選擇。
2. There are a few options.	有幾個選擇。

■ 沒有選擇的餘地。

3. You have no other choice [option].	你沒有其他的選擇了。
4. There's no alternative.	沒有其他選擇了。

■ 問題是，要選擇哪一個。

5. It's (the choice) between ... and...	問題在於要選……還是選……。
6. There are two ways of... [There are two options here.]	關於……有兩個辦法。〔現在有兩個選擇。〕
7. We have two alternatives.	我們有兩個選擇。
8. We have two options.	我們有兩個選擇。
9. We can ... or we can...	我們可以……或是……。

■ 只有一個方法。

10. The only solution is...	唯一的方法是……。
11. There is no way but to...	除了……之外別無他法。
12. The only logical thing to do is to...	唯一合理的做法是……。
13. ... will [can] ... only if...	唯有在……的狀況下，……可以……。

■ 還有一個方法。

14. If ... not..., the next option [choice] is to...　　如果……無法……，其他選擇是……。

15. If ... not..., the final option is to...　　如果……無法……，最後的選擇是……。

■ 句型解說

. . . .

2. 請看以下對話。

情境對話

A: I'm looking for a single room.

B: Fine. Let me see. *There are a few options.* The first one is the Blue Boar Hotel. It has a comfortable room with a view of the sea.

A: How much is that?

B: It's fifty pounds.

A: It's a little too expensive. What about another one?

B: There is a hotel near the station. It's less expensive, but the view from the rooms is not so good.

A: I prefer a room with a good view.

B: Your final option, then, is the White Horse Hotel. It's thirty pounds. It's some distance from the city center, but it is located in a beautiful part of the town.

A：我要一間單人房。

B：好的，我看看。有幾個選擇，首先是藍豚飯店。藍豚飯店有舒適而且面海的房間。

A：價格呢？

B：50 英鎊。

A：有點太貴了。其他飯店呢？

B：車站附近有一家飯店，房價比較低，不過房間看出去的風景就不怎麼好了。

A：我比較想住在視野好一點的房間。

B：那您最後的選擇是白馬飯店。30 英鎊，距離市區稍遠，但位於鎮上一個風景優美的地點。

. . . .

6～8. 後面可以接 One is... The other is...（一個是……，另一個是……。）

---

13. 在某個前提下才能成立。

- The trouble with the computer *will* be solved *only if* we install a new hard disk.
  只有換顆新硬碟，才能解決這台電腦的問題。

■ 重點提示

　　上述的句型都用來提出各種方法選項，選擇可以只有一個，也可以有很多個。句型中以 we 為主詞者表示提案，以 you 為主詞者，是幫對方出主意或提出建議的說法。另外，choice 和 option 指的是一般的選項，alternative 是指二擇一的情況。

指出利弊得失　　　　　　　　　　　⦿ MP3 169

■ ……的優／缺點是……。

1. ... has the advantage [disadvantage] of...	……的優點〔缺點〕是……。
2. The advantage [disadvantage] of ... is...	……的優點〔缺點〕是……。
3. One of the advantages [disadvantages] of ... is that...	……其中一個優點〔缺點〕是……。
4. One advantage [disadvantage] is that... Another advantage [disadvantage] is...	優點〔缺點〕之一是……。另一個優點〔缺點〕則是……。
5. It is an advantage [disadvantage] to...	……比較有利〔不利〕。
6. ... has two [three] advantages [disadvantages].	……有兩個〔三個〕優點〔缺點〕。
7. There are two [three] advantages [disadvantages] to...	……有兩個〔三個〕優點〔缺點〕。

8. There is little advantage in...　　　……幾乎沒有好處可言。

9. ... has both advantages and　　　……有利有弊。
   disadvantages.

■ 句型解說

1. 例如：

- The machine *has the disadvantage of* making too much noise.
  這台機器的缺點就是太吵了。

情境對話

A: We have a choice between two candidates for the post at our London branch: Mr. Morris and Mr. Greene. Which one would you support?

B: I would support Mr. Greene because he *has the* great *advantage of* having a good command of English.

A：關於倫敦分公司的職缺，目前有莫里斯先生和葛林先生兩個人選，你會選哪一位？

B：我會選葛林先生，因為他有英語的優勢。

2. 例如：

- The President is going to take strong action in foreign affairs, but *the disadvantage of* his situation *is* that his term of office is running out.
  總統將在外交事務上採取強硬手段，但不利的是，他的任期即將屆滿。

3. 請看以下對話。

情境對話

A: I am thinking about applying for a school in London. I have two schools in mind. Which would you recommend, School Y or School Z?

B: School Z may be worth applying for. *One of the advantages of* the school *is that* it has a computerized teaching system.

A：我想要申請倫敦的學校，目前屬意兩所。你會推薦哪一所？ Y 學校還是 Z 學校？

B：Z 學校可能比較值得申請，那所學校的優點之一在於擁有電腦教學系統。

5. 例如：

- *It is a* great *advantage to* have someone on our staff who has a good command of English.
  擁有一位英語能力強的同仁，對我們而言是一大利多。

---

8. 例如：

- *There is little advantage in* approaching him if you know he is hostile to your plan.
  如果你知道他反對你的計畫，那麼接近他可真是一點好處也沒有。

■ **重點提示**

討論時，提出各個方法的利弊得失十分重要，可以善用上述 advantage 和 disadvantage 的句型。

指出規定的內容 ● MP3 170

■ **按照規定，……。**

1. The rule is that...	規定是……。
2. The rules say that... [The law says that...]	規定是……。〔法律規定……。〕
3. The rules require that...	規定要求……。
4. ... agrees with...	……和……一致。
5. It's against the rules [law] to...	……是違反規定〔法律〕的。
6. ... doesn't agree with...	……和……背道而馳。

▪句型解說

1. 例如：

- *The rule is that* students should attend more than two thirds of the whole course.
  學校規定學生全學期出席率需達三分之二以上。

2. 例如：

- *The* British *law says that* if you have been wrongfully convicted of a criminal offence, you can apply to the Home Secretary for compensation.
  根據英國法律，如果你因司法誤判而被定罪，可向內政大臣求償。

4. ... agrees with... 是指「（決定、行為、見解）和（規則、法律）一致」。

- The decision of this meeting *agrees with* our school rules.
  會議的決議和校規一致。

5. 例如：

- *It's against the law to* counterfeit money.
  印製偽鈔是違法的行為。

09

第9章
論證

明確的理論與適當的論證，是討
論的根本之道。本章將介紹相關
基礎句型，順利說出讓對方認同
的論證。

Useful English Expressions
for Communication

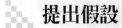 **提出假設**　　　　　　　　　　　　　　　　　◉MP3 171

■ 如果……的話。

1. If..., what...?	如果……的話，會是……？
2. (Let's) Suppose..., what...?	（我們）假設……，會是……？
3. (Just) Imagine [Try to imagine]...	想像一下〔試著想像〕……。
4. (Let's) Say...	（我們）假設……。
5. One [You] might say [argue] that...	或許有人〔你〕會說〔爭論說〕……。

■ 句型解說

1. If..., 用來陳述假設的條件，以下列的形式表現：

- *If..., what* would happen?
  如果……的話，會發生什麼事？
- *If..., what* would be the consequences?
  如果……的話，會有什麼後果？
- *If..., what* shall I [we] do?
  如果……的話，我〔我們〕該怎麼做？

2. Suppose..., 和 If ..., 一樣用來陳述假設的條件。

- *Suppose* we failed, *what* would be the consequences?
  要是我們失敗了，結果會如何？
- *Suppose* you were right, *what* would be the difference?
  就算你是對的，又有什麼差別？

3. 用想像的方式描繪假設的情況。

- *Imagine* you were the President of the United States, what action would you take?
  想像一下如果你是美國總統，你會採取什麼行動？

4. 和 Let's suppose... 同義，但較爲婉轉。

- *Say* he is telling the truth. How can he prove it?
  就算他說的是眞的好了，他要怎麼證明呢？

---

5. 表達出一種不信任他人的態度。

- *One might say* there is something in the English language itself that makes it an international language, but I think the reason for its popularity is chiefly political.
  或許有人會說是因爲英語本身有一種特質，才會變成國際性的語言，但我認爲英語的普及主要跟政治有關。

■ 重點提示

上述的假設句型主要用於提案、提出問題及警告三種情況。

1. 提案

- *If* we stop our project right now, we'll be able to keep our losses to a minimum.
  如果馬上停止這項企劃，我們就可以把損失減到最低。

2. 提出問題

- *If* your second point is true, what about the first point? Your two points seem to contradict each other.
  假設你提出的第二點是正確的，那麼第一點呢？這兩個論點看來互相矛盾。

3. 警告

- *If* you hesitate too long, you'll lose your chance to come to an agreement.
  猶豫太久的話，你就會失去達成協議的機會。

取決於某個條件

■ 取決於……。

1. ... depends on...	……取決於……。
2. ... is up to... [That's up to you.]	……是由……決定。〔決定權在你。〕

■ 句型解說

1. 類似的說法還有 Everything hangs on ...'s decision.（一切都看……的決定而定。）、The choice rests with you.（由你來選擇。）

• Our view of nature *depends on* our view of mankind.
   我們對自然的看法是根據我們對人類的看法而來。

情境對話 1

A: What's the meaning of this word?

B: That *depends on* the context.

A：這個字的意思是？

B：要看前後文。

depend on 還可以接疑問詞所構成的名詞子句，如 depends on whether [what/when/where]...。

情境對話 2

A: Will you go on to college?

B: That *depends on whether* I can find financial support.

A：你會繼續唸大學嗎？

B：那要看我有沒有辦法找到經濟支援。

It depends on...（那要看……。）也是常見的句型，例如：

• *It depends on* several factors.
   那由很多因素決定。

- *It depends on* where you stand.
  那要看你站在什麼立場。
- *It depends on* where you look.
  那要看你的著眼點在哪裡。
- *It depends on* how much you're prepared to pay.
  那要看你有多少預算。
- *It depends on* who you're talking to.
  那要看你是跟誰說。

也可以在 depend 的前面加上 all 來加強語氣，如 It all depends on...（那完全要看……。）

----

2. That's up to you. 意思是交由對方決定。

指出判斷的依據 　　　　　　　　　　◉MP3 173

■ 從……來判斷，……。

1. From..., ...	從……來看，……。
2. Judging from [by]..., ...	從……來判斷，……。
3. You can tell by...	從……你會發現……。
4. My instinct tells me...	直覺告訴我……。
5. As far as I can see [judge] by [from]..., ...	就我從……可以看到〔判斷〕的，……。

■句型解說

----

1. 例如 from the way...（從…的方式來看）、from what I heard（從我聽到的）、from the evidence（從證據來看）、from the context（從前後文判斷）等等。

- *From* what I read in the newspapers, I have a feeling that the prime minister will soon resign.
  從我在報紙上讀到的，我有預感首相不久之後就會辭職。
- It is clear *from* the context that the author doesn't mean that.
  從文章的前後文可清楚看出作者的意思不是那樣。

---

5. 請看以下對話。

情境對話

A: I wonder where he comes from. Is he an American?

B: *As far as I can judge from* the way he speaks, he is English, not American.

A：我很好奇他從哪裡來的。他是美國人嗎？

B：從他說話的方式來判斷，他是英國人，不是美國人。

■ 重點提示

　　提出判斷的根據（包括具體的證據、外表的印象或直覺）和判斷的材料（例如既有的知識或典故）時使用。

▩ 陳述理由　　　　　　　　　　　　　◉MP3 174

■ 理由是……。

1. The reason for ... is that...	……的理由是……。
2. The reason (why) ... is that...	（為什麼）會……，是因為……。
3. It's because...	是因為……。
4. For one thing, ..., and for another,...	一個原因是……，另一個原因是……。
5. ... That's why...	……。因此……。
6. ... After all,...	……。畢竟，……。

7. That being so [being the case],...　　　正因為那樣，所以……。

句型解說

1, 2. that 子句說明理由，the reason why 的 why 經常省略。

- More and more students take Chinese courses at our university. *The reason for* the increase *is* obviously *that* students have begun to realize that China, particularly the southern part of the country, is making remarkable economic progress.

  我們學校有愈來愈多學生選修中文課程，學中文的學生人數之所以增加，顯然是因為他們開始了解中國的經濟正呈現驚人的成長，尤其是中國南方。

- *The reasons* I want to study biochemistry *are that* it is a new field of science, and it has wide applications.

  我之所以選擇攻讀生化，是因為生化是一門新興的科學，而且應用範圍相當廣。

3. 請看以下對話。

情境對話

A: Why did the experiment fail?

B: In my opinion *it's because* we didn't maintain the correct temperature.

A：為什麼實驗會失敗？

B：我認為是因為沒有維持在正確的溫度。

4. 原因有兩個。

- I'm honored I was offered the position, but I'm afraid I can't accept your offer. *For one thing,* I don't think I'm suitable for the job, *and for another*, I'm happy with my current position and am not interested in changing my job.

  能受到青睞是我的榮幸，但我恐怕無法接受您的邀請。原因之一是我覺得我並不適合這份工作，另一個原因是我很滿意現在的工作，並沒有轉換跑道的打算。

5. That's why... 前面的內容即原因所在，此句型僅適用於對話。

- A hard disk can be damaged easily. *That's why* we have to be careful handling it.
  硬碟很容易損壞，所以拿的時候要小心。

------

6. After all 後面所陳述的內容即爲前一句的理由，多用於說明某個理所當然的原因。

- You shouldn't have said that to him. *After all,* he is your boss.
  你不該跟他說那些的，畢竟他是你的上司。

------

7. 例如：

- *That being the case,* I have decided to offer my own valuable paintings for sale.
  正因爲那樣，我決定出售我所擁有的珍貴畫作。

▚ 提出可能性　　　　　　　　　　● MP3 175

■ 有……的可能。

1. There is a possibility of [that]...	有……的可能。
2. One possibility (of ...) is that...	（……的）其中一個可能是……。
3. ... can [may]...	……可能……。

■ 或許……。

4. ... could [might]...	……也許……。
5. Possibly [It's possible that]...	說不定〔有可能〕……。
6. Perhaps [Maybe]...	或許……。
7. We can't ignore [overlook] the possibility of...	我們不能忽略……的可能性。

■ 句型解說

1. possibility 後面也可以接 that 子句，請參考句型 7 的解說。

- *There is a possibility that* the patient will get better, and we can't ignore it entirely.

  患者的症狀是有可能改善的，我們不能完全忽略這個可能性。

4. could 表示從某個合理觀點來看的可能性，但這樣的可能性並不高，意思是「理論上有可能，但實際上不太可能」。might 表示可能性不高，是一種推測的說法。

情境對話 1

A: As I said before, the deposit is not refundable.

B: Just a moment. I *could* be wrong, but I don't think you told me anything about that.

A：如同我先前所說的，押金是無法退還的。

B：等等，我可能記錯了，但我不記得你提過這點。

情境對話 2

A: How long does it take from Narita to London?

B: About thirteen hours.

A: He *might* be in London by now.

B: I don't think he would have arrived yet.

A：從成田機場到倫敦要多久？

B：大概 13 個小時。

A：他可能已經在倫敦了。

B：我覺得他應該還沒到。

5. possibly 是「說不定」的意思，用來表達可能性較低的情況，不要和 probably 或 perhaps 搞混了。

情境對話

A: Have you decided on the topic of your thesis?

B: I'll be writing on "Romeo and Juliet," or *possibly* "The Merchant of Venice."

A：你決定好論文主題了嗎？

B：我要以《羅蜜歐與茱麗葉》為主題，或者也有可能是《威尼斯商人》。

• *It's possible that* the yen will soon go down, but I think it's likely to stay high for the next few months.

雖然日圓不久後可能會下跌，但我認為接下來幾個月仍然會持續在高點。

---

6. 英國人多用 perhaps，美國人多用 maybe，兩者的可能性皆高於 possibly。

情境對話

A: Why don't you stay here for another year to pursue your research?

B: I have to go back to Taiwan because I don't have enough financial support.

A: *Perhaps* there's a research grant available from the government. You'd better check it out.

A：為什麼不多待一年繼續做研究？

B：因為沒有足夠的經濟支援，只好回台灣了。

A：政府也許有提供研究補助，你最好去問問看。

---

7. 可能性雖低，但也不能忽略。類似的說法還有 The possibility (of...) cannot be put aside completely.（不能完全排除……的可能性。）

表示合乎邏輯 ● MP3 176

■ ……是合乎道理的。

1. It's logical to think [suppose/say/ conclude] that...	認為〔推測／說／下結論〕…… 是合乎邏輯的。
2. It's reasonable to think [suppose/ say/conclude] that...	認為〔推測／說／下結論〕…… 是合理的。
3. It follows that...	理論上可以……。
4. It follows logically that...	理論上，當然可以……。

■ 理論上，可以說……。

5. It's logically possible to think [suppose/assume] that...　　可以合理認為〔推測／假設〕……。

6. Technically it's possible to...　　技術上，……是有可能的。

7. In theory,...　　理論上，……。

句型解說

1. 也可以在 logical 前面加上 more 而成為 It's more logical to think...（……想更符合邏輯。），否定則是 It's not logical to think that...（……想不合邏輯。）

7. 用來提出和現實無關的論證，後面接 but in practice,...（但實際上，……。）會更有效果。

  • *In theory,* the train can run at a speed of 250 kph, *but in practice*, 200 kph is the fastest that it can attain.
  理論上，這輛火車的時速可達 250 公里，但實際上 200 公里已經是極限了。

重點提示

句型 1 到 4 用來描述符合邏輯的情況，句型 5 和 6 則用來提出和現實不符的推論。

舉例　　◉MP3 177

■ 舉例來說，……。

1. For example [instance],...　　舉例來說，……。

2. Look at..., for example. [Take ... for example.]　　以……為例。

3. Let me give you [Let me take/Let's take] an example.　我舉個例子給你聽〔讓我舉個例子 / 我們來舉個例子〕。

4. To take an example,...　舉例來說，……。

5. An example of this is...　關於這個的例子是……。

6. ... is an example. [... are examples.]　……是其中一個例子。〔……是其中的例子。〕

7. Let's take the case of...　我們以……為例。

8. Let's take any..., say,...　我們以……，譬如……，為例。

9. ... This is just an example.　……。這只是個例子。

10. Let me just give you one figure.　讓我給你一個數據。

■ 句型解說

1. 可放在句首或句尾。

- There are a number of renowned professors on our teaching staff. Professor Jones, *for example*. He is an outstanding scientist in the field of biochemistry.
  我們的師資團隊中有許多知名的教授，以瓊斯教授為例，他是生化學界傑出的科學家。

3. example 前面可以用形容詞修飾，例如 specific example（具體的例子）。

- *Let me give you* a number of *examples*.
  我舉一些例子給你聽。

4. 若要再舉一個例子，可用 To take another example,...（再舉一個例子，……。）或 Let's take another example.（我們舉另一個例子。）

6. 例如：

- As a rule, a capital city is the cultural center of a country as well as the seat of its government. London, Paris, Tokyo *are* notable *examples*.

一般而言，首都是一國的文化中心，也是中央政府的所在地。倫敦、巴黎、東京都是很有名的例子。

---

7. 請看以下對話。

情境對話

A: The test of a genius is whether he is short-lived or not.

B: I don't agree. *Let's take the case of* Picasso. No doubt he was a genius, but he lived to his nineties.

A：要看一個人是不是天才，就看他的壽命是不是比較短。

B：我不同意。以畢卡索為例，他無疑是個天才，但他可是活到 90 幾歲。

---

8. 表示同一類的人事物中，任何例子都適用，say 是一種簡略的表現。

- To be able to become successful as a pianist, you have to start your career very early in life. *Let's take any* pianist, *say*, Richter, Horowitz, or Brendel. They had all made their debuts by the age of twenty.

   要成為一個成功的鋼琴家，必須很早就開始以彈鋼琴為業。我們拿幾個鋼琴家來說好了，李希特、霍洛維茲和布蘭德爾等等，他們都是 20 歲的時候出道的。

■ 重點提示

　　討論時，適時舉出具體的例子非常重要，尤其在一般的論述之後利用上述句型來舉例，效果更佳。

指出例外　　　　　　　　　　　　　　　 ●MP3 178

■ ……是例外。

1. But some ... are...	但有些……是……。
2. But there are (some) exceptions.	但有（一些）例外。
3. But ... is an exception.	不過……是例外。

4. The only exception is...　　　　　　唯一的例外是……。

5. But ... cannot be applied to...　　　但是……不適用於……。

句型解說

1. 請看以下對話。

情境對話

A: Companies everywhere are suffering from a considerable decrease in profits because of the recession.

B: *But some* companies *are* making even bigger profits in spite of the recession.

A：因為不景氣，各地的公司都為收益大幅減少所苦。

B：雖然景氣低迷，但有些公司卻是逆勢成長。

5. 表示不符合原則，用來表現例外。

情境對話

A: As a rule, the cultural center of a country as well as the seat of its government is its capital city. London, Paris, Tokyo are notable examples.

B: *But* this rule *cannot be applied to* New York.

A：一般而言，一國的文化中心以及中央政府的所在地是首都。倫敦、巴黎、東京都是很有名的例子。

B：但紐約不在此例。

導出結論　　　　　　　　　　　　　　◉MP3 179

■ 結論是……。

1. Let me conclude by saying...　　　　讓我以……作結。

2. I would like to conclude by saying...　我想以……作結。

3. I conclude that...　　　　　　　　　　結論是……。

4. My conclusion then is that...　　　　　因此我的結論是……。

5. It's my conclusion that...　　　　　　我的結論是……。

6. I think we can conclude from this ...　　我想我們可以從這個……得
   that...　　　　　　　　　　　　　　　出……的結論。

7. There is only one conclusion.　　　　只有一個結論。

8. In conclusion, let me just say this.　　最後，讓我這麼說。〔我想說
   [I'd like to say...]　　　　　　　　　　……。〕

■ 因此，結論是……。

9. Our conclusion then is that...　　　　因此我們的結論是……。

10. That seems to be the only logical　　那似乎是這次討論唯一合理的
    conclusion of our discussion.　　　　結論。

11. That seems to be the conclusion of　　那似乎是這場會議的結論。
    this meeting.

12. That sums it up.　　　　　　　　　結論就是那樣。

■ 讓我以……作結。

13. Let me close this meeting by saying...　讓我以……來結束這場會議。

14. Let me finish by saying...　　　　　讓我以……作結。

■ 句型解說

1 ~ 8. 用來陳述結論。句型 2 除了提出結論，也可以做為話題結束前的陳述。此
外，如果不得不以某個結果來下結論，可以用 I'm obliged to conclude that...
（我不得不做出……的結論。）

- I've considered all aspects of the accident and *I'm obliged to conclude that* it was a man-made disaster.

  我已經全面調查過這場意外，不得不說這是一場人爲的災難。

4, 9. then（因此）用來帶出目前爲止根據論證或調查所產生的結論。

---

9 ~ 12. 常見於開會時主席根據討論脈絡、順勢提出結論的情況。句型 10 到 12 用來指接受他人提出的結論或要點，並以該結論或要點作結。

---

13. 主席結束會議的表現方式。除了做結論外，也用來做最後的補充。

歸納總結   ◉MP3 180

■ 總而言之，……。

1. Let me sum up.	讓我來總結一下。
2. Can I sum up by saying...?	我可以以……來作結嗎？
3. Let me summarize my [our] argument [main points].	讓我歸納一下我〔我們〕的論點〔要點〕。
4. To summarize my [our] argument [main points], ...	我〔我們〕的論點〔要點〕歸納如下，……。
5. So, to sum up, ...	所以，總而言之，……。
6. In summary, ...	總之，……。

■句型解說

---

3. 類似的說法有 Let me summarize what we have agreed on.（讓我歸納一下我們已達成的共識。）

明確、清楚提出論點或意見的句型　　●MP3 181

one thing.../There is something that...

不直接描述一件事，而是先有一個緩衝，再帶出現況。用來當做緩衝的話一句或兩句以上都可以。

- There is *one thing* that is very clear. The room was locked last night.
  有件事情是很確定的，昨晚房間是上鎖的。

- *Two things* have come to my mind. One is that the route goes on the west side of the mountain, and there is less danger of avalanches down there. The other is that the slope is much less steep on that side of the mountain.
  我想到兩件事。一是那個路線是沿著山的西坡，而西坡比較不會有雪崩的危險；一是西坡的坡度要緩得多。

- *There's something that* I don't understand in your statement. Why do you use the word "internationalization" so often?
  你的說明之中有個地方我不太明白，為什麼你這麼常用「國際化」這個詞呢？

... is this. ...

先用 this 來代替要說的內容，結束句子，接著另起新的句子，說明主要的內容，例如：

- My opinion/suggestion/problem/position *is this*. ...
  我的意見／建議／問題／立場是，……。

- What I can do *is this*. ...
  我能做的是，……。

- What he said *was this*. ...
  他說的是，……。

這種用法除了能避開冗長的句子，也比較容易引起對方的注意，專注於 this 所指的內容。

- What I'd like you to do *is this*. You'll offer me maintenance service for three years.
  我希望你做的是，提供三年的維修服務。
- My fear *is this*. If we don't realize how important it is for Japan to try to cooperate with Asian countries, we will be in great trouble in the future.
  我害怕的是，如果我們不了解日本和其他亞洲國家合作的重要性，那麼前途堪慮。

... That is...

為前句做出總結，前述內容用 that 取代。

- ... *That's* the advantage.
  ……。那就是優點所在。
- ... *That's* my view.
  ……。那就是我的看法。
- ... So, the yen will keep rising. *That's* my view.
  ……。因此，日幣會持續攀升。那是我的看法。

10

第10章
理解與誤會

交換意見時,有時會聽不懂對方
的話,或者對方誤解自己的意
思,這種情況並不少見。本章將
帶你透過各種句型修正彼此的誤
解,讓溝通更為順暢。

Useful English Expressions
for Communication

表示無法理解

■ 我不懂你所說的。

1. I'm sorry, I can't follow you.   抱歉，我不懂你的意思。

2. I don't understand what you're saying.   我不了解你說的話。

3. Excuse me [Sorry], I don't understand.   抱歉，我不明白。

4. I'm not quite with you.   我不太懂你的意思。

5. I don't know what you mean.   我不懂你的意思。

6. I don't understand what you mean by...   我不懂你提到的……。

7. I don't quite follow what you said about...   我不太懂你所說的……。

■ 我不懂。

8. I don't understand.   我不懂。

9. I'm not sure that I fully understand your point.   我不確定是否完全了解你的重點。

10. I'm not sure I get everything that's on your mind.   我不確定是否了解你的想法。

11. I don't understand the point you're making.   我不了解你的重點在哪。

12. So, what is [what seems to be]...?   所以，……是什麼？

13. Could you be more precise?   能不能說得更具體一點？

■ 我不清楚……。

14. I'm not clear about...   我不太清楚……。

15. One thing that's not clear to me is...   我不清楚的是……。

16. I don't understand why [how]...   我不了解為什麼〔如何〕……。

句型解說

---

8 ~ 11. 無法理解對方陳述的內容或主張。如果對方提出的論點不合邏輯（或對方的論點在多數的情況下並不合理），可以說 I don't follow your argument.（我不懂你的論點。）

---

12. 雖然了解對方的說法，但不明白重點為何。例如對方熱烈地陳述某個議題，但身為聽者的我們卻很難有共鳴，又或是對方不擅言詞，話講得不清不楚，這個時候就可以用 So, what is...? 來發問。句首的 So 是重點，意思是「所以呢？」暗示「你說的這些我都知道了，請說重點」。

- *So, what is* your suggestion?
  所以呢？你的建議是什麼？
- *So, what seems to be* the problem?
  所以呢？問題是什麼呢？

---

14. 對於事實的理解不夠清楚。類似的用法有 I'm not clear whether [what]...（我不太清楚是否〔什麼〕……。）

情境對話

A: Those are the details of the English courses at our school. Have I made myself clear?

B: Well, *I'm not clear about* what you said on tuition. When do I have to pay the entrance fee?

A：那就是本校英文課程的細節。這樣清楚了嗎？

B：嗯，你說的學費部分我不太清楚。什麼時候要付呢？

---

15. 對於事實的認知，提出疑問或不清楚的地方。類似的說法有 It's not clear to me why [how]...（我不清楚為什麼〔如何〕……。）、There is one thing that's not clear to me.（有件事情我不太清楚。）

- Thank you for your instructions, but *there's one thing that's not clear to me.* What exactly do you mean by...?
  謝謝你的指導，但有件事情我不是很清楚。你說……是什麼意思？

---

16. 類似的說法有 What I don't understand is why [how]...（我不了解的是為什麼〔如何〕……。）

▮重點提示

上述句型主要是在無法理解對方描述的內容，或請對方進一步說明時使用。另外，在句子前面加上 I'm afraid（我恐怕）會讓整句話變得比較婉轉，例如 I'm afraid I don't quite follow you.（我恐怕不太了解你的意思。）

▮ 確認對方理解的程度 ◉MP3 183

▮ 你了解嗎？

1. Do you follow me so far?	到目前為止了解嗎？
2. Are you with me so far?	到目前為止聽得懂嗎？
3. Do you see what I mean?	你了解我的意思嗎？
4. Do you understand what I am saying?	我說的你了解嗎？

▮ 清楚嗎？

5. Have I made [Did I make] myself clear?	我說的你清楚嗎？
6. Is everything clear?	都清楚嗎？
7. Is that clear?	清楚嗎？

▮句型解說

1. 類似的說法還有 Do you follow my argument?（你了解我的論點嗎？）。

3. see 就是 understand 的意思。

4. 也可以直接說 (You) Understand?（懂了嗎？），是比較口語的說法。

5. 講完重要或複雜的內容後，詢問對方是否了解。

情境對話

A: That's how to operate the machine. *Have I made myself clear?*
B: I think so.
A：這就是機器的操作方式，我說的你懂了嗎？
B：應該懂了。

重點提示

　　當陳述的內容較爲複雜時，不要只是自己一味地講個不停，應該適時詢問對方是否理解。說明即將告一段落時，也要問對方「了解了嗎？」，給對方提問的機會。

確認自己的理解是否正確　　　　◉MP3 184

■ ……是這個意思嗎？

1. ... Is that the point you are making?	你想說的是不是……？
2. Am I correct that your point is...?	你的重點是……，我的理解正確嗎？
3. Am I right in thinking [saying]...?	我……的想法〔說法〕是正確的嗎？
4. Do I understand that to mean...?	那是……的意思嗎？
5. Is your argument [point] that...?	你的論點〔重點〕是……嗎？
6. If I understand you correctly, you are saying that ... Am I correct?	如果我的理解正確的話，你的意思是……，對嗎？
7. Let me check [see] if I understand you correctly.	讓我確認一下我的理解是否正確。

■ 句型解說

- -

1. 用自己的話重述對方的看法，並詢問「這樣的理解正不正確」。

- -

4. 也可以說 Do I understand you correctly that...?（你是說……，我的理解正確嗎？）。

- -

6. 用自己的方式重新整理對方的看法，最後再用 Am I correct? 確認。

- -

◈ 表示理解　　　　　　　　　　　◉ MP3 185

■ 我明白了。

1. (Oh,) I see.	（喔，）原來如此。
2. I see what you mean.	我懂你的意思。
3. I see what you are trying to say.	我了解你說的。
4. Now I see what you mean.	現在我懂你的意思了。
5. Ah, now I understand.	啊，我懂了。
6. I see what you want to say [do], (but)...	我了解你想說〔想做〕的，（但是）……。
7. I understand up to a point, but...	到某部分為止我都了解，但是……。

■ 句型解說

- -

6. but 後面多半接相反的意見。

- -

7. 能理解部分的看法，但並非全部。也可以說 I understand you up to the point that...（關於你提出的……，我能了解。）

確定重點

◉MP3 186

■ 我想說清楚……。

1. Let me ... to make sure that...	讓我……，以確定……。
2. Let me make one thing very [perfectly] clear.	讓我徹底說清楚一件事情。
3. Let's be clear about...	關於……，讓我們說清楚。
4. I would like to make it very clear that...	我想說清楚……。
5. One thing that I would like to make (absolutely) clear is that...	我想（徹底）說清楚的是……。
6. I would like to make one thing (absolutely) clear. That is...	我想（徹底）說清楚一件事，那就是……。
7. Let me repeat your points to make sure...	讓我複述一次你的重點，好確定……。

句型解說

1. 例如：
   - *Let me* ask a few questions *to make sure* there is no misunderstanding on either side.
   為確保雙方不會產生誤解，讓我問幾個問題。

2. 類似的說法是 Let me clarify...（讓我弄清楚……。）
   - *Let me make this very clear*. I won't support the party's decision.
   讓我把話說清楚，我是不會支持黨的決定的。
   - I locked the door. *Let me make that perfectly clear*. I had definitely locked the door when I went out, but on my return I found it was open.
   我有鎖門。讓我徹底說清楚。出門前我確實上鎖了，但回家的時候發現門是開著的。

7. 例如：

- *Let me repeat your points to make sure* I fully understand what's on your mind.
  讓我複述一次你的重點，好確定我完全了解你的想法。

▪重點提示

　　討論時，可能在不知不覺中產生誤解。這個時候必須即時確認重點，了解雙方的看法。

▨ 說明要點 ◉MP3 187

■ 我想說的是……。

1. I mean...	我的意思是……。
2. What I mean is that...	我的意思是……。
3. The point I would like to make is that...	我想說的重點是……。
4. What I'm trying to say is that...	我想說的是……。

▪句型解說

---

1. I mean 可用來清楚表明前述的內容、進一步說明重點，或者換句話說，是十分簡便的說法。

情境對話　**1**

A: Do you know him personally?

B: Yes, indeed. He is a friend of mine. *I mean* he used to be my business partner.

A：你跟他私底下有來往嗎？

B：有，他是我朋友。我的意思是說，他以前是我的事業伙伴。

情境對話 2

A: Japan is one of the richest countries in the world.

B: Well, the Japanese are rich as a nation, but not as individuals. *I mean* their standard of living is not high. Most of them can't afford to take a long vacation. The prices, particularly in big cities like Tokyo and Osaka, are extremely high.

A：日本是全世界最富有的國家之一。

B：嗯，以國家來看的確如此，但個人的情況就不同了。我的意思是，日本人的生活水準不高，大部分的日本人沒有放長假的餘裕。物價高得嚇人，特別是東京或大阪等大都市。

4. 例如：

• Why are you bringing up others' faults? It's no good speaking ill of others here. *What I'm trying to say is that* you should take some responsibility.
你為什麼提起別人的錯？在這裡道人長短不是什麼好事。我想說的是，你自己該負點責任。

■ 重點提示

　　覺得自己說得不夠清楚時，藉由「我想說的是……」說明重點為何是十分重要的。此外，上述句型也可以用來排除對方的誤解。其他請參考以下「釐清誤會」的句型。

▨ 釐清誤會 (I) ●MP3 188

■ 我的意思不是……。

1. This is not to say...	我的意思不是……。
2. I'm not (really) saying...	我（真正）的意思不是……。
3. I don't mean [wish] to imply that...	我並不是〔並不想〕要暗示說……。

> 4. I don't want to appear to be saying [criticizing]... 　　我不是要讓人覺得我在說〔批評〕……。
>
> 5. I'm not denying that... 　　我沒有否定……。
>
> 6. I'm not [No one is] disputing... 　　我不是要〔沒有人要〕質疑……。
>
> 7. I wouldn't say... 　　我不會說……。

■ 句型解說

2. 類似的說法有 I'm not really criticizing you, but...（我不是眞的要批評你，但是……。）

---

4. 例如：

- *I don't want to appear to be criticizing* him, but I think he was a little careless in his statement that there would be a tax-increase in the near future.
  我不是要讓人覺得我在批評他，但我認爲他說不久之後稅率將調高的發言有點隨便。

---

5. 先姑且同意對方的看法，再陳述其他論點，達到反駁的效果。

情境對話

A: I don't agree that he is the best singer in the choir.

B: Why not? He is a talented singer.

A: *I'm not denying* he is talented, but he is not very dedicated to music. I can see it in the way he sings.

A：我不認爲他是合唱團裡唱得最好的人。

B：爲什麼？他是個很有天分的歌手。

A：我沒有否認他很有天分，只是他對音樂並沒有很投入。從他唱歌的方式就知道了。

---

6. dispute 在這裡有「質疑」的意思。

情境對話

A: We tried our best. We made a strong effort to solve the problem, but...

B: *No one is disputing* your effort.

A：我們盡力了，用最大的努力想解決問題，但是……。

B：沒有人質疑你們的努力。

類似的說法還有 I wouldn't dispute [question]...（我不會質疑……。）

- *I wouldn't dispute* the authenticity of the manuscript.
  我不會質疑這份手稿的可信度。

- *I wouldn't question* his sincerity.
  我不會懷疑他的誠意。

---

7. 也可以說 I don't say...（我不是說……。）

情境對話

A: Do I have to learn Latin grammar in order to study English etymology?

B: *I wouldn't say* you have to study it, but I think you ought to know something about Latin vocabulary.

A：如果要研究英語的語源，是不是一定得學拉丁文文法？

B：我不會說一定得學，不過我覺得你多少要懂一些拉丁文字彙。

■ 重點提示

　　這部分的句型，是預想對方可能產生誤會，換個方式重新確立重點。要排除他人的誤解，記得先表明「我要說的不是……」。

請對方不要誤會

● MP3 189

■ 請不要誤會。

1. Just a moment. You misunderstood [misunderstand] me.	等等，你誤會我了。
2. (Please) Don't misunderstand me.	（請）不要誤會我。
3. (Please) Don't be misled.	（請）不要被誤導了。

4. There seems to have been a
   misunderstanding (about...).

（對於……）似乎有所誤解。

■ 我的意思不是那樣。

5. I'm not saying that.

我的意思不是那樣。

6. I didn't say that. [I've never said that.]

我沒有那樣說。〔我從沒說過那
種話。〕

7. That's not what I'm saying [what I
   said].

我要說的〔我說的〕不是那樣。

8. That's not what I mean. [I don't mean
   that.]

我的意思不是那樣。

9. That's not true.

不是那樣的。

10. No, you're wrong. I didn't say that.

不，你錯了。我沒有說過那種
話。

11. No, not really. Now, let me clarify that.

不，不是那樣的，讓我解釋清
楚。

■ 我不是在說……。

12. I'm not talking about [referring to]...

我不是在說〔在指〕……。

■句型解說

1. Just a moment. 用來制止對方繼續說下去，類似的說法還有 Hold on.，不過比
   較口語。

2. 類似的說法有 Don't get me wrong.（不要誤會我。），是比較口語的表現方式。

4. 用 seem 比較不會太直接，類似的說法還有 There seems to have been some kind of mistake.（這其中似乎有些誤會。）

* *There seems to have been a misunderstanding about* the terms on your side.
  你對協議的內容似乎有所誤解。

5, 6. 用 I'm not saying that...（我的意思不是⋯⋯）針對對方誤解之處提出解釋。而 I haven't said...（我從來沒有說⋯⋯）則是引用對方的說詞，強調自己沒有說過那樣的話。

情境對話 1

A: I just don't understand why we should stop the project when we've tried very hard to achieve our goal.

B: Just a minute! You misunderstand me. *I'm not saying* we should stop the project. What I'm saying is that we should modify the plan to suit the situation.

A：我不懂，我們明明這麼努力想要達到目標，為什麼必須中止這項企劃呢？

B：等等！你誤會了。我沒說要中止企劃。我的意思是，我們應該調整企劃內容來配合現在的情況。

情境對話 2

A: So, would you please sign here? You are interested in our campaign, aren't you?

B: *I haven't said* "yes." I just asked you questions about what you've been doing.

A：那麼，麻煩您在這裡簽名好嗎？您對我們的活動感興趣對吧？

B：我從來沒有說感興趣，只是針對活動內容問了幾個問題而已。

7, 8. 類似的說法是 That's not exactly what I mean.（我的意思不是那樣。）

---

10. 請看以下對話。

情境對話

A: But you said you're going to renew the contract for another two years.

B: *No, you're wrong. I didn't say that*.

A：但你說你會再續兩年約。

B：不，你錯了。我沒有說過那種話。

---

11. 除了 Let me clarify that. ，還可以說 Let me make it very clear. （讓我把話講清楚。）

情境對話

A: Are you saying that all the employees above the age of fifty should go?

B: *No, not really. Now, let me clarify that.* I just wanted to suggest that some of them may wish to leave.

A：你的意思是說 50 歲以上的員工都該走人？

B：不，不是那樣的，讓我解釋清楚。我只是要說，他們之中可能有些人想離開。

- -

■ 重點提示

意識到對方有所誤解時，先用 Hold on!、Just a moment!、Wait a minute!、No, no. 等方式制止對方，接著再說 You misunderstood me.。然後指出對方誤解的地方，並告知正確的內容（請參考接下來的句型）。

▓ 釐清誤會 (II)　　　　　◉MP3 190

■ 我說的是……。

1. What I said was...	我說的是……。
2. What I'm saying is that...	我的意思是……。
3. What I'm trying to say is that...	我想說的是……。
4. What I (exactly) mean is that...	我（真正）的意思是……。
5. I am just [simply] saying that...	我的意思是……。（我只是在說……。）

■ 重點提示

不清不楚的敘述容易造成誤會。如果發現對方有所誤解，應該先請對方不要

誤會（請參考前項句型），並告知正確的內容。關於這方面的表現，有兩種說法。
一是否定對方誤解的內容，如 I didn't say that...（我沒有說……。），另一個是
把話說清楚，如 What I exactly mean is that...（我真正的意思是……。），兩種說
法也可以同時使用。

- I didn't say that. What I said was that...
  我沒有那樣說，我說的是……。
- I'm not saying that... What I'm saying is that...
  我的意思不是……，而是……。

表示自己不是在開玩笑　　　　　◉MP3 191

■ 我是認真的。

1. I meant it seriously.	我是認真的。
2. I mean what I say. [I mean it.]	我是說真的。
3. I'm serious.	我是認真的。
4. I'm not joking.	我不是在開玩笑。

句型解說

2. 例如：
- Don't laugh! *I mean it!*
  不要笑！我是說真的！

重點提示

認真討論卻被他人當做玩笑看待，這時便可用上述句型表達自己的立場。

為自己的玩笑話道歉

◉MP3 192

■ 我是開玩笑的。

1. I'm sorry. I meant it as a joke.   對不起。我是開玩笑的。

2. That was meant to be a joke.   那是個玩笑。

3. I was just [only] joking.   我只是在開玩笑。

重點提示

如果對方把你的玩笑話當真,可用上述句型化解誤會。

對誤解感到抱歉

◉MP3 193

■ 抱歉我誤會你了。

1. I'm sorry I must have misunderstood you.   抱歉,我一定是誤會你了。

重點提示

誤會對方時,表達歉意的說法。

確認對方真正的意思

◉MP3 194

■ 你的意思是……嗎?

1. Do you mean...? [You mean...?]   你的意思是……嗎?

2. Does that mean...? 　　　　　　　　　意思是⋯⋯嗎？

3. Are you saying...? 　　　　　　　　　你的意思是⋯⋯嗎？

4. Are you trying to say...? 　　　　　　你是不是想說⋯⋯？

5. Are you implying [suggesting] that...? 　你是不是在暗示〔建議〕⋯⋯？

6. Is your point that...? 　　　　　　　　你的重點是⋯⋯嗎？

■ 你想要說什麼？

7. What do you mean by...? 　　　　　　你說⋯⋯，是什麼意思？

8. What are you trying to say? 　　　　　你想說什麼？

9. What is your point? 　　　　　　　　你的重點是什麼？

■ 你指的是什麼？

10. What [Who] do you have in mind? 　　你想到什麼〔誰〕？

11. What [Who/Which one] are you
    talking about? 　　　　　　　　　你在說什麼〔誰／哪一個〕？

12. What [Who/Which one] are you
    referring to? 　　　　　　　　　　你指的是什麼〔誰／哪一個〕？

■ 你想說的是⋯⋯嗎？

13. ... Is that what you mean? 　　　　　⋯⋯。你的意思是那樣嗎？

14. ... Is that what you are saying? 　　　⋯⋯。你想說的是那樣嗎？

15. (You're saying)... Is that right? 　　　（你說的是）⋯⋯，對嗎？

■ 句型解說

1. 對於他人想表達的意思感到困惑，進而詢問對方。

情境對話 1

A: We have to charge you an extra ten pounds.

B: *Do you mean* that even though I have paid twenty pounds, I still have to pay another ten pounds?

A：我們必須加收 10 英鎊。

B：你的意思是說，雖然我已經付了 20 英鎊，但還得再付 10 英鎊？

另外，肯定句語尾的語調上揚，可以表現出一種確認的語氣。

情境對話 2

A: I need certain types of assistance from you.

B: *You mean* money?

A: Uh, yes.

A：我需要你某種形式的協助。

B：你是說錢嗎？

A：嗯，是的。

---

2. 也可以用 You said... Does that mean...?（你說……，意思是……嗎？），先重複對方的話，再確認對方的意思。

---

7. 也可以用副詞 exactly（到底）來加強語氣，即 What exactly do you mean by...?（你說……，到底是什麼意思？）。

---

15. 先說出自己的理解，再向對方確認。Is that right? 也可用 Am I right? 替代。

- You saw the man coming out of the house. *Is that right*, Mrs. Brown?
  布朗太太，妳看到那個男人從屋子裡走出來，對吧？

■ 重點提示

　　無法理解對方所說的內容而想確認對方的意思時，首先先提出疑問 Do you mean...?（你的意思是……嗎？），等對方解釋完後，再用 I see. So...（我明白了。所以意思是……。）來回應。如此便能減少誤解的情況。

請對方再說一次

◉MP3 195

■ **請再說一次。**

1. Sorry?	抱歉，你說什麼？
2. Excuse me?	不好意思，你說什麼？
3. Pardon (me)?	抱歉，請再說一次。
4. I beg your pardon.	請再說一次。
5. Could you say that again?	可以再說一次嗎？
6. Sorry, I don't quite follow you. What did you say?	對不起，我跟不太上，你剛剛說什麼？
7. Could you repeat that, please?	能不能請你重複一次？
8. I couldn't hear (you).	我聽不到（你的聲音）。

■ 句型解說

1. 沒聽清楚想請對方再說一次，是非常口語的說法。英國人多用 Sorry?，美國人較常用 Excuse me?。

4. 句尾音調上揚，表示請對方再說一次。由於是較為強調的說法，隨著語調不同，甚至會有「你說什麼？」的質問語氣，所以使用時要特別留意。

6. I don't follow. 指的是跟不上對方的說話速度，或聽不懂對方所說的內容。

8. 因為環境太吵以致於聽不見對方的話，或是場地太大，聽不見另一邊的人在說什麼。另外，聽演講時如果坐得比較後面，聽不清楚講者的話時，可以說：
   • Could you please speak up? We can't hear you at the back.
   能不能大聲一點？我們坐後面的聽不到。

沒有聽到對方的重點

◉ MP3 196

■ 我沒有聽到……。

1. I didn't catch...	我沒有聽到……。
2. Could you repeat..., please?	可以請你再說一次……嗎？
3. What [Which/Where/When/Who] did you say...?	你說……是什麼〔哪一個／哪裡／什麼時候／誰〕？
4. I couldn't hear. What did you say after "..."?	我聽不到。「……」之後你說了什麼？

■句型解說

1. catch 的原意是「抓住」，在這裡當「聽到，了解」解釋。

- *I didn't catch* your name.
  我沒聽清楚你的名字。

- *I didn't catch* what you just said.
  我沒聽到你剛才說的。

- *I didn't catch* what you said after "..."
  「……」之後你說了什麼我沒聽清楚。

2. 例如：

- *Could you repeat* the spelling, *please?*
  能不能請你再拼一次？

- *Could you repeat* the last word, *please?*
  最後一個字能不能請你重複一次？

3. did you day 當做插入句使用，置於疑問句當中。

- *What did you say* his name is?
  你說他叫什麼名字？

▌重點提示

　　請對方再說一次自己沒聽清楚的內容。如果只是要求「再說一遍」，對方可能會把說過的話再重說一遍，非常浪費時間。因此，指定某個聽不清楚的部分，請對方再講一次即可。

確認特定內容　　　　　　　　　　　　　◉MP3 197

■ 你說的是「……」嗎？

1. (Excuse me, but) Did you say "..."?	（不好意思，）你是說「……」嗎？
2. "...," did you say?	你是說「……」嗎？
3. "..." Is that what you're saying?	「……」，你說的是那樣嗎？
4. (Excuse me.) Do you mean...?	（抱歉。）你的意思是……嗎？
5. Who, me?	誰？我嗎？

▌句型解說

- -

1. 確認沒聽清楚的話。也可以用來表示不太相信對方的說詞，要求再說一次。

情境對話

A: I talked to Barack Obama at the party, and...

B: *Excuse me. Did you say* you met Barack Obama, the President of the United States?

A: Yes, I talked to him.

A：我在宴會上和歐巴馬說話，然後……。

B：抱歉，你是說你遇到歐巴馬嗎？美國總統歐巴馬？

A：對啊，我和他聊了一下。

- -

2. 和句型 1 一樣用來請對方重複一次自己沒聽清楚的內容，是非常簡便的說法。

情境對話

A: I went to Uganda last week, and...

B: "Rwanda," *did you say?*

A: No, Uganda. I went to Uganda.

A：上禮拜我去了趟烏干達，然後⋯⋯。

B：你是說「盧安達」嗎？

A：不是，是烏干達。我去了烏干達。

---

3. 重複對方說的話，確認其可信度，尤其是在確認內容時使用。

情境對話

A: In case of emergency, do not try to rush into the elevator. Take the stairs, instead, on the east side of the building. Just go downstairs. It leads you to the back door which opens on to the street outside.

B: I shouldn't take the elevator. I should go down the stairs on the east side. *Is that what you're saying?*

A：如果遇到緊急情況，不要搶搭電梯。改從大樓東側的樓梯下去。只要一直往下走就好，樓梯會通到後門，出了後門就是外面了。

B：不要搭電梯、要從東側的樓梯下去，你的意思是這樣嗎？

---

4. 用來確認對方話中的意思。如果沒有把握自己的理解是否正確，可以這麼說：I'm not sure I understand. Do you mean...?（我不確定我有沒有聽懂，你的意思是⋯⋯嗎？）。

---

5. 一時之間不知道對方是不是在說自己，進而提出疑問。

■重點提示

　　如果聽不懂對方的話，可以用上一個句型請對方再說一次。如果聽了似懂非懂，用這個部分的句型適時提出疑問、加以確認才是上策。

詢問對方話中的意思

◉MP3 198

■「……」是什麼意思？

1. (Excuse me, but) What does "..." mean?	（不好意思，）「……」是什麼意思？
2. (Excuse me, but) What do you mean by "..."?	（不好意思，）你說的「……」是什麼意思？
3. (Excuse me, but) What is "..."? [Could you tell me what "..." is?]	（不好意思，）什麼是「……」？〔可以告訴我「……」是什麼嗎？〕

■句型解說

1. 請見以下對話。

情境對話

A: Wrongful dismissal applies to this case.

B: *Excuse me, but what does* "wrongful dismissal" *mean?*

A：非法解雇適用於本案件。

B：不好意思，「非法解雇」的意思是？

2. 請見以下對話。

情境對話

A: The manager is suffering from a kind of megalomania.

B: *What do you mean by* "megalomania"?

A: It's the excessive belief that one is more important than one really is.

A：經理有誇大妄想症。

B：你說「誇大妄想症」是什麼意思？

A：就是把自己看得太重，覺得自己很重要。

3. What is...? 用來詢問某件事背後代表的意義，而不是字面上的意義。句子前面加上 Could you tell me 比較婉轉。

■ 重點提示

　　對方用了較難的字詞時，雖然可以從前後文猜出意思，但若真的不懂也不要裝懂，利用上述句型找機會發問，才不會愈聽愈不知所以然。句型 1 和 2 都用了動詞 mean，不過句型 1 的主詞是未知的內容，句型 2 則是用第二人稱的 you 為主詞。

請對方說清楚　　　　　　　　　　　　　◉MP3 199

■ 請慢慢說。／請大聲一點。

1. Please speak slowly.	請慢慢說。
2. Could you speak more slowly?	能不能請你說慢一點？
3. Could you speak a little louder?	能不能請你稍微大聲一點？

■ 句型解說

1. 以下是另一種婉轉的說法。

- I can't follow you. So, *please speak slowly.*
  我跟不上你的速度，所以，請說慢一點。

■ 重點提示

　　雖然 Could you speak more clearly?（可以說得更清楚一點嗎？）沒什麼不對，但可能會讓對方誤以為是不是自己的發音不清楚。因此，跟不上對方說話的速度或對方聲音太小時用 Could you speak more slowly [a little louder]? 比較恰當。

11

第11章
道歉與解釋

道歉是一門大學問。不了解事情輕重就草率地道歉，事後不但會覺得不舒服，甚至因為先道了歉而得負起全責。因此，面對他人的責難時，必須清楚解釋自己的立場和事態的發展，以獲得他人的理解。當然，如果是自己的錯，必須勇於承認錯誤、適時表達歉意。

Useful English Expressions
for Communication

承認錯誤

■ 我錯了。

1. I made a mistake.	我錯了。
2. I'm very sorry (for the mistake).	很抱歉（我犯了那個錯誤）。
3. That was my mistake.	那是我的錯。
4. I'm sorry. It's my fault. [It's my fault, I'm afraid.]	對不起，是我的錯。〔恐怕是我的錯。〕
5. I was wrong (about...).	（關於……，）我錯了。
6. I supposed [believed] wrongly that...	我以為是〔相信是〕……，但我錯了。
7. My ... was wrong.	我的……錯了。
8. I'm sorry I didn't ... enough.	抱歉我不夠……。
9. I should [shouldn't] have...	我應該〔不應該〕……。
10. It's a pity I [I didn't]...	抱歉我〔我沒有〕……。
11. It was a mistake to [not to]...	做了〔沒做〕……是錯的。

句型解說

1. 坦承錯誤。使用範圍很廣。如果想表達犯下很嚴重的錯誤，可以說 I made a terrible mistake.。

4. fault 是「過錯，責任」的意思，it's my fault 表示「是我的錯」、「我來負責」。類似的說法還有 That's entirely my fault.（那完全是我的責任。）

5. 判斷錯誤。也可以說 I'm afraid I was wrong.（我恐怕錯了。），如果要表現出勉強承認錯誤的態度，可以改用 I admit 而成為 I admit I was wrong.（我承認是我的錯。）

- *I was wrong about* his character.
  我對他的性格有所誤解了。

wrong 還可以這樣使用。
- *I got* your name *wrong*.
  我記錯你的名字了。

---

7. 以自己錯誤的思考或行為當做主詞，表達「我所做的……是錯的」。

- *My* assumption that women are not apt for the job *was wrong*. She has done a very good job indeed!
  我以為女人不適合那份工作，但我錯了。她的表現確實非常出色！

---

8. 例如：

- *I'm sorry I didn't* think carefully *enough* about that.
  很抱歉，關於那件事我考慮得不夠周詳。

也可以說成：
- I didn't give enough thought to that.
  我考慮不夠周詳。

---

9. 例如：

- *I should have* given a little more thought to that.
  我應該考慮周全一些。

---

11. 一時失去判斷而做了某事，事後發覺是個錯誤。

- *It was a mistake to* criticize the director at the meeting.
  在會議上批評主任是不對的。

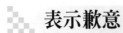 ## 表示歉意

●MP3 201

■ 對不起。

1. I'm sorry (for...).	（對於……）我感到抱歉。
2. I (really must) apologize for...	我（真的必須）為……致歉。
3. (Please) Forgive me (for...).	（請）原諒我（……）。
4. I'm sorry, I'll never do that again.	對不起，我絕對不會再那樣做了。
5. I'd like to apologize on behalf of...	我要代表……向你致歉。
6. I have no excuse for...	對於……，我沒有什麼好辯解的。

■ 句型解說

1. 其他說法包括 I'm sorry that...（我對……感到抱歉。）、I'm sorry to...（……，我很抱歉。）此外，可以用 indeed, very, really, terribly 等副詞來加強語氣。
   - *I'm sorry to* cause you so much trouble.
     對不起，給你添了這麼多麻煩。

   情境對話

   A: The next speaker for today is Professor John Brighton.

   B: Excuse me. My name is John Bryant.

   A: Oh, *I'm terribly sorry*.

   A：今天下一位主講人是約翰‧布萊頓教授。

   B：不好意思，我的名字是約翰‧布萊恩。

   A：喔，真的很抱歉！

2. 也可以單用 I apologize.，意思和 I'm sorry. 和 Forgive me. 相同。
   - *I apologize for* the delay.
     對不起我耽擱了。

另外，apologize 的名詞 apology 也很常用，例如 Please accept my apologies for...（關於……，請接受我的道歉。）

4. 類似的說法還有 I hope it won't happen again.（希望不會再發生了。），不刻意提起自己的錯誤，只是表達遺憾。

5. 代表公司或團體致歉。
   - *I'd like to apologize on behalf of* the company.
     謹代表公司向您致歉。

6. 承認錯誤，不做任何辯解。
   - *I have no excuse for* losing your typescript.
     弄丟你的打字稿，我沒有什麼好辯解的。

■ 重點提示

　　道歉前，必須先弄清楚道歉的對象，以及道歉的程度為何。I'm sorry 後面除了可以接 for...，也可以接 that 子句。如果要表達深切的歉意，有以下說法。
   - I can't tell you how sorry I am.
     我無法形容我有多抱歉。
   - It won't happen again, I promise.
     我保證不會再發生了。

　　因為給別人造成麻煩而致歉時，有以下的說法。
   - I'm sorry to have troubled you.
     很抱歉給你帶來麻煩了。
   - I'm very sorry about all the trouble I've caused.
     我對我造成的麻煩感到非常抱歉。
   - I'm sorry I have caused you so much trouble.
     很抱歉，給你添了這麼多麻煩。

 提出解釋　　　　　　　　　　　　　　　　　◉MP3 202

■ 對不起，那是因為……。

1. I'm sorry, but...	對不起，但是……。
2. I'm sorry, I didn't realize that [what/how]...	抱歉，我不知道〔我不知道什麼／怎麼〕……。
3. I wasn't aware...	我沒有注意到……。
4. I meant [intended] to..., but unfortunately...	我的確是想……，但可惜的是……。
5. I tried to [I was going to]..., but...	我試著要……，但是……。
6. I wish I could..., but...	我希望我能……，但是……。
7. I didn't mean (to) [I had no thought/intention to/of]...	我不是故意要……。
8. I didn't know I was doing something wrong.	我不知道自己做錯了事。
9. I know ... I can only say that...	我知道……，我只能說……。

■ 不過，那是因為……。

10. Well, you see,...	嗯，事情是……。
11. Well, the thing is...	嗯，事實是……。
12. I'm sorry, I must apologize. But you must understand...	對不起，我得道歉。但是你必須了解……。
13. That's just...	那只是……。
14. I'm sorry, but I just...	對不起，但我只是……。

■ 我正試著……。

15. I'm [I have been] trying to...	我〔一直〕試著要……。
16. I'm working on it now.	我正在努力。

句型解說

1. 辯解的基本句型。

情境對話

A: Why didn't you tell me the truth?

B: *I'm sorry, but* I was afraid you'd be angry.

A：為什麼不告訴我真相？

B：對不起，但我怕你會生氣。

突然有事耽擱了原計畫因而造成他人的不便時，可以用以下句型來表達歉意。

* I'm sorry, but some urgent business occurred, and I couldn't...
  對不起，可是那時突然有急事，我沒辦法……。
* I'm sorry, but some unexpected business came up, and I couldn't...
  對不起，可是那時突然有事情發生，我沒辦法……。

2, 3. 沒有注意或意識到某件重要的事情。如果忘得一乾二淨了，可以用 I'm sorry I forgot to...（對不起，我忘了……。）表示。

情境對話

A: What do you mean by throwing away the envelope? My important notes were inside it.

B: *I'm sorry. I didn't realize that* they were so important.

A：你把信封扔了是什麼意思？裡頭有我重要的筆記啊。

B：對不起，我不知道那有這麼重要。

5. 原本計畫要完成某事，但沒有達成。

情境對話

A: I thought you were going to finish it soon.

B: *I was going to, but* I was interrupted by a visitor.

A：我以為你會盡快完成這件事。

B：我本來是這麼打算的，但是被訪客打斷了。

7. 表示自己並無惡意。

* *I didn't mean* any harm.
  我不是故意要傷害人的。

- *I didn't mean to* cause trouble.
  我不是故意要製造麻煩的。

- *I had no intention of* hurting your feelings.
  我不是故意要傷害你的感情的。

情境對話

A: I'm sorry I touched you. *I didn't mean to.*

B: That's all right.

A：對不起碰到了你。我不是故意的。

B：沒關係。

---

9. 先用 I know 來承認自己的缺失，再以 I can only say that... 說明理由。

- *I know* my term paper was terrible. *I can only say that* I didn't have much time to do it.
  我知道我的學期報告寫得很糟，只能說我沒有太多時間好好寫。

---

10. 表示會犯錯是理所當然的，接著提出原因。

情境對話

A: You didn't put a list of references at the end of your paper.

B: *Well, you see*, you didn't tell me anything about the format.

A：你的報告最後沒有附上參考文獻。

B：嗯，因為你沒有告訴我該用哪一種格式。

---

13. 對於個性、興趣等他人視為問題的點，加以反駁。

情境對話 1

A: Why are you so quiet?

B: *That's just* the way I am.

A：你怎麼這麼安靜？

B：我本來就是這樣。

情境對話 2

A: Why do you stay up so late?

B: *That's just* my lifestyle.

A：你為什麼那麼晚睡？

B：我的日常作息就是那樣。

---

14. 請看以下對話。

[情境對話]

A: Did you break the vase?

B: *I'm sorry*, *but I just* touched it, and it fell.

A：花瓶是你打破的嗎？

B：對不起，我只是摸一下而已，花瓶就掉下去了。

---

16. 請看以下對話。

[情境對話]

A: Haven't you finished it yet?

B: I'm sorry for the delay. *I'm working on it now*.

A：還沒完成嗎？

B：抱歉拖到進度了，我正在努力。

■ 重點提示

　　句型 1 到 9 主要是道歉並加以解釋的表現。句型 10 到 14 是說明原因，15 和 16 則表示正在努力彌補。如果要請對方給自己一個解釋的機會，有以下說法。

- Please listen to my side of the story.
  請聽我的解釋。
- Please hear what I have to say.
  請聽一下我的說法。

▓ 承認自己粗心大意　　　　　◉MP3 203

■ 我沒有想過……。／我不知道……。

1. It never crossed my mind (that...).	我從沒想過（……）。
2. It never occurred to me (that...).	我從沒想過（……）。
3. I didn't know that.	我不知道。

句型解說

1, 2. 表示事情在預料之外，也可以用在有欠考慮或疏忽的情況下。

情境對話

A: The patient has become worse over the last few days. However, I don't see any particular cause for his condition.

B: Have you considered the possibility of nosocomial infection?

A: *It never crossed my mind!* I'm going to check it.

A：過去幾天來，患者的病情惡化了，但是我找不出特定的原因。

B：有想過院內感染的可能性嗎？

A：完全沒想過！我來查查看。

3. 請看以下對話。

情境對話

A: Why didn't you greet the president?

B: Who? That gentleman? Is he the president? *I didn't know that.*

A：你為什麼不跟校長打招呼？

B：誰？那位男士嗎？他是校長？我不知道啊。

重點提示

上述句型用來表現說話者粗心大意、思慮不周，雖然也有為自己辯解的意味，但從字面上來看也可以單純表示說話者忘了某件事情，不一定有承認疏失的意味。若要承認自己的疏失，有以下幾種說法。

- I'm sorry for my carelessness.
  請原諒我的疏失。

- How careless I was!
  我怎麼這麼不小心！

- I was careless indeed!
  我真的太不小心了！

要求對方解釋

◉MP3 204

■ 你有什麼要解釋的嗎？

1. Do you have anything to say for yourself?　　你有什麼要為自己辯解的嗎？

2. Do you have any excuse for...　　對於……，你有什麼藉口嗎？

句型解說

2. 例如：

• *Do you have any excuse for* being so late?
遲到這麼久，你有什麼要解釋的嗎？

請對方不要找藉口

◉MP3 205

■ 不要找藉口了。

1. There is no excuse for...　　……沒什麼好解釋的。

2. Stop making excuses!　　別再找藉口了！

句型解說

1. 例如：

• *There is no excuse for* such behavior.
這樣的行為沒什麼好解釋的。

表明自身的清白　　　　　　　　　　◉MP3 206

■ 我沒有錯。

1. I'm innocent of...	我沒有做……。
2. I can't accept your charge that...	我無法忍受你關於……的指控。
3. I have no idea...	我不知道……。
4. I did nothing wrong. [I didn't do anything wrong.]	我沒有做錯事。
5. You do me an injustice to say...	你說我……，這樣並不公平。
6. No one can accuse me of...	沒有人可以指控我……。
7. (I didn't...) I just...	（我沒有……）我只是……。
8. What's wrong with me? [Where am I at fault?]	我做錯什麼了？
9. Where am I wrong?	我哪裡錯了？
10. It's not my fault.	不是我的錯。
11. I don't think [I don't understand why] I should be blamed for that.	我不認為〔我不懂為什麼〕我該為那件事負責。
12. Why should I...?	為什麼我應該……？

◼ 句型解說

1. 例如：

　● *I'm innocent of* violating the regulations.
　　我沒有違反規定。

2. 例如：

　● *I can't accept your charge that* what I did was tantamount to theft.
　　我無法接受你指控我的行為跟偷竊一樣。

3. 請看以下對話。

情境對話

A: I'm really angry with you!

B: *I have no idea* what I did wrong.

A：我真的很氣你！

B：我不知道我做錯什麼了。

---

5. 請看以下對話。

情境對話

A: You gave me an empty box for two hundred dollars. You cheated me.

B: *You do me an injustice to say* I cheated you. I just didn't check inside the box. I'm sorry about that, but I didn't cheat you on purpose.

A：我付了兩百塊美金，結果你給我一個空箱子！你騙我。

B：說我騙你並不公平。我只是沒有確認內容物而已。關於這點我感到很抱歉，但我沒有故意騙你。

---

7. 帶有辯解的意味。

情境對話

A: The machine is broken. Did anyone touch it? Peter, what did you do?

B: *I didn't* do anything to the machine. *I just* passed by it, and it fell.

A：機器壞了。有誰碰過它？彼得，你幹了什麼好事？

B：我沒有碰那台機器，只是從旁邊經過，機器就掉下來了。

---

12. 請看以下對話。

情境對話

A: You should take all responsibility for the accident.

B: *Why should I?*

A：這個意外你要負起全部的責任。

B：為什麼我要負責？

■ 重點提示

遇到別人故意找麻煩，或是明明沒錯卻被誣賴的情況下，可以使用上述句型堅定地表達自己的立場。I'm innocent of... 雖然有點正式，但遭受重大的冤屈時反而能派上用場。總之，對於沒做過的事，就要清清楚楚地表示自己沒做過。

把矛頭指向對方   ◉ MP3 207

■ 那你呢？你又如何？

1. What about you [yourself]?	那你〔你自己〕呢？
2. But you also...	但你還不是……。
3. Let me ask you then.	那我問你。

■ 句型解說

1. 面對指責，反過來把矛頭指向對方。

情境對話

A: You're to blame for the accident that happened in the playground. You should have watched the children more carefully.

B: But *what about yourself?* You had a visitor then and you were talking with him all the time.

A：在操場發生的意外你要負責，你應該把小朋友看好才對。

B：那你自己呢？那時你有訪客，你一直在和訪客聊天。

2. 反過來指責對方。句子後面接 Isn't that...?（那不是……？）或 It is..., isn't it?
（那是……，不是嗎？）效果更強。

情境對話

A: You spent too much money on your research last year. You deserve to be
reprimanded.

B: *But you also* spent too much. Your telephone bill is very high every month.
Isn't that a waste of money?

A：你去年花太多錢在研究上，被罵也是應該的。

B：但你還不是花了一大筆錢。你每個月的電話費帳單都很驚人，這難道就不是浪費
錢嗎？

----

3. 請看以下對話。

情境對話

A: I won't tolerate your mistakes.

B: *Let me ask you then.* What do you think about the terrible mistake that you
made with the invoices last week? How can you blame others?

A：我不會原諒你的錯誤。

B：那我問你，上禮拜處理發票時發生的嚴重疏失你怎麼說？你有什麼資格責怪別人？

■ 重點提示

若對方不知反省自己，只是一味指責別人，可以用上述句型反擊。

12

第12章
遣詞用字

溝通討論藉由語言文字達成，因此，由語言文字組成的各種表現相當重要。而在以英文溝通的場合，適當合宜的遣詞用字也是一門不簡單的學問。

Useful English Expressions
for Communication

改口 ●MP3 208

■ 我是說，……。

1. I mean,...	我是說，……。
2. ..., indeed...	……，其實是……。

■ 句型解說

1. 說錯話時用來補救的說法。另外，如果先前的敘述有誤，也可以用 I mean 傳達正確的訊息。其他請參考「說明要點」的部分 (p. 272)。

- At the party, I had a chance of speaking to the prime minister, *I mean* the former prime minister.
  在宴會上，我有機會和首相說了幾句話，我是說前首相。

情境對話

A: Are you sure you lost your wallet in the room?

B: Yes. Um, *I mean*, no. I'm not really sure where I lost it.

A：你確定錢包掉在房間裡？

B：對。嗯，不對。我其實不確定掉在哪。

2. indeed 是「其實」，帶有「說得更清楚一點」的意思。

情境對話

A: Would you tell me what the decision of the committee was?

B: I cannot, *indeed* I shouldn't tell you anything about it at the moment.

A：可以告訴我委員會的決定嗎？

B：不行，應該是說我現在什麼都不該說。

換個說法

◉MP3 209

■ 換句話說，……。

1. ..., in other words,...	……，換句話說，……。
2. ..., or...	……，也就是說……。
3. ..., that is,...	……，也就是說……。
4. ..., namely,...	……，就是……。
5. Let me put it this way:...	我這麼說吧：……。
6. Let me put it another way.	我換個方式說。
7. This means that...	這意味著……。
8. ... which means...	……意思是……。
9. To put it the other way round,...	換個方式來說，……。

句型解說

1. 以提綱挈領的方式，將先前的內容重述一次。
   - With this computer, you can have access to the book search system of the National Library. *In other words,* you can search for most of the titles published in Taiwan.
   有了這台電腦，你就可以連線到國家圖書館的館藏檢索系統。換句話說，你可以查詢全台灣大部分已出版的書目。

2. 將前面說過的話用另外的方式敘述。
   - Ren, *or* "the sense of compassion," has deep roots in Chinese culture.
   仁，也就是「憐憫心」，是中華文化中根深蒂固的觀念。

3. that is 雖然和 in other words 同義，但如果用來取代特定字詞，特別能凸顯說話者想表達的內容。
   - I'm a specialist in psychology, *that is,* the study of the human mind.
   我專攻心理學，也就是人類心理的研究。

4. 和 that is 同義，用來指出某個特定內容。

- In the first half of the eighteenth century, there were two great composers in Europe, *namely*, Bach and Handel.

18 世紀前期，歐洲出現了兩位偉大的作曲家，也就是巴哈和韓德爾。

5, 6. 這兩個句型都能將複雜的內容簡化。句型 5 的 this way 指冒號後面的內容。除了換個方式陳述自己的想法，也可就自己所理解的說出對方想表達的意思。

---

7. this 指的是剛剛說過的內容。

- About twenty thousand people a year take the judicial examinations, but only five hundred are able to pass. *This means that* only 2.5 percent of those who take the examination are successful in getting into the Training Institute for Judges and Prosecutors.

每年約有兩萬人參加司法特考，但只有 500 人能通過考試。這意味著參加考試的人當中只有 2.5% 能順利進入司法官訓練所。

---

8. 帶有為對方說明內容的意味。

- The man committed larceny, *which means* theft.

那個人犯了竊盜罪，就是偷了別人的東西。

■ 重點提示

敘述的內容太複雜以致於對方不清楚時，換個說法使對方明白是非常重要的。上述句型有兩種表現方式，一是從別的觀點切入，一是直接換個說法。

適切的表達 ●MP3 210

■ 這樣說也可以。

1. ..., I should say,...   ……，可以說……。

2. ..., one might say,...　　　　　　……，或者可以說……。

3. ..., if I may say so,...　　　　　　……，如果可以這樣說的話，
　　　　　　　　　　　　　　　　　　……。

4. ..., if I may put it that way,...　　……，如果可以那樣說的話，
　　　　　　　　　　　　　　　　　　……。

5. The right [best] word [phrase/way] to　最適合用來形容……的字
describe ... is "..."　　　　　　　　〔詞／方式〕是「……」。

6. ... (and) I use the word [phrase]　……，（而且）我刻意使用這個
deliberately.　　　　　　　　　　　字〔詞〕。

■句型解說

1. 可置於句首、句中或句尾。句型 2 到 4 亦同。
   - It was indeed a difficult job, but the project turned out to be a success, *I should say*.
     這確實是一項艱鉅的任務，但企劃的結果可以說非常成功。

2. 不想下斷言的情況下使用，用 might 來表現婉轉的態度，藉由泛指一般人的 one，說話者的立場也就不那麼鮮明強烈了。
   - He is indeed a talented poet, a genius, *one might say*.
     他確實是個才華洋溢的詩人，或者可以說是個天才。

3. 和句型 4 同義，但較為正式。

4. put 在這裡是「說」的意思。
   - Throughout its history, Japan has been protected by the sea, *if I may put it that way*.
     從古到今，日本一直受到海洋的保護，如果可以那樣說的話。

5. describe 是「描述」的意思，這裡可用 apply to 取代。

- *The* Englsih *word to describe* the fresh, comfortable feeling after taking a bath *is* "refreshed."
  英文中用來形容洗完澡後通體舒暢的感覺的單字是「refreshed」。

情境對話 1

A: Chikamatsu is one of the greatest dramatists in Japanese history.

B: Certainly. I think *the best phrase to describe* him *is* "the Japanese Shakespeare."

A：近松門左衛門是日本最偉大的劇作家之一。

B：的確。我認爲「日本的莎士比亞」最適合用來形容他。

情境對話 2

A: The manager is a cunning old man.

B: Yes, indeed. *The best name to apply to* his character *is* "crafty old fox."

A：經理眞是老奸巨猾。

B：沒錯，「狡猾的老狐狸」最適合用來形容他。

情境對話 3

A: What's happening in the new plant?

B: "All hell let loose" *are the best words to describe* the situation.

A：新廠房發生了什麼事？

B：「一塌糊塗」這幾個字最適合用來形容目前的狀況。

---

6. 表示用字遣詞小心斟酌，仔細想清楚才說出口的。

- The pipeline burst and we walked in a river of oil. *I use the word* "river" *deliberately* because we were knee-deep in the oil.
  管線破裂，結果我們在油河裡行走。我刻意用「河」這個字來形容，因爲膝蓋以下眞的都浸在油裡了。

■ 重點提示

　　想要把意見傳達給對方時，除了既定的說法，從其他角度切入可以讓整句話更加鮮活。上述句型除了表示自己對某事物的觀察之外，透過各種形容方式也間接表達了自己的看法。另外，or whatever you call it（任何你想得到的說法）用

在不拘泥特定說法的情況。

- "Transience," "solitude," "sorrow," *or whatever you call it*, there seems to be a kind of sadness which underlies Japanese literature.
  「短暫」、「孤獨」、「哀愁」或任何你想得到的詞，日本文學似乎以悲傷爲基調。

邊道歉邊說出自己的想法　　◉MP3 211

■ 這麼說很失禮，但……。

1. ..., if you don't mind my saying so,...　　……，如果你不介意我這麼說的話，……。

2. ..., excuse me for saying so,...　　……，請容我這麼說，……。

3. I'm sorry, but...　　我很抱歉，但是……。

4. I must say...　　我必須說……。

句型解說

1, 2. 都可置於句首、句中或句尾。

- Your research was, *excuse me for saying so,* a complete failure.
  你的研究，請原諒我這麼說，完全失敗。

3. 另一種說法是 I'm sorry to say that.，意思是「很抱歉這麼說」。

- I understand you're trying hard, but you expect too much. *I'm sorry*, *but* it's true.
  我知道你很努力，但你的期望太高了。我很抱歉，但這是事實。

4. 說出令對方無法承受的事實。

- Now that you've spent more than fifty thousand dollars without any commendable result, *I must say* that you failed.
  你都已經花了五萬多美金卻沒有什麼值得一提的成果，我必須說你就是失敗了。

■ 重點提示

討論時，難免會說出一些比較不中聽的話，這時別忘了多用婉轉的語氣。

說法不恰當   ● MP3 212

■ 這樣說並不恰當。

1. It's too much to say...	說是……太過分了點。
2. That's a strong way to put it.	那樣的說法太過了。
3. I think ... is not the right [best] word to describe [to apply to]...	我認為……不是最適合形容……的字。
4. You can hardly call it "..."	你不能說是「……」。
5. Do you use the word "..." deliberately?	你是刻意用「……」這個字嗎？
6. You seem to confuse the words "..." and "..."	看來你好像搞混了「……」和「……」的意思。

■ 句型解說

1. 指對方說得太過。

情境對話

A: People involved in the project are simply wasting money.

B: *It's too much to say* we are wasting money.

A：參與這項計畫的人只是在浪費錢。

B：說我們浪費錢太過分了點。

如果要引述第三者的話，並表示其言過其實，可以用 go so far as to say... （甚至說……。）

• He called the plan rubbish. He *went so far as to say* that the people involved in the project were simply wasting their money.

他說這個計畫根本是垃圾，甚至說參與其中的人只是在浪費錢。

另外，指責他人玩笑開過頭時，可用以下說法。

- You carried the joke too far.
  你玩笑開過頭了。

---

4. 請看以下對話。

[情境對話]

A: The office is quite near the city center.

B: *You can hardly call it* "near" to the city when it is located twenty minutes by car from the city center.

A：公司離市中心蠻近的。

B：開車到市中心要 20 分鐘不能說是「蠻近」的吧。

---

5. 發現對方用詞不當時，語帶確認地詢問。

[情境對話]

A: Mozart was a childish man.

B: *Do you use the word* "childish" *deliberately?* I think you mean "childlike" in fact.

A：莫札特蠻幼稚的。

B：你故意用「幼稚」這個詞嗎？我想你的意思應該是「像孩子一樣天真無邪」吧。

---

6. 請見以下對話。

[情境對話]

A: I understand "loneliness" is the most important concept in Basho's haiku school.

B: Just a moment. *You seem to confuse the words* "loneliness" *and* "solitude."

A：我知道「孤寂」是芭蕉派俳句的中心思想。

B：等等。你似乎把「孤寂」和「閑寂」搞混了。

▍重點提示

指對方歪曲事實或誇大其詞時都可使用上述句型。其他請參考第 3 章「言過其實」的部分 (p. 62)。

▓ 請求協助

● MP3 213

■ 請問……英文怎麼說？

1. What's ... in English?	請問……英文怎麼說？
2. What's the English word that means...	要表示……的話，英文用哪個字？
3. What do you say in English if you (want to say) ...	如果你（想說）……的話，英文怎麼說？
4. What's the right way to say ... in English?	……的英文怎麼說才是對的？

▓ 重點提示

　　有時候腦袋裡突然冒出一句話，卻不知道該如何用英文表達，這時，直接詢問對方才是最好的解決之道，沈默或支吾其詞的話，話題是沒辦法繼續的。

▓ 明確指出話中的意思

● MP3 214

■ 我的意思是……。

1. When I said..., I meant [I didn't mean]...	我說……時，我的意思是〔我的意思不是〕……。
2. When I say..., I (don't) mean...	我說……時，我的意思（不）是……。
3. I used the word ... in the sense that...	我用……，是取其……的意思。

句型解說

1, 2. mean 可用 imply（意味著）或 suggest（暗示）替代。

3. sense 的前面可以看情況接各種形容詞，如 in the specific sense that...（是取其特定的…之意）、in the broad sense that...（是取其廣泛的…之意）、in the scientific sense that...（是取其科學上…的意思）等等。

  • The candidate for the post is quite good *in the sense that* he has experience in the field.
  該職位的人選相當不錯，意思是說他在這個領域有經驗。

▓ 詢問對方話中的意思 ◉MP3 215

■ 你的意思是？

1. You mentioned... Could you tell me what it is?　你提到……。可以告訴我是什麼嗎？

2. You said something about... I'm not sure what it is.　你說到……，我不太確定是什麼。

句型解說

1, 2. Could you tell me 和 I'm not sure 後面除了 what it is 之外，也可以接 who he [she] is（他〔她〕是誰）、where it is（在哪裡）等等。

情境對話

A: When I read Shakespeare I often consult the *Oxford English Dictionary.* Shakespeare's English is quite different from modern English.

B: Excuse me. *You mentioned* the name of a dictionary. *Could you tell me what it is?*

A：閱讀莎士比亞的作品時，我經常查《牛津英文字典》。莎士比亞的英文和現代英文很不一樣。

B：抱歉，你剛剛提到一本字典的名字，可以告訴我是哪一本嗎？

■ 重點提示

　　對方提到一個陌生的字詞而自己第一時間沒能掌握時，可以用上述句型來詢問。由於大部分的情況都是自己不太確定聽到的內容為何，因此下列說法也能派上用場。

- You mentioned a word like...
  你提到……之類的字。

- You mentioned a word that sounds like...
  你提到一個聽起來像是……的字。

- You mentioned ... or something like that.
  你提到……，又或者跟那個很像的字。

打破沈默的利器　　◉MP3 216

　　大部分的人講話講到一個段落時會稍做停頓，很少人能夠滔滔不絕。但若討論時停了下來，很容易讓對方有機可乘。沈默代表的意義很多，在歐美文化中，有時不發一語甚至是很不禮貌的。

　　換言之，沈默不見得是金，如何填補話跟話之間的空白就變得很重要了。就算只是發出一個無意義的音也好，在還沒想到下一句話該怎麼說之前，利用某個音或某些感嘆詞、發語詞等來填補空白，趁機思考接下來該如何應對。以下提到的 Well, I mean, um 等就是打破沈默、爭取時間常見的用法。

Well

接近中文的「嗯」、「這個嘛」，用法如下。

(1) 回答對方前的停頓語氣。

情境對話 1

A: Professor Smith, could I ask you some questions concerning what you talked about in today's lecture?

B: *Well*, you see, I'm very busy at the moment. I'll try to see you tomorrow.

A：史密斯教授，關於今天上課的內容，我有幾個問題想請教一下可以嗎？

B：這個嘛，我現在很忙，明天再說吧。

情境對話 2

A: What do you think about his paintings?

B: *Well*, quite honestly, I don't like them.

A：你認為他的畫如何？

B：嗯，老實說，我不喜歡。

(2) 不知道該怎麼回答對方時的緩衝口氣。

情境對話 3

A: How old is she?

B: *Well*, I don't know.

A：她幾歲啊？

B：嗯，我不知道。

(3) 開啓新話題。

• *Well*, I think we may break for lunch now.

　嗯，可以休息吃個午飯了。

(4) 表示讓步，接著發表意見。

情境對話 4

A: You are to blame. You should take all the responsibility.

B: *Well*, I don't think I'm solely responsible for it.

A：都怪你。你應該負起所有的責任。

B：嗯，但我不認爲只有我該負責。

(5) 表示驚訝或懷疑。

情境對話 5

A: The total price is twenty thousand dollars.

B: *Well*, are you sure? It's twelve thousand, isn't it?

A：總價是兩萬美金。

B：嗯？你確定嗎？應該是一萬二才對吧？

I mean...

　接近中文的「嗯，我的意思是」，有以下兩種用法，是相當好用的表現方式。

(1) 修正先前的說法，帶有「不是這個意思」的意味。

- You can find the title in Pelican, *I mean*, uh, Penguin Books.
  你可以在鵜鶘出版社的書中找到那本書，不對，嗯，我是說企鵝出版社。

(2) 說明先前的敘述，給說話者多一點時間準備接下來要說的話。

情境對話

A: Why did you keep silent throughout the meeting?

B: I thought there was no need for me to speak. Well, *I mean*, I was not interested in the discussion.

A：為什麼你在會議上一直保持沈默？

B：我想沒有我發言的必要。嗯，我的意思是，我對討論不感興趣。

Let me see

接近中文的「嗯，我想想」。表示有某種發想或發現。

- Shakespeare died, *let me see*, in 1616.
  莎士比亞是在，嗯，我想想，1616 年去世的。

情境對話

A: Where can I find a picture of a pyramid?

B: I think it's somewhere around page fifty.

A: *Let me see* ... Oh here it is.

A：哪裡有金字塔的照片？

B：我想應該在 50 頁左右的地方吧。

A：我看看，喔，在這裡。

What [How] should I say?

腦袋裡想不出恰當的詞句，或對話不知如何繼續下去時使用，意思都是「怎麼說才好」。

- There is a kind of overestimation of Western cultures ... *what should I say?* ... a craze for the West.
  現在普遍存在著一種對西方文化的過高評價，該怎麼說呢？一種對西方的狂熱。

國家圖書館出版品預行編目（CIP）資料

如何提升英語溝通能力：關鍵句 1300 / 崎村耕二著；劉華珍譯 . -- 初版 . -- 臺北市：眾文圖書，
2010.12 面；公分
ISBN 978-957-532-392-9（平裝附光碟片） 1. 英語 2. 句法
805.169   99020036

OE019

如何提升英語溝通能力：關鍵句1300

定價 380 元
2015 年 4 月　初版 2 刷

作者　　　　崎村耕二
英文校閱　　Michael Wattie
譯者　　　　劉華珍
責任編輯　　蔡易伶

主編　　　　陳瑠琍
副主編　　　黃炯睿
資深編輯　　黃琬婷・蔡易伶
美術設計　　嚴國綸
行銷企劃　　李皖萍・莊佳樺
發行人　　　黃建和
發行所　　　眾文圖書股份有限公司
　　　　　　台北市 10088 羅斯福路三段 100 號
　　　　　　12 樓之 2
網路書店　　www.jwbooks.com.tw
電話　　　　02-2311-8168
傳真　　　　02-2311-9683
郵政劃撥　　01048805

"EIGO NO GIRON NI YOKU TSUKAU HYOGEN (Useful
English Expressions for Discussion and Debate)" by
Koji Sakimura. Copyright © Koji Sakimura 1996. All
rights reserved. Original Japanese edition published by
Sogensha, Inc. This Complex Chinese edition published
by arrangement with Sogensha, Inc., Osaka in care of
Tuttle-Mori Agency, Inc., Tokyo, through Keio Cultural
Enterprise Co., Ltd., Sanchong City, Taipei County,
Taiwan.

ISBN 978-957-532-392-9
Printed in Taiwan